FRACTURED FRAME

Robert Archibald

Cactus Mystery Press
an imprint of Blue Fortune Enterprises LLC

For information contact :
Blue Fortune Enterprises, LLC
Cactus Mystery Press
P.O. Box 554
Yorktown, VA 23690
http://blue-fortune.com

Book and Cover design by BFELLC

ISBN: 978-1-961548-11-4
First Edition: May 2024

DEDICATION

To Kirk Lovenbury, a gentle critic and stalwart friend.

Fiction by Robert Archibald:
Roundabout Revenge
Guilty Until Proven Innocent
Crime Might Pay
Who Dung It?
Illusion of Truth

Reviews for *Roundabout Revenge*

Fascinating plot, thoughtfully developed. Looking forward to what story twists his next book will bring.
Fred Cason, Amazon review

I loved Roundabout Revenge. Author Robert Archibald is a retired college professor whose writing demonstrates that he is a scholar not only in his professional field of study, but also in his observations on society. In this engrossing novel, he sheds light on why law and justice are sometimes at odds with each other. There also are wonderful discussions among the characters about sports, diversity in schools and society, and about how conservatives and liberals have come to hold their beliefs. I look forward to the sequel.
CW Stacks, Amazon review

Reviews for *Guilty Until Proven Innocent*

Another Archibald masterpiece... This quality page-turner encompasses a number of adventures that sometimes end not as anticipated. The expected becomes the unexpected...
If you enjoyed "Revenge," you'll enjoy this too. If you missed "Revenge" pick it up with the knowledge that you'll have two enjoyable books to occupy your time.
Wilford Kale, Virginia Gazette review

Reviews for *Who Dung It?*

Interesting twists and turns... This is the fourth of Robert Archibald's novel I have read. Each one has had an interesting plot and surprises. He interweaves his stories with some short sentences that at first seem innocuous, but that lead to a change in a story's direction. I can never predict the twists and turns that will occur.
Amazon review

Acknowledgments

Fractured Frame is a work of fiction. Any resemblance between characters in the book and anyone I have known or met is a complete coincidence.

This book had a lengthy gestation period. I wrote a partial draft several years ago, but other projects got in the way. When *Fractured Frame* finally worked its way to the top of the pile, I couldn't determine why it had been shoved aside. My friend Kirk Lovenbury read the manuscript and gave me useful comments. Unlike my other books, I did not have my writers' group read *Fractured Frame*. Still, echoes of their advice—show don't tell, give more description, ugh, passive voice, and others—rattled around in my brain as I worked on this book. As a result, the Silver Quill Writers Group: Tim Holland, Elizabeth Lee, Caterina Novelliere, Peter Stipe, and Susan Williamson, deserve some credit but no blame. Finally, I would like to thank Stacia Chapman and Narielle Living for an excellent editing job. Their efforts were exceedingly helpful.

Finally, everything I do benefits from the help of my wife, Nancy.

Chapter One
Walter Cunningham, October 25, 1980

Newspapers called Walter Cunningham the perfect candidate for governor. He was photogenic, standing six feet two, with strong cheekbones, wavy brown hair, and a ready smile. In his short career he'd been a successful mayor and state senator, so he checked the experience boxes. The polls had him with a double-digit lead over his older, tired-looking opponent. Two weeks before the election, everyone was sure he was headed for an easy win. Cunningham was poised to bring progressive policies to the state.

He didn't think his job at today's outdoor rally involved changing minds. The task today was energizing his base. Walter didn't want his people becoming overconfident. He knew his lead in the polls would be inconsequential if his voters didn't turn out on election day. On the ride from Springfield, Cynthia Opal, his top campaign aid, prepped him on the people he'd be sharing the stage with. He knew most of them, which made things easier. The local mayor, Joel Henderson, was a long-time friend. Sally Givens was a colleague in the state senate. The only unknown was the leader of the county party. Walter figured he must have met him a couple of times. Still, he didn't know if he would recognize William Morris. Fortunately, Cynthia provided a photo, which made his job easier.

Cunningham's station wagon slid into its parking place in front of the fruit stand. Walter considered it an unusual setup. A large natural amphitheater loomed behind the fruit stand—a grassy slope now filled with people. The weather was splendid, warm with a bright blue sky and only had a few fluffy white clouds—perfect for this kind of rally. As they'd approached the fruit stand, Walter passed by fields converted into temporary parking lots, and he'd seen several buses parked among the cars. His brief glimpse of the large crowd suggested the advance team had done an excellent job. Walter made a mental note to thank them.

Walter exited the station wagon to a scattering of applause from those on the hill who could see him. A pair of large birds flew over the crowd. He didn't think they were "hawks making lazy circles in the sky" like in *Oklahoma*. These were buzzards or vultures; he never knew which. He hoped it wasn't an omen.

All thoughts of birds disappeared when his older brother Horace walked up to him with his arms open for an embrace. He shouldn't have been surprised. Horace ran a factory in Tyndall, only twenty miles away. The brothers embraced briefly and exchanged a few words. Cynthia, ever concerned about keeping things on schedule, pulled Walter away so he could greet the other people selected to be on the candidate's side of the ropes. He greeted all the donors and other local worthies before his staff hustled them off to their reserved seats in the front row.

After the others were seated, Walter, the mayor, Senator Givens, and Morris walked from behind the fruit stand and mounted the podium. The crowd went crazy. Walter stepped to the front of the stage and acknowledged the applause with a wave. He still got a thrill during these events. Thousands of people chanted his name, applauded, and cheered for him. He pointed to people he knew and waved to the rest. His smile lit up. The rally would make a great lead for the local news all over the state.

After the applause waned, Walter retreated to his seat. For the next twenty minutes, he appeared interested in the speeches of the other three. Their job was to energize and excite the crowd without exhausting anyone. They performed admirably, and he rose when he heard Morris, the last to speak, introduce him as, "the next governor of the great state of Missouri!"—an applause line for sure—and as Walter walked to the podium to shake Morris's hand, the crowd rose again. After a few minutes, Walter motioned them to sit down and said, "Thank you. Thank you so much." While some continued to applaud, in short order he calmed the crowd.

"Wow," he said. "I love the enthusiasm." As he dug his prepared remarks from his inside coat pocket, a puff of smoke rose high on a hill to his left. Things escalated after that. First, a bullet tore into Walter's left shoulder. He spun to the floor behind the podium, bleeding profusely. Second, after a stunned pause, people began screaming. Some of the people in the front row dove on the ground to take cover, and the state police detail rushed to the podium, weapons drawn.

Newspapers the next day led with the story of the shooting. They all shared that only one shot had been fired, striking Senator Cunningham in the shoulder, and details about the extent of the injuries were not available. The senator had been rushed to the university hospital where surgeons completed a long and difficult surgery. The most information the papers could get from the hospital was that the senator was in intensive care. The prognosis was unknown at the time the paper went to press. Despite camping out at the hospital all night, journalists could not provide additional information. They simply repeated the horrific footage they'd taken at the rally.

Chapter Two

Ho Narwhal, April 13, 1968

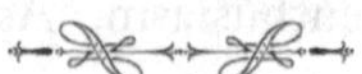

As Horace Narwhal paced behind the counter at the Quick Stop convenience store, a bead of sweat rolled from his armpit down his ribcage. *I guess nervous energy can make a person sweat,* he thought. Horace, who liked to be called Ho, was a sandy-haired seventeen-year-old slightly pimpled high school dropout working the late shift. His buddies, Sam and Henry, had assured him the robbery would be a piece of cake—like taking candy from a baby. He checked the clock. It was only 11:15. They told him they'd arrive at 11:30. He was ready. He'd been careful to block the view of the video camera when he stashed most of the twenties behind the tens, not in the lockbox where they were supposed to go. If everything went well, Sam and Henry should be in and out of the store in no more than three minutes. They'd have to point a gun at him to make things look real—*no big deal. Everything should work out fine.*

A bunch of Mexican guys in painter's clothes came in at 11:25. Ho knew them. They were putting the first coat on the new condos. Usually, they came in a little later. Of course, tonight, here they were. They finally finished shopping at 11:35.

Five minutes later, Sam and Henry rushed in the door. With panty hose covering their faces, they were unrecognizable. Ho almost laughed. Sam drew a pistol from his belt, pointed it at Ho, and yelled, "Empty your cash register!" Ho raised both hands and backed away.

"I said empty your cash register!" Sam yelled even louder as he gestured toward the bag Henry was holding.

Ho lowered his hands, opened the cash register, and handed the bills to Henry, who stuffed them into the bag. "Here. There isn't any more. I don't want any trouble. Take it," Ho said. He carefully maneuvered himself as he spoke and stepped on the alarm button on the floor behind the counter. The store owner had expended the cost of the system to be hard wired to the police station, and Ho had known this was an important part of the operation.

Sam and Henry ran out and jumped in Sam's car. They hurried because they knew the police had been notified. Ho had explained to them he'd have to step on the button. They figured they could deal with it. They'd worked out a foolproof escape route.

A minute after Ho stepped on the button, patrolman Bill Jones, who was headed to the Quick Stop for coffee, heard the alert over his radio and saw a car fly out of the parking lot. He turned on his flashers and siren and gave chase. When the car accelerated instead of pulling over, Bill grabbed his radio. "In pursuit of Quick Stop robbers south on Forty-Eight. Request backup."

Sam and Henry were desperate. *How had the police responded so quickly?* They'd only paused to pull off the panty hose before backing out of the parking lot. "Pull over," Henry said. "There's no way we'll outrun them in this piece of junk. It's slower than a horse with a stomachache."

"Very funny. I can't stop. We've got to get away."

Henry turned in his seat to look at the cop car. "He's right on our tail. I'll throw the bag out the window and then pull over. He's probably called for backup already. There's gonna be cops all over the place."

Officer Jones saw something flung out of the car, and the vehicle slowed and moved over to the side of the road. He parked behind them and waited for backup.

Mario, in the other cruiser, came to a halt in front of the car Bill had stopped. Bill climbed out, walked up to Mario, and told him the story. "Let's find out who they are, and then I'm going to figure out what they threw out back there."

The two policemen went to Sam and Henry's car. Bill asked for their driver's licenses. After he gave the licenses to Mario, he asked the boys what they were doing, and why they'd initially sped up when he'd turned on his siren and flashers.

Sam said, "We were driving home. Your lights startled me, and I must have stepped on the gas when I meant to step on the brake."

"Where were you coming from?"

"We'd been at a movie. At the mall in Sheffield," Sam replied.

"I saw your car coming out of the Quick Stop. What were you doing there?"

"Oh, we stopped for Cokes."

"Where are the cups?"

"We finished them at the store."

"Okay, boys, sit tight. I'll be back to you. Meanwhile Officer Lopez is running your IDs."

Bill hopped in his cruiser and reversed to where he thought he'd seen the thing thrown out of the car. With the help of his flashlight, he found a bag beside the road after only a few minutes. He opened the bag and saw lots of cash. These guys had held up the Quick Stop, no doubt about it. He was lucky he'd been headed there just after the robbery occurred.

When Bill returned to the other two cars, he said to Mario, "Get them out of the car. We need to cuff them, read them their rights, and take them in. They're the ones who held up the Quick Stop. I found the bag of cash they threw out before I stopped them."

Bill and Mario handcuffed the two boys and put them into Mario's cruiser. After Mario left with them, Bill turned his cruiser around and headed to the Quick Stop. When he arrived, he saw two people inside. He recognized the store owner, Mr. Rodriquez, a short, black-haired man who looked like he could be Mexican or Latino. The other was the teenager, a short, slightly chubby kid with a pimply face. He had one of those haircuts like a British rock-and-roll star. Bill didn't know his name.

When he entered, he said, "Mr. Rodriquez, I was headed this way to get a cup of coffee just as the robbers pulled out of the parking lot. I caught the two who did it."

"Wonderful," Rodriquez responded. "It's good to see you, Bill."

Bill held up the bag. "I even recovered the money they took."

He handed the bag over to the store owner, and then said, "I'll have to take it back in a minute. After we count it and log it, someone will return the money to you. Right now, it's evidence in a crime. Were you here when the robbery happened?"

"No, Ho was the only one here. He called me right after he alerted the police with the security alarm, exactly like I tell them to. I tell them not to try to be heroes. It's only money."

The officer turned to Ho. "Ho, what kind of name is that?"

While Ho was incredibly nervous, he responded after a short pause. "My name is Horace, but everyone calls me Ho. I don't know when it started, must be before I can remember."

"Okay, Ho, give me your full name and address."

"Horace Narwhal, 602 South Beaver Street."

"In Viceroy?"

"Yes."

"Okay, tell me what happened."

"At about 11:30, two guys came into the store. They were running, and they had panty hose or something over their faces. One of them pulled a gun on me. They yelled at me to empty the cash register, so I did. Like Mr.

Rodriquez said, it's what we're supposed to do."

"So, you put the cash in the bag," the policeman said, pointing to the bag Mr. Rodriquez was pawing through.

"Yeah, one of them had the gun and the other one had the bag."

"Can you describe the two guys?"

"Like I said, they had panty hose over their heads. It would be hard to describe them."

"Where they white or back? How tall were they? Were they thin or fat? What were they wearing? You should have seen those kinds of things."

"Sure," Ho responded. "They were white guys. The guy with the gun was tall, maybe over six feet and skinny. The other guy was shorter and fatter. I think they had on sweatshirts and jeans."

"What color were the shirts?"

"Gosh, I don't know. One was red I think, maybe Nebraska? I'm not sure. The whole thing happened in a hurry."

"Did you see what kind of car they were driving?"

"No, I guess I should have. I was pretty shook up. No one's ever pointed a gun at me before. I saw you take off after them, you know with your lights and siren. I'm not sure I even saw their car."

The policeman closed his little notebook and said, "Ho, you've done a good job. I know it's scary to have a gun pointed at you. Your description fits the two guys we picked up. Thanks."

Mr. Rodriquez spoke up. "I looked through this cash. I saw more than ten twenty-dollar bills in the bag. It's too many."

"What?" the policeman asked.

"The clerks are supposed to have no more than five twenties in the cash register at any time. The rest of them go in the lockbox so if we're robbed, it's only small stuff."

Ho, who was sweating profusely, stammered, "Gosh I must have forgot. It's really busy here sometimes, and this group of guys all had twenties."

Mr. Rodriquez interrupted, "You've never forgotten to separate out the twenties before. Are the two guys who pulled this thing off buddies of yours?”

"No," Ho said. "Like I said, they had panty hose over their heads. I couldn't tell who they were."

Silenced greeted Ho's response. Mr. Rodriquez and the policeman gave each other a look. Finally, Mr. Rodriquez asked, "Ho, did you know the guys who robbed you?"

"No… I don't know. Maybe I do. Like I said, I didn't recognize anyone."

"Mr. Rodriquez, he pushed the button pretty fast. Would he do that if they were his buddies? And I caught those two. You're going to get your money back. Maybe we should cut Ho some slack."

Mister Rodriquez shook his head. Giving Ho a stern look, he said, "I'm not sure. These kids. You don't know if you can trust them. I'm still bothered by all the twenties in the bag."

"I'll take the bag. It has to go to the station as evidence. Ho, I arrested those guys. If they're your friends, and you were in on it, I'll be back."

Chapter Three

Kenny Sturgis, September 3, 1980

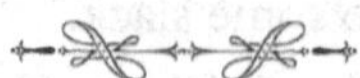

Kenny Sturgis parked his Jeep and made his way through the vacant lot across the street from his mother's new house. It was morning and builders were already at work on the house going up in the adjacent lot, so he had to be careful. The six-foot-two, seventeen-year-old blond silently walked through the wooded lot and settled down where he could see her house from across the road. Her new house was a strange looking modern design, not anything like the log cabin Kenny lived in. Nothing happened until 8:15 when her husband left. At 8:30, the school bus came by to pick up the little kid who waited. He could see his mother in the front yard with the toddler waving goodbye. He guessed the two kids were his half-brother and half-sister. He'd never met them. His mother had deserted Kenny and his father a long time ago when Kenny was eight or nine, he couldn't remember. He didn't know what he was doing spying on her like this. His mother had made it clear. She wanted nothing to do with him or his father.

After his mother herded the little girl back into the big house, Kenny sat back and thought things over. He changed his mind. He wouldn't go up to the door like he'd planned. Honestly, he couldn't figure out what he'd say, and he knew he wouldn't be welcome.

Kenny understood why his mother had walked out on his father. His dad was a hard man. It couldn't have been easy to live like hermits squirreled away in the woods so far from any neighbors. Then there were his crackpot political views. His dad, William Sturgis, was an anarchist, a complete anarchist. He thought of all government as evil. It pained him to ride on county roads or use government-issued money. He even opposed a standing army.

Kenny understood leaving his weird father. What he couldn't understand was why she hadn't taken him with her. At eight or nine years old, what had he done? This question had haunted Kenny for years. Now he'd found her. Still, he didn't have the nerve to go up to the door and ask her. He sat there for twenty minutes trying to figure out why he'd bothered to make the fifty-mile trip from his home. He checked his watch. It was 9:15. *My father is going to be furious at me for taking off like this. I better head home.*

As Kenny drove his Jeep into the parking area at the end of the long gravel driveway lined with trees, he thought he might be in trouble. When he saw the big green truck from High Trail Outfitters parked in front of the log cabin, he was sure his dad would be angry with him. His father had warned him to be there when the truck arrived. Unloading the truck with all the tents and other gear for hunting season was a big job.

"Where the hell you been boy?" his father yelled when Kenny came walking beside the truck.

"Weren't they supposed to come tomorrow?"

"You know damn well today was the day. Get back here and help. They only sent Joe. I don't know why they don't send someone with him."

When Kenny got to the back of the big truck, his father slapped him on the back of the head. "You thought it was tomorrow. Idiot."

The slap hurt, but Kenny had learned not to let on. Also, he knew enough not to fight back. His father had a couple of inches and probably fifty pounds on him. His hair and full beard were white. It made him look old, but Kenny knew from experience he was in great shape. His dad's muscles were rock hard. Kenny took his punishment and went to work.

Two hours later, they'd unloaded the truck. Kenny's dad was a hunting guide. Being the way he was, he wouldn't be anyone's employee. He had an arrangement with High Trail. They lined up the clients and furnished the gear and the supplies: the tents, the cook stove, the sleeping bags, and the food. Kenny's dad organized the hunting trips and made sure the clients had a great experience. High Trial paid him in cash, completely off the books. William wouldn't have paid any taxes even if there were a record of his earnings. This arrangement made it easier.

When Kenny turned 16 last year, his dad could legally take him out of school, so his dad forced Kenny to quit. Actually, he didn't mind that much. He didn't do well at school, and he didn't have many friends. Usually, he liked working with his father. His dad wasn't a bad guy if he'd only be quiet about his crackpot political opinions. This past year Kenny had been working full time. In previous years, he'd worked on weekends and some in the summers. Kenny had become a good hunter—an excellent shot with his thirty ought six.

After they'd finished unloading the truck and stacked everything in the lean-to beside the cabin, they said goodbye to Joe, the High Trail driver, and went inside. Joe had given William a list of the hunters who'd reserved space at the Sturgis camp. The Sturgis house was a sparsely furnished six-room log cabin: two bedrooms, living room, kitchen, bathroom, and a storage room that doubled as an armory. William's father, Kenny's grandfather, had built it after his wife died. Kenny never knew either of his grandparents. They were gone before he was born. As he understood it, his dad's bizarre politics came straight from his father. He'd built the cabin to escape from government and civilization.

When William finished transferring the list to the big calendar he used to keep his schedule, he announced, "It's going to be a good season. We have those same archery guys who came last year, then two groups of turkey hunters, and we're booked solid for deer season. We'd better take the stuff out to the camp soon. We only have a week 'til the first group."

"Okay. I guess I'll go to town to check on the weather forecast. We don't want to try to transfer all the gear in the rain if we can help it."

"Good thinking."

Kenny knew he'd get nowhere with his next plea. Still, he gave it a shot. "You know, you and me could save a lot of time and money if we put up an antenna and bought a TV. I wouldn't have to drive into town to check on the weather all the time, and wouldn't it be good to know more about what's going on?"

"There you go again. You know the answer. No, we ain't getting no TV. All you're going to get on a TV is government propaganda and nonsense. You know I go into Willy's in town every once in a while. He's got those TVs at both ends of the bar, and there's never anything worth watching. Usually it's a baseball game, and you know I don't give a shit about no baseball."

Kenny knew his dad didn't give a shit about most things. Deciding to end the conversation, he said, "Okay. I'll go into town and check the paper for the weather later. Right now, I'm making me a sandwich and then going out to do some shooting."

His dad didn't say anything.

After he finished his sandwich, Kenny collected his rifle, a scope, and a box of ammo from the storage room and headed out to the shooting range. He liked shooting. On this day, he decided to practice long-range shots.

At the range, a twenty-foot-wide cleared space with a berm at the far end, he headed downrange to set up his targets. A bunch of mangled beer cans were scattered around. They'd all been used as targets many times, so most of them had gaping holes. He found four cans that pretty much hung together and set them on the bullet-scarred shelf resting against the berm. After making sure his targets would stand up, he retreated to the 300-yard mark toward the far end of the range. When clients came to do their practice shots, they shot much closer to the targets.

Kenny loaded his rifle and checked the way the scope was mounted. When he was satisfied with his equipment, he lay down in the prone position. He checked the wind by looking at the rustling of the leaves. Any little thing, the wind, his breathing, or his heartbeat, could be enough to make him miss at this distance. He calmed himself, stopped breathing, sighted at the far-left target, and squeezed the trigger. The target stayed still as a statue. The puff of dust that rose on the berm indicated he'd been a little high and right. He adjusted his aim, fired another shot, and sent the target dancing. All the targets were down after six shots. The two misses irked Kenny.

Kenny made the trip to the far end of the shooting range four more times to set up targets. As his practice progressed, finding intact beer cans became more and more difficult. *I'd better get more beer cans before the clients come.* He hit four targets in four shots and on the fifth try and decided to call it a day. Satisfied, he returned home and cleaned his rifle before putting it up.

Chapter Four

Ho Narwhal, April 24, 1968

Ho's father, Ray Narwhal, a slightly balding fifty-five-year-old, rolled out of bed when he heard a knock on the front door at nine o'clock the next morning. After throwing on some clothes, he opened the door and found two policemen standing on his porch.

"What can I do for you officers?" Ray said. He'd learned the hard way you were better off being polite with the police.

"Does Horace Narwhal live here?" the black policeman asked. He was taller than the white guy and seemed to be in charge.

"Yes, he's my son. He's asleep now. He works the night shift at the Quick Stop out on Forty-Eight. What do you want with him?"

"Wake him up. We have a warrant for his arrest. He was involved in a robbery last night."

"What?"

"We picked up two of his friends last night. Caught them red-handed. When we questioned them, they came clean. Your son was part of the deal. We've come to arrest him. Wake him up."

Ray left the policemen on the front porch and went back inside. He thought maybe he should have invited them in, but the house was in no shape to receive company. They could stay outside. Heading down the hallway, he barged into Ho's room without knocking. Ho didn't stir. Ray poked his shoulder, and Ho roused.

"A couple of people are at the front door for you. You'd better come see them," Ray said with a smile on his face.

"Who is it?" Ho mumbled.

"It's the police, two of them. They said they're here to arrest you. You'd better get dressed and get out there."

"You told them I was in here?"

"Sure, I did. I'm not lying for you. Whatever you did—a robbery, one of them said. You'd better straighten it out."

"I didn't do it. Heck, whoever they were, they robbed me. Two guys came into the store. They pulled a gun on me. I emptied out the cash register and gave them the money like I was supposed to."

"Don't tell me. Tell the guys at the front door."

Ho climbed out of bed and started dressing. Meanwhile, Ray returned to the front room and hollered through the door, "He's getting dressed. He'll be out in a minute."

Still drowsy, Ho ran his fingers through his hair, put on his jeans, a yellow shirt, and sneakers before going out to meet the policemen on the front porch. One of them said, "You're Horace Narwhal, right?"

Ho nodded.

"I'm placing you under arrest," the policeman said. "Turn around so Officer Middleton can handcuff you. We're taking you to the station."

Ho backed away. "I didn't do anything. Heck, I'm the one who was robbed."

"Look son. Save it for the detective at the station. We're simply doing our job, and we have a warrant for your arrest. Want to see it?"

Ho stopped arguing and turned around for the cuffs.

At the police station, an officer made him empty his pockets, took his fingerprints, and photographed him before putting him in a cell. He didn't know what was happening, but it couldn't be good. He paced around the cell in the cold dim light. *I should have put on a sweatshirt,* he thought. There was an odd smell. The whole scene made him nervous—scared and nervous. After half an hour, a detective opened the cell and guided him into a small room, just like on TV. The cop read from a card, "You have the right to remain silent and refuse to answer questions. Anything you say may be used against you in a court of law. You have the right to consult an attorney before speaking to the police and to have an attorney present during questioning now or in the future."

Ho zoned out as the detective finished the Miranda warning but said, "Okay, I understand. I don't want a lawyer. I don't need one. I don't understand why you're arresting me. The way I see it, I got robbed. I'm the victim here. Two guys came into the store where I work, pulled a gun on me, and robbed me."

"So, you don't know the guys who robbed you?"

"Like I said to the policeman last night, I might know them. I know a lot of people. I didn't recognize them. They had panty hose over their faces and a gun pointed at me. The whole thing shook me up. I tried to do what our boss told us to do. I emptied the cash register, gave them the cash, and stepped on the alarm button as quick as I could."

"Do you know Sam Heflin and Henry Worthington?"

Ho's eyes widened. "Was it Sam and Henry last night?"

"You damn well know it was Sam and Henry last night. The three of you are tight as ticks. It didn't take a half hour last night before they said you were in on the robbery. We found eighteen twenty-dollar bills in the bag you filled for them. You're supposed to put excess twenties in the lockbox. Last night you didn't. You knew they were coming."

Ho responded, "I told the police about that last night. The store was really busy. I forgot. It happens sometimes."

"No, it doesn't," the detective said. "Mr. Rodriquez, your boss, said you always do things right. You only slipped up last night. Except we're sure it wasn't a slip up. Your two partners in crime told us about keeping the twenties in the cash register."

Ho hung his head. He couldn't think of anything to say.

"Look Horace, you need a lawyer, or you need to admit what you did. If you plead guilty, the judge might take pity on you. Denying it isn't going to work. You weren't the one who pulled the gun. Maybe you'll get off as an accessory."

After more silence, Ho asked, "Okay. I'll cooperate. What do I have to do?"

Later in the morning, Ho's father came to see him in the jail. When they were alone in a room, Ray started in on him. "You really fucked up. You and your buddies got caught. Ho, everything's stacked against people like us. I've been telling you all your life. You have to keep your head down, or they'll be all over you. Now you go and give them a chance to really land on you. Look, the world has its foot on your throat. There's no reason to give them a chance to put on any extra weight."

Ho got mad. "You're one to talk! Why'd you lose your job at the plant? For drinking. For not showing up to work. And for stealing. I know the world's stacked against me. I'm only trying to get a little ahead. I don't need you lecturing me."

His father shook his head and stalked out.

Early in the afternoon, Ho gave his so-called friends a dirty look as he joined Henry and Sam when the police escorted them to the courthouse, one building over from the police station. The whole look of the place was different. The jail had been painted light green and everything was close. The courthouse had dark wood paneling and high ceilings. Only a scattering of people were in the courtroom seats. When their turn came, the judge, a big, bald guy, imposing in his robes, had the three boys approach the bench. He said, "I'm going to be quick with you boys. The evidence is overwhelming, so I know what I'm going to do. Mr. Heflin, step forward."

When Sam stepped closer, the judge said, "Samuel Heflin, I'm remanding you over for trial. Use of a firearm in the commission of a robbery is a felony. Bail is set at $10,000."

Then he had Henry and Ho step forward. "Henry Worthington and Horace Narwhal, I could remand you over for trial too. You're not in as much legal jeopardy as Mr. Heflin. Still, you're in plenty of trouble. As it turns out, it's your lucky day. I've decided to make you an offer. If you'll volunteer to be drafted, I'll drop these charges."

Henry and Ho looked at each other. Then Henry spoke up, "Your honor sir, I'm 4-F. The army won't take me."

The judge sat back. "Let me think about it for a minute. Mr. Narwhal, what's your draft status?"

"I-A probably," Ho said. "At least, I think. I've never taken a physical."

"Okay, you go to the back of the courtroom. Mr. Brady from the draft board, the one with the red tie, is there. He'll sign you up if you want to take my offer."

"Yes, I do. I'll go see Mr. Brady. Can I leave?"

"Yes, but before you go, I want your solemn promise you'll follow through with what the draft board wants. You'd better pray you pass the physical. If you're 4-F like your buddy here, come back and check in with me. And if you don't show up to be drafted, there will be a warrant out for your arrest. I can still bring charges. If you mess up again, you won't get any breaks from this court. I don't want to see you back here. Understand?"

"Yes sir. Can I go now?"

The judge nodded.

Ho hustled to the rear of the courtroom and found Mr. Brady. After they shook hands, Mr. Brady led him out of the courtroom to the Selective Service office, around a corner in the same building. It didn't take much paperwork before they finished. He had three days before he was supposed to show up at the bus station for the ride to the St. Louis induction center.

As Ho walked out of the courthouse, he wondered what lay ahead of him. Initially, he thought he'd dodged a bullet. It appeared Sam was in for some jail time and maybe Henry too. He wouldn't do any jail time and wouldn't have a record. Still, he knew what the army had in store for him. He'd be sent to Viet Nam for sure. The judge acted like he'd done Ho a favor. The more he thought about it, the more he thought it wasn't anything of the kind.

His father always said things were stacked against him. Maybe he was right. Nothing so far told him his dad was wrong. The teachers at school didn't give him any breaks, so he'd dropped out. The Quick Stop job was all he could get, and it was a dead-end. *Now what kind of choice has life given me? Jail or Viet Nam. What wonderful options.*

Chapter Five

Kenny Sturgis, September 3, 1980

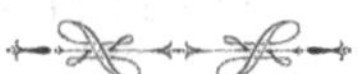

Kenny made it into Sheffield at five-thirty in the evening. Sheffield wasn't much of a place. He'd gone to school there, so he knew the setup. As he drove slowly down Main Street, he didn't see anyone he knew. It was quiet. A bunch of the stores were closed already. It made sense. On Wednesdays the Baptists and Methodists had mid-week meetings at night. Not many people were going to be shopping.

After checking out Main Street, Kenny went to the library. It closed at six-thirty, so he had plenty of time. Nothing seemed to be happening there either. The only librarian sat behind the check-out desk, and she didn't look busy. Kenny knew where they kept each day's *St. Louis Post Dispatch*. The weather section took up the back of the sports section. Kenny turned right to it. Though the long-range forecast often wasn't accurate, it was the best they could do. It showed rain the next day, and Friday didn't show any weather headed their way. They'd better move everything Friday.

Kenny gazed at the front page. Most of it was dedicated to stuff about the presidential election. He didn't see how anyone could pick between the two guys. One was a movie star who'd been the Governor of California, and the other was the current President who'd been a peanut farmer. He didn't know why he bothered to think about it. His father wouldn't welcome any talk about the election. All politicians were horrible, according to his father. Also, talking politics with the clients was completely out of bounds.

Kenny's stomach growled. He'd get a steady diet of his father's cooking when the hunting season started so he decided to go to the A&W. His friend Jesse, whose father owned the place, would probably be working. Knowing Jessie would give him a large order of fries and charge for a small one helped Kenny choose the A&W. Actually, there was only one other option, a McDonald's out by the freeway, but it was a five-mile drive in the wrong direction, so he headed for the A&W.

When Kenny approached the A&W, he could see they were busy, with three cars out front. He recognized one of them, a big station wagon with a confederate flag decal covering its back window. It was a Wilcox car. Given the other cars, Kenny figured Joan Wilcox must be there. Joan was the prettiest girl in Sheffield by a long shot, and she attracted boys like flies. Lots of rumors floated around about who'd been to how many bases with her. Kenny didn't think half of them were true. Anyway, he knew she was out of his league.

As he pulled into a parking place, he recognized one of the cars. It belonged to the Lewellen boys, the black guys who were big-time basketball players. Kenny had some history with them. He'd always been tall—six foot in eighth grade. He'd been the best player on the junior high team. Then the Lewellen brothers moved into town, and they were six-four and six-six. Kenny thought it would be great to play with them in high school. They did win most of their games. But with them on the team, no one passed the ball to Kenny. Sure, the Lewellen brothers were good. What bothered Kenny was, even when he was open under the basket, he rarely touched the ball. The other black players on the team always passed it to the Lewellens. In frustration, Kenny had a run-in with the other players and got kicked off the team.

Kenny didn't acknowledge either of the groups of teenagers as he went inside but he nodded to his friend Jessie.

"Hi Jessie," Kenny said. "Looks like Joan Wilcox is good for business."

"It's not all I figure she's good for," Jessie said with a smirk.

"She not going to think about either one of us twice and you know it."

"Yeah, but a man can dream. So, what do you want?"

"Make it a cheeseburger, fries, and root beer. And remember you know I like French fries."

After he paid for his food, Kenny sat at the inside table in the corner away from the Wilcox group. He could see them clearly. Sure enough, all the teenagers surrounded Joan Wilcox. She wore short shorts and a little orange crop-top exposing her belly button. Kenny had to admit she was gorgeous, a teenage goddess. Even so, somehow he didn't like her. She seemed too impressed with herself. He thought she always had to be the center of attention.

Kenny was happy to see the Lewellen crew clearing out and heading toward their car. A few minutes later, much to Kenny's surprise, a white girl walked away from where the black kids' car had been and headed to the Wilcox group. He recognized his former girlfriend, Mary Beth Sizemore, who joined the clutch of teenagers surrounding Joan Wilcox. Mary Beth had dumped Kenny when he dropped out of school. She'd called him a loser and told him he'd never amount to anything. While it hadn't been much of a romance, it still hurt. Since he wasn't in school anymore and spent so much time helping his father, Kenny hadn't hooked up with anyone since Mary Beth. He tried to tell himself it didn't bother him, but he knew it did. Now it looked like she was hanging around the Lewellen brothers. And he didn't like it.

As Kenny finished his burger and started in on his fries, the door opened, and Joan's older sister came in. Kenny didn't know her name. Much to his surprise, she came over to his table, pointed to the seat across from him, and asked, "Mind if I sit here?"

Kenny said, "Sure."

"I'm Maybell Wilcox."

"Kenny Sturgis." He couldn't help staring at her. She was tall for a girl, close to six foot. She had short, curly brown hair and a sort of odd face. Maybe her head was too big. She had large ears and a slightly off-center mouth. What grabbed Kenny's attention most was her boobs, which spilled out of her only partly buttoned red-checked top.

"Checking out my front, are you there Kenny."

Kenny blushed. "I guess I was. Sorry, it doesn't bother you, does it?"

"I guess you wouldn't be a boy if you didn't, so you pass the test."

Kenny filled the brief silence that followed. "Do you come here often? I don't think I've seen you here before."

"My dumbass sister, you know Joan, is between boyfriends. No one to drive her around, so she had me drive her. She's on the hunt for her next sucker."

"I'm sure there'll be many candidates."

"You don't want to put your hat in the ring, Kenny. You're a good-looking guy in the right age range."

Kenny blushed again. "No way, she wouldn't look at me twice. And besides, she's too stuck on herself for me. I'm not interested in a flashy girl like Joan. I bet Joan doesn't ever walk by a mirror without checking herself out."

"You're a smart boy, Kenny. Joan's my sister, and I love her. Still, you've got her pegged right. She's stuck up, always has been."

Kenny pushed over his half-finished bag of French fries. "Want one?"

"Thanks." After eating a few French fries, Maybell continued, "I saw you looking at the Sizemore girl as she walked away from the Lewellens' car. Didn't you used to go out with her?"

"Mary Beth. Yeah, a long time ago."

"Still, it bothered you seeing her with them, didn't it?"

Even though he knew Maybell was right, he said, "Nope. What she does is her business."

"It's not natural hanging out with blacks. Don't you think?"

"You're right. It's not, but I'm not doing nothing about it. She dropped me. It didn't surprise me. I was about over her anyway."

"How old are you, Kenny?" Maybell asked after a pause.

"Seventeen. I turn eighteen in two months. How about you?"

"I'm twenty-one and I turn twenty-two in January. You're not in school, are you?"

Kenny shook his head.

"So, what do you do? Do you have a job?"

"I work with my father. He's a hunting guide. Me and him work with an outfitter in St. Louis called High Trail. They get us clients, and we take them on hunting trips. The season's about to start. We have a bunch of guys coming next week. The bow hunting season starts before they let in the people with the rifles."

"Sounds interesting. What exactly do you do?" Maybell leaned in closer.

"I help around the camp. There's a lot to do. My biggest job comes when we get the regular hunters. I'm in charge of checking out their rifles and getting them sighted in on the rifle range behind our house. And I lock the rifles in a special cabinet in my tent at the camp site."

"Do you hunt too?"

"Not when we're leading groups. Dad and me hunt after they're gone. Actually, don't tell anyone. We don't let things like hunting season bother us. We eat a lot of the things we kill."

"Are you a good shot?"

Kenny didn't know what was going on. Maybell had switched seats to his side of the table when she asked the last question. "Yes, if I do say so myself, I'm a real good shot. I was practicing from three hundred yards early this afternoon, and I could hit the beer cans down range pretty regular."

"Wow, from three hundred yards away." Maybell laid her hand on Kenny's knee.

Kenny jumped a little at the first touch. Then he looked at her and she smiled back while her hand started to rub his knee. "I always wanted to learn how to shoot a gun. Do you think you could teach me?" She slid closer to Kenny.

As she leaned toward him, all Kenny could see were her breasts. "Sure, sure, I have some time between the bow hunters and the regular season. Maybe you could come out to our house," he stammered as Maybell's hand crept up his leg. "Like I said, we have a shooting range."

"That would be great." She smiled at Kenny's gasp when her hand reached his crotch and rubbed his erection through his jeans. "Yeah, it would be great." As she continued to stroke him, Kenny's face flushed a deep crimson and he was about to burst. In a panic, he grabbed her hand and put it on the table. "Okay please stop." He shifted away from her and tried to slow his breathing.

"Impressive," she said.

"Huh?"

"Big," Maybell replied as she reached for her purse. She took out a pen, turned his hand over, and wrote a phone number on his palm.

"It's my number. Call any time after five-thirty if you want to see me again."

She gave his knee a squeeze and walked out of the restaurant. Kenny stared at her as she walked. When she reached the outside group, she turned and gave Kenny a little wave. She was something. He wondered why she'd come on to him. Maybe his height had something to do with it. As big as she was, lots of guys were shorter than her. Kenny felt good about being taller.

Kenny took his time with his remaining French fries. He had to get rid of his erection before walking anywhere. The Wilcox bunch left before things calmed down, which was just fine as far as he was concerned.

Maybell Wilcox thought about Kenny Sturgis as she drove home. She liked the way he jumped when she started touching him. She'd have him eating out of her hands in no time. His old girlfriend, Mary Beth, had told her about his shooting. If Kenny worked like she hoped, Maybell may have found the secret ingredient. She was eager to get home to tell her father.

Chapter Six

Ho Narwhal September 15, 1968

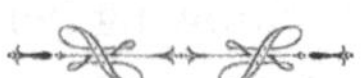

Ho had time on the plane ride to Viet Nam to think about what had happened since the judge gave him the option to volunteer for the draft. Most of the time he'd been in some kind of Army training—basic and then AIT, advanced infantry training. Sure enough, they assigned him to the infantry—a gun toting soldier. Just prior to the plane ride, he'd finished a two-week home leave.

Several surprises on his leave put things in perspective for Ho. First, Henry was about to be a free man. During basic training, he'd heard Henry had to stand trial, and he'd plead guilty. His six-month jail term ended right when Ho was going to land in Viet Nam. Though Henry had a six-month sentence, he was getting time off for good behavior. Ho had always suspected Henry had been lucky to be 4-F. He just didn't know how lucky. The way Ho figured it, because he was relatively healthy, he faced a two-year sentence in a war zone. The way guys were dying in Viet Nam, it could turn out to be a death sentence. Second, even Sam, who'd gotten a two-year sentence, would probably be free before Ho returned from Viet Nam. This comparison with his old buddies confirmed Ho's suspicion. Just like his father said, the world had it out for the Narwhals.

The change in his little sister was another surprise. Linda was fifteen, three years younger than Ho. When she first saw Ho, she gave him all sorts of compliments about how he looked. He had to admit he'd grown maybe a half inch in height, lost several inches around his waist, and put on some muscle. Actually, the changes in Linda shocked Ho. She'd changed a lot. She'd developed boobs and her backside had become more rounded too. Ho guessed it was inevitable. What bothered Ho most was the way she dressed— way too flirty. She seemed to be throwing herself at boys. When he tried to have a talk with her, she wouldn't listen. She yelled at him for deserting her. Still, she promised to send letters to Viet Nam. They both knew their dad wouldn't.

The final surprise was how few of his so-called friends wanted to talk to him. Maybe they didn't recognize him with his GI haircut, but he thought there was more to it. Most of them treated him like he had a contagious disease. Ho knew lots of people thought being in Viet Nam was a big mistake, and they seemed to be taking it out on him. Hell, he didn't make the decisions. It wasn't his fault lots of guys were dying for no good reason. Some older folks were different. They came up to him and said, "Thank you for your service." Ho didn't know how to react, since he didn't see how he'd been of service to those folks.

Ho looked down the rows of seats in the airplane in front of him, a regular passenger plane with no first-class section packed with guys in olive drab. Lots of them were probably headed for safe jobs: clerks, supply people, mechanics and so on. Not him. Ho was headed for an infantry unit. He'd be what they called a "grunt". It pointed out another way the world had it out for him. Heck, as a high school dropout, you'd think the army would have given him some kind of skill. No way. He was going to be carrying a rifle.

Basic training had been eye opening for Ho. The group of them who'd passed their physicals and been inducted in St. Louis all expected they'd be sent nearby to Fort Leonard Wood. They weren't. The seven of them were put on a plane. It was Ho's first plane ride, and when the plane encountered turbulence, he almost threw up. The plane landed in California, and they were sent to Fort Ord near Monterey. He went through basic with a bunch of guys from California, Colorado, and Arizona. He ended up being the only one from Missouri in his basic training platoon.

His father told him someone had stacked the deck against people like the Narwhals. Nothing about basic training made Ho doubt his dad. Every time he turned around, they were crapping on him. While he couldn't figure out why, something about him made the drill sergeants pick on him. He didn't have any trouble with the other guys, only the drill sergeants. They were all over him all the time. Every little misstep brought down a load of shit heavier than the last. Ho was sure he did more KP than anyone in his platoon. The drill sergeant made him do the stupid low crawl a bunch of times because he supposedly did it wrong.

He got along with the other trainees. One of the odd things was his clean-up job in basic. Lots of things had to be done to get the barracks ready for inspection. One day in the second week, Ho had been assigned to polish brass. There were brass plates and handles on the doors at both ends of the barracks. They had to be shined every day. Though Ho had never liked cleaning at home, he found he liked polishing brass. It was strangely rewarding. You could see instant progress. Since he'd let it be known a judge had sentenced him to the draft, everyone thought he was a badass, so no one complained when he said he'd do the brass each day. He volunteered for the same job in AIT.

Ho didn't figure there'd be any brass to polish in Viet Nam. He was really scared about going. He didn't read newspapers or watch the news, but he couldn't help hearing about the Tet Offensive. The war seemed to be changing and not for the better. He figured he'd be sent to a unit with places to fill because they'd lost a lot of people. Ho had never been political. Still, he couldn't see the point of the war. Hell, he didn't think one out of a hundred people could have found Viet Nam on a map before the whole thing started. It didn't matter. He was going, and he couldn't get out of it.

When Ho's plane landed at Ton Son Nhat International Airport in Viet Nam, he thought he's stepped right into hell. It was incredibly hot—like an oven. The plane had taxied onto a steel grid, not pavement. Ho and the other troops had to stand out on the blazing steel grid until everyone exited the plane and claimed his duffle bag. If all of Viet Nam was going to be like this, the year would be unbearable.

Three days after he arrived, Ho was assigned to a unit. A sergeant took him and another guy, Jerry Kimball, in a Jeep to join their new company. The Jeep trip was the first time he'd been off the base and had a chance to see the country. The entire place was flat, with lots of rice paddies. There were mountains further inland, but he wasn't headed there. The people he saw wore black silk pajamas and funny pointy hats, what he'd call coolie hats. There didn't seem to be civilian cars. People were either walking on the road or riding bicycles. They didn't seem to notice the Jeep as it went past. Ho guessed they'd seen plenty of US soldiers.

When the Jeep reached his company, they were camped out beside a dirt road a little way off the main paved road. The GIs looked weird to him. Basic training and AIT were all about having everything clean and polished. He didn't see anything like that. Most of the guys in his new unit weren't in full uniforms. They had long hair, and one of them appeared to be trimming his impressive Fu Manchu mustache with a Bowie knife. Some of the machine gunners had strings of bullets across their chests. They looked like Poncho Villa or something out of a movie. Like he'd suspected, Viet Nam didn't contain any brass for Ho to polish.

Ho figured he'd better keep his opinions to himself. When the Jeep stopped, he hoisted his enormous pack, and the sergeant led him and Jerry over to the company commander to report in. He and Jerry were assigned to the third platoon and taken to where they were camped. Nothing in particular seemed to be happening. The platoon sergeant welcomed them.

"Good. Fresh meat. What are your names?"

"Jerry Kimball."

"Horace Narwhal. Everyone calls me Ho."

"Where you guys from?"

"Missouri, Viceroy, Missouri," Ho responded. "It's a small place. Next to no one's heard of it."

"Pueblo, Colorado," Jerry said.

"Okay, I'm going to put both of you in the squad with Vargas. He's been here six months. He can show you the ropes." Then he yelled, "Vargas, get over here. I want you to show these new guys what to do."

The platoon members stared at him and Jerry. He returned the stares. They were a motley group. He felt like he stood out in his new uniform. A Mexican guy came over to them with his hand outstretched. "Hank Vargas," he said as he shook hands with Jerry and Ho.

"Horace Narwhal. I like to be called Ho."

"Jerry Kimball."

"Okay, come on over, and I'll show you where you can put your stuff."

Chapter Seven

Kenny Sturgis, September 4, 1980

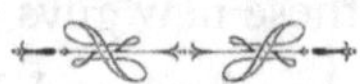

Kenny had a hard time waiting until five-thirty on Thursday. He thought it would have been cooler to make Maybell wait for two days, but he and his dad would be busy moving gear on Friday. The meeting he wanted so much had to be today. Once again, he cursed his father. They didn't have a phone at the cabin, so he had to use the pay phone at the bowling alley. Luckily the rain had stopped a couple of hours ago.

The phone rang four times before someone picked it up. A male voice said, "Mobile grooming, can I help you?"

Kenny didn't know how to respond. He knew he had the number right, so he stammered, "I'm looking for Maybell Wilcox. Is this the right number?"

"Yup, it's right. Maybell's not available right now. Can I have her call you?"

"When do you expect her?"

"Any minute now. Give me your number. She'll call right back."

"No, I'll call in a little while," Kenny said, hanging up.

What the hell? "Mobile grooming," with a guy answering? He felt like a fool not being able to give a number. He couldn't give the bowling alley number; he didn't know it. *Even if I did, sure as shooting, someone else would come to use the phone while I'm waiting for Maybell to return the call.*

Kenny cooled his heels in the bowling alley and watched a bunch of adults arriving for their league games. Their uniforms were dorky. Why the hell would grown people get dressed up in matching shirts with their names on the back? They weren't really athletes, only bowlers.

After fifteen minutes, Kenny tried the number again. This time Maybell answered, "Mobile grooming, can I help you?"

"I think you can. It's Kenny. You said to call if I wanted to see you."

"Oh, Kenny. I thought you might be eager. When did you have in mind?"

"Tonight, if it's okay. I have to help my father tomorrow. We might have to sleep out at the camp, and I could be tied up on Saturday. Would tonight work?"

"I can make it work. Come by our place at seven o'clock. You know where it is?"

"Off Overlook Road?"

"Yeah, a couple of hundred yards past the gas station. There's a confederate flag on the mailbox."

"See you at seven."

At seven on the dot, Kenny pulled into the Wilcox's long driveway. When he finally came to a clearing, a bunch of vehicles were parked in front of a ranch-style house. One of them was a big van with "Mobile Grooming" and a picture of a dog painted on its side. Maybell stood beside it, and she waved for Kenny to park behind the van.

As Kenny pulled up, he thought Maybell looked good. She had on a short skirt, low-cut green blouse, and a big smile. "Hi, stud," she called out as Kenny climbed out of his Jeep.

"Hi yourself," Kenny said as he walked up to Maybell, enjoying the view.

"Want to see where I work?"

"Sure."

Maybell opened the van's back door and said, "Welcome to my office," motioning for Kenny to enter.

While Kenny had to stoop a little to get through the door, he had no problem standing once he was inside. He glanced around. It was all set up for dog grooming—a little area to bathe the dogs and other areas where they could be cut. There were also a bunch of covered bins. Kenny figured grooming supplies were in them.

"Neat set up," Kenny said as Maybell came in behind him and closed the door.

She sidled close to him and said, "I didn't think you'd be so interested in the van. I thought you'd be more interested in me."

Kenny turned and smiled at her. She was incredibly hot. Her blouse revealed lots of cleavage, and the blue denim skirt was real short. "You know I'm interested in you."

Maybell responded, "I thought so," and leaned into him. She wrapped her right arm around his waist and at the same time, her right breast poked into his side. Kenny wasn't sure which point of contact made him jump. At least one of them did.

"Stay calm," Maybell said. Her left hand came up and she pulled Kenny's head closer so they could kiss.

Kenny kissed her back. It was nothing like kissing his old girlfriend, Mary Beth. Maybell opened her mouth and pressed her body into his in a way Mary Beth never did. After breaking off the kiss, Maybell stepped back a little and her hand went around to Kenny's crotch. She started to rub.

Kenny smiled at Maybell. "You don't waste much time, do you?"

"Why waste time. We both know why I wanted you to call, and we both know why you did."

"Yeah, we do." Partly to stop the effect of the rub and partly because he wanted to, he reached out to kiss Maybell again. This kiss was even longer and deeper. They both were panting when they broke apart.

"You'd better drop those clothes fast," Maybell said, as she pulled her top over her head. "I'm ready for action."

Kenny had a hard time paying attention to unbuttoning his shirt because he was too interested in watching Maybell disrobe. When she was completely nude, and Kenny was still working on his pants, Maybell said impatiently, "Come on stud, get with it."

When he finished undressing, Maybell wrapped herself around him. They hardly came up for air again until they were both spent. Obviously, she had used the grooming van for this kind of activity in the past. She knew just where they should position themselves.

After they finished, and his breathing returned to normal, Kenny said somewhat sheepishly, "Oh God, I brought a rubber. It happened so fast, I forgot all about it."

"Don't worry, I've got an IUD. And you're right; it was fast. Next time we can go a little slower. Let's get dressed and go for a little walk."

"Sure," Kenny said, wondering if the next time would be tonight.

All dressed, they exited the van, and Maybell showed Kenny a path. They took the path, walking side by side. Kenny grabbed her hand, and she started to laugh.

"What's so funny?"

Maybell turned to him. "So it's supposed to start out like the Beatles' song, you know, *I Want to Hold your Hand.* But we have it all backwards. We've already fucked, and now you want to hold my hand."

"Yeah, I guess we skipped a few steps." Kenny started walking again, still holding her hand. After a few moments of silence, he asked her how she got into the dog grooming business.

It turned out to be easy to talk to Maybell. She told him how she'd taken out a loan to outfit the van, and how the business worked. She got her big break when she'd taken over the customers of a woman who'd retired and moved to Florida. Since Maybell was better than the other woman, both at showing up on time and at grooming dogs, she'd been able to expand the business.

The path ended at a lake, where there was a bench. "This lake yours?" Kenny asked after they sat down.

"Yeah, it belongs to my family."

"Me and my dad have lots of property too, but nothing like this lake. Our land is just lots of forest. The lake looks like it's big enough to put a boat in. Do you guys have a boat?"

"We sure do. There's a dock around the corner. You can't see the Rebel Yell from here."

"What's up with all the confederate flags and a boat called the Rebel Yell? You guys have a thing about the civil war?"

"We do. My dad's folks fought for the South, and he thinks it's terrible the way they lost." After a pause, she continued. "And you know what? I agree with him. Things would be different if the South had won."

"How?"

"For one thing, there wouldn't be any blacks at the A&W bothering white girls like your old girlfriend. What's her name?"

"Mary Beth Sizemore."

"If the South had won, the races would be kept separate. There would be none of the racial mixing the federal government keeps forcing on us."

"I can see. Yeah, I guess that makes sense."

"You're not too political, are you, Kenny?"

"I guess not. My dad's so against any kind of politics, him and me never talk about it. Still, I can see what you're saying. The races ought to be kept separate. It's not natural for them to mix."

"You've got some real potential there, Kenny," Maybell said with a smile.

Kenny pulled Maybell to him and kissed her. When they broke apart, she said, "Ready to go again already?"

Kenny blushed. "You are so good looking. I just wanted to kiss you."

"So, you're not ready?"

"I didn't say that."

"Okay. Let's get back to the van. I don't like doing it out here. Too much dirt and too many bugs."

At ten o'clock, Kenny hopped into his Jeep. It had been incredible. Maybell had been right; the second time wasn't as fast, and it turned out to be better. He didn't know exactly what he'd expected, but this whole visit exceeded his wildest dreams. On top of it all, Maybell made it clear she was eager for more. He was coming back Sunday night.

As Kenny's Jeep pulled away, Maybell smiled. She had him hooked for sure. Kenny's naïveté made it easier. While she'd always been with men who were older, she liked that Kenny was younger. After a couple more bouts like tonight, he'd be willing to do anything she asked. He was a little clumsy when it came to sex, but she could teach him. As she'd told him, he had lots of potential. She walked back to the house, immensely pleased with herself.

Chapter Eight

Ho Narwhal, September 15, 1969

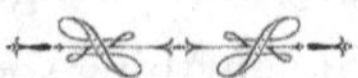

After twelve months and mounds of paperwork, Ho and Jerry finally filed onto the plane that was taking them home. They had a hard time not breaking out into big grins when they reached their seats. They weren't alone. Smiling GIs filled the rest of the plane. When the plane lifted off, all the passengers clapped and cheered. They were all thrilled to be leaving Viet Nam.

Ho sat back and thought about what he'd experienced. Luckily for him, he'd managed to get through his year without being in any pitched battles. They'd seen plenty of action in ambushes and small fire fights. Those fire fights were over in a hurry because they could call in air strikes, and the Viet Cong couldn't. While a few people in his company had been wounded, they didn't lose anyone. He knew he'd been lucky. Not everybody was going home in such good shape.

Ho reflected on his earlier thoughts back when he was on the plane to Viet Nam. He'd been convinced the cards were stacked against him. He'd had a rough time in basic and AIT, and he'd put it down to the drill sergeants picking on him. Now he wasn't so sure. His whole attitude, straight from his father, had been that the world was out to get him. For the last few months, Ho started to wonder if it wasn't a self-fulfilling prophecy. If you thought you were going to be a loser, didn't you start to act like one? If you thought the world was out to get you, didn't it put you in a position to be got?

Ho looked over at Jerry, who was trying to sleep. Jerry had been a big help. They'd arrived at the company the same day, so they were thrown together at the start. While their relationship had been a little awkward at first, after they had a chance to get better acquainted, they found they had a lot in common. Ho had never really had a close friend like Jerry, and it helped. Jerry suggested Ho should write to his sister, Sarah. After Jerry's introduction, Ho had written to her, and she responded immediately. Ho didn't know what to think would happen, but he was going home with Jerry after they were discharged. He was eager to meet Sarah. He suspected he was too hopeful. Sarah hadn't led him on in any way. Still, Ho allowed himself to fantasize about what could happen. Jerry had shown Ho a picture of his family, and Sarah, a petite blonde, looked really cute.

The way he saw it, everyone in his company had two objectives. The first was to survive. The second was to help everyone else survive. Maybe the higher-ups, the people directing the whole thing, had other ideas. Maybe they were interested in body counts, but Ho, Jerry, and their fellow soldiers weren't. When they were shot at, the higher-ups wanted them to "maintain contact," which was the last thing we wanted. Maintaining contact meant the bad guys were still shooting at us, and someone could get hurt. We wanted to break off contact. The less contact with the enemy the better. A guy could get hurt if he maintained contact.

This experience made him doubt another thing his father had always preached: the only way to advance was by stepping on someone else. In Ho's father's view, he'd always been the steppee, never the stepper. Ho, Jerry, and their fellow soldiers didn't want to step on anyone. They wanted to help each other. Some of them were promoted. On the main and on the whole, they were the ones who should have been promoted. Heck, Ho and Jerry were "spec fours" now. It didn't matter. No one tried to get ahead at anyone else's expense. They were interested in pulling together to survive. Of course, they had their complaints about the Army, about being in Viet Nam, about being away from home, and about C-rations. Still, they were happy lots of the time.

Another thing struck Ho about three-quarters of the way through his tour. Most of his fellow troops were wildly happy about eventually going home, particularly Jerry. It was different from wanting to get out of Viet Nam. They all wanted out. It was more than that. They wanted to get home. Some of them had wives and girlfriends. Jerry showed Ho most of his letters from his girlfriend, Suzanne. Reading the letters and seeing a picture of her made it clear why Jerry wanted to get home. While others didn't have a girl waiting, they had jobs or plans to go to college. The few who weren't happy about going home were thinking about reenlisting. Ho didn't fit. He was sure he was through with the army, but going home didn't hold much appeal either. It offered him nothing. Ho wondered where he could find a better future than the one waiting for him.

No matter what he wanted, he knew he had to go back to his father's house. His sister needed him. Her letters had been full of complaints about their father. Though Ho found it hard to believe, Linda said his drinking was worse. He'd lost another job. As far as Ho knew, his father was still collecting unemployment. On top of it all, two months ago Linda had injured her leg in a car accident. Ho didn't know the details. It worried him. He couldn't be there, and she needed help. While apparently she'd gotten better, she said the leg still hurt at times.

When the plane landed, they were taken to Oakland to be officially processed out. Even though Ho, Jerry, and the rest of the draftees hadn't served their full two years, the army didn't need or want them. They were getting early outs.

Dressed in their formal green uniforms, Ho and Jerry were dropped at the San Francisco airport with a bunch of other guys. They only had standby tickets, not reservations. All the colors Ho saw at the airport dazzled him.

He'd been in a sea of olive drab for more than a year. People wore red, yellow, blue, purple, and bright green. He noticed the girls, too. He'd seen a few American women in his year in Viet Nam, but not many. There were certainly not any women in the short skirts he saw in the airport. He couldn't believe the clothes the hippie girls were wearing. It was almost a culture shock. Finally, he noticed the way people looked at him. As far as he could tell the looks were disapproving, like he'd done something wrong. He and Jerry weren't welcomed home as war heroes by any means.

They were lucky enough to get seats on the second flight they tried and made it to Denver. In Denver, it took a while to find a bus to Pueblo, but they succeeded. When the bus stopped, Ho let Jerry get off first and hung back while he greeted his parents.

"You must be Ho," Jerry's mom said after she released her son. "Welcome back."

Ho shook Jerry's mom's hand and then his father's. Meanwhile a young woman came running up and leaped into Jerry's arms.

"Must be Suzanne," Ho commented.

"You're a good guesser," Jerry's dad laughed.

The five of them agreed on a restaurant for dinner and after they'd loaded their duffle bags into Jerry's folk's car, Ho and Jerry rode together in Suzanne's car. While Ho had seen pictures of her, Suzanne was different in person. She'd cut her brown hair shorter, and she was taller than he'd expected. As he sat in the back seat, he began to realize he'd probably not see much of Jerry during this visit. Suzanne was almost sitting in Jerry's lap as he drove.

At dinner, Jerry's mom told them Sarah and a friend were driving in from Boulder the next day. Ho knew Sarah was at the university from her letters. Because she was in college, the fact that he was a high school dropout didn't make him feel good about his chances with her. Still, her letters had been encouraging.

Sleeping in the Kimball's guest room turned out to be a luxury for Ho. He hadn't slept in a bed with sheets and a pillow the entire time he'd been in Viet Nam. Breakfast the next morning was great too. The eggs were real, not the powdered eggs he'd been fed at the mess hall at base camp. Actually, anything would have been better than C-rations. Ho envied Jerry's family life. He couldn't remember the last time he and Linda had eaten breakfast with their father—like a "real" family.

After breakfast, Jerry took Ho on a tour of Pueblo. First, they picked up Suzanne. Then they stopped to see some of Jerry's friends. Everyone had been alerted of his return by Suzanne, so the people weren't surprised. Still, they seemed thrilled to see Jerry.

Ho knew he was a fifth wheel for sure. Also, he felt self-conscious in the one set of civilian clothes he'd purchased at the San Francisco airport, so he asked to be dropped off at a shopping mall. The two love birds agreed to pick him up at noon.

Back at Jerry's house, his mother fixed lunch. After a while, Ho recognized what was going on. They were all waiting around for Sarah's arrival. At two o'clock a car pulled up and two people stepped out. One was Sarah, and the other, her friend, was a guy. The guy escorted Sarah up the front walk with his arm around her. Ho's heart sank.

Two days later, Ho said goodbye to the Kimball family and rode a bus back to Denver. Despite the warm welcome, the stay in Pueblo had been a disaster for Ho. While he liked seeing where Jerry lived and meeting some of his friends, clearly Jerry wanted to spend more time with Suzanne than with Ho. He'd fantasized about Sarah in Viet Nam, but the reality was completely different. She hardly spoke to him. He reverted to his old thought patterns. *The world is stacked against me.*

Ho hit some luck back in the Denver airport. He got a seat on the first plane leaving for Missouri. In St. Louis, he rode a bus into the city and checked into a cheap hotel. After he dumped his duffle bag beside the bed, he looked at himself in the mirror. He liked what he saw. He was now a tall, slim, muscular guy. Miracle of miracles, his face had cleared up in Viet Nam. Also, it was apparent that he'd grown an inch or two. He hadn't liked the steady diet of C-rations, but it probably helped take off the weight. Also, carrying the heavy backpack all the time was real exercise. His brown hair was a reasonable length, though probably too short to be fashionable in 1969. He'd never thought of himself as good looking, and he probably wasn't. Still, he thought his appearance had improved during his year in Viet Nam.

The next morning, he returned to the bus station and found a bus with a stop in Viceroy. Right before the bus took off, he watched the bus driver load the last remnant of his Army days, the olive drab duffle bag. The trip home took about four hours. He'd called Linda on a pay phone in the bus station to tell her his scheduled arrival time. At least she seemed excited to have him coming home.

The scenery on the bus ride wasn't anything to get excited about and his fellow passengers all seemed to want to sleep. The whole thing bored Ho. When they pulled away from their stop in Tyndall, a little city about an hour from Viceroy, something he saw excited him—a help-wanted sign at a brass bed factory. Up to this point, Ho didn't have the faintest idea what kind of work he could find. Working with brass again might be interesting. He cursed himself for not having a piece of paper or a pen. He couldn't write down the phone number. He tried to memorize the stores around and the name of the street. He had really liked polishing the brass in basic and AIT. He decided to try to get back here as soon as he could.

Ho was the only one who exited the bus in Viceroy. Linda, who'd been there waiting for him, ran to him as he retrieved his duffle bag from under the bus. She jumped into his arms and gave him a big hug. When he put her down, she winced a little. She could tell he noticed, so she said, "It still hurts sometimes. I guess I should have been more careful jumping on you like that. Step back, let me get a look at you."

"Do you think I changed in Viet Nam?"

"No silly. It's because I haven't seen you in a year, but you've changed and in a good way. You grew over there, didn't you? And you've lost weight! You look great."

"You look good too," Ho said, suppressing what he really thought. Linda had put on some weight, and it wasn't a good look. Her blue dress was too tight. Maybe it had been hard for her to exercise because of the accident.

"I guess we'd better get home," Linda said. "Dad almost came with me, but then he backed out at the last minute. He'll want to see you."

Ho felt funny getting in a car and having his sister drive. She drove his dad's old Chevy, and compared to the Kimball's cars, it was a little trashy. When they arrived home, Ho could tell his dad had been drinking, and it was only noon.

"Good to see you, son," his father said, holding out his hand. Ho shook his father's hand.

"Is my old room still available?"

"Yeah, your sister cleaned it out this morning."

"Thanks," Ho said as he lugged his duffle bag into his old room. He found it depressingly the same.

After putting up his duffle bag, Ho returned to the front room. "I'm going to take you two out to eat and catch up on what's happened."

"Whoa, you're going to take us out. You mister money bags now?" his father asked.

"I have some money. They paid us, but there was nothing to spend it on, and my checking account got ten percent interest. They gave me combat pay on top of my salary, and I got promoted a couple of times. I'm in pretty good shape right now."

At the restaurant, Ho heard all the gossip. It didn't seem like much around Viceroy had changed. As usual Ho's father continued to be sour about everything. He'd lost his last job because his boss was unreasonable about the couple of times he'd shown up late. He had another three weeks of unemployment checks, so his job search would start in a week. Linda was starting her senior year in high school. She said she hated school. Ho told her to stick it out through graduation. He said dropping out of high school was about the dumbest thing he'd ever done. By the end of the meal, Ho had the impression things were much the same in Viceroy. While the town hadn't changed, he had.

After they returned from lunch, Ho asked to borrow the car so he could go to the bank. He had a certified check from his Viet Nam bank, and he wanted to open a checking account. Ho found driving weird. He hadn't driven since his leave before Viet Nam. When he finished at the bank, he had an account with over $6,000 in it. For one of the first times in his life, he felt like he had real money and maybe even a good shot at something.

Before going to bed, he planned the next day's events. Ho said he'd drive Linda to school, so they could have the car. Then he and his father planned to go to the used car lot to see if they could find something for Ho. They figured the lot would be open by nine-thirty. Ho was eager to get going. His father seemed less than happy with the arrangement, but none the less, he agreed.

His father hadn't awakened when Ho returned from taking Linda to school. By quarter to ten, he still wasn't awake. Ho checked the trash. There was an empty rum bottle on top. He'd seen the same bottle the night before. It had been half full when Ho turned in last night. At ten o'clock, Ho left a note for his father and went off to the car lot.

At the car lot, Ho didn't like the options. He knew he didn't want to spend more than half of his money on a car. He test drove two of the cars in his price range and finally decided he wanted the blue four-year-old Plymouth, two-door coupe with 63,000 miles on it. Ho figured it would last him for a while. He bargained with the guy a little, threatened to leave once, then finally agreed on a price three-hundred dollars under the starting price. The guy had to call the bank to be sure Ho's check was good. In the end, Ho went out to the lot and put a sold sign on the car. He drove his dad's car home and got his father to take him back to the lot so he could pick up his new car.

The next morning, Ho took Linda to school in his new car and headed for Tyndall. He hoped the help-wanted sign was still up. He had no trouble finding the place and the sign was still there. He'd put on his best civilian outfit. Unfortunately, it was a little wrinkled, but he couldn't find an iron at his house. He spotted the sign over the factory: Cunningham Brass Beds. As he opened the door, he wondered if he would be talking to Mr. Cunningham.

He walked up to the middle-aged secretary at the front desk. After greeting her, Ho asked about the help-wanted sign. She smiled at him and said, "Yes, the job's still open." After she shuffled some papers around on her desk, she held one out. "Fill out this application. It will get the process started. You can sit over there at the empty desk."

Ho started on the application. It didn't take him long to fill out most of it. He didn't have much work history, only the job at the Quick Stop and the army. The references section stumped him. As he puzzled over what to do, a man in a light brown business suit and a paisley tie came through the front door. He gave Ho a smile and went over to the secretary. Ho overheard her tell the man Ho was a job applicant.

The man turned to Ho and said, "Son, why don't you bring the application back to my office. We can talk things over."

Apprehensive but encouraged, Ho followed the man into his office. The man was medium height, bald, and a little overweight. The little wisp of remaining hair was reddish, and he had a red complexion. He sat behind a big desk and motioned for Ho to take a chair facing the desk. "I'm Horace Cunningham," he said. "I own this place, and I understand you're looking for a job."

"What are the odds? I'm Horace Narwhal. I don't run into many other Horaces."

The two shook hands. "No," Mr. Cunningham said, "I can't say as I meet many other people named Horace."

"People call me Ho."

"Okay, Ho. Let me see the application."

"It's not finished. I got hung up on the references part."

"Let's see it anyway."

Mr. Cunningham perused what Ho had written. "So, you're a high school drop out?"

"Yes. The stupidest thing I've ever done."

"And you recently mustered out of the army?"

"Yes sir, I finished up my tour in Viet Nam a week ago. I made it home day before yesterday."

"You don't list any criminal record."

"Technically no. Let me explain. A judge said he'd drop the charges for a botched robbery if I'd volunteer for the draft. I chose the Army over jail and a record. I want to be up front about my past."

"Good, I like your attitude. So, you're just out of the army. What did you do?"

"I was in the infantry. I made it to Specialist Fourth Class. I don't think it prepared me for any job, but I'm willing to learn, and I know how to work hard."

Mr. Cunningham took a long look at Ho and then said, "I'm going to take a chance on you, Ho. Veterans usually make good employees. You don't do drugs, do you?"

"No sir. I don't even drink much."

"The job pays the minimum wage. If you work out, you'll get raises. Also, I'm going to put one condition on you. I want you to enroll in a GED course. I want you to have the high school equivalency within a year of starting here. I'll give you time off work if you need it. Sound okay?"

"Yes sir, yes sir. You won't regret taking a chance on me."

"All right, go out to Sally, and she'll have the paperwork for you. I'm not promising you a cushy job. While it's hard work out on the factory floor, I bet it's going to be easier than being in the infantry in Viet Nam."

Chapter Nine

Kenny Sturgis, September 7, 1980

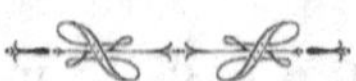

Kenny and Maybell met up Sunday morning in the dog grooming van. Like the previous meeting, they didn't talk much before they took off their clothes and tore into each other. After a satisfying twenty minutes, they agreed Kenny should show Maybell the hunting camp.

Once dressed, Kenny said, "As much as I like your short skirt, it's not going to work good at the camp. You might want to change into jeans."

"Listen to you, giving orders."

"I'm only looking out for you."

"Okay, don't go anywhere. I'll be back in a flash."

Kenny was waiting next to his Jeep when Maybell came running out of her house. She'd changed into jeans and still had on the skimpy red top showing a lot of cleavage. Kenny liked it. She also had a six-pack of beer with her.

The drive to the camp took forty-five minutes. They didn't talk much because of the road noise. The last ten minutes of the drive was on dirt roads. Luckily the rain a couple of days ago kept the dust to a minimum. Kenny had to unlock a couple of gates before they reached the parking area.

The camp had seven big tents in a circle around an open area with a fire ring in the middle. The tents were made of heavy green canvas.

Maybell did a circuit of the tents. "It smells a little funny."

"It's the wet canvas, I think. The smell goes away after a while, or maybe I just get used to it. Come here and look at this tent. It's the cook tent. It even has a stove and an icebox."

Maybell poked around in the cook tent. "You get ice somewhere, so you can keep stuff cold?"

"Yeah, at the start of the week. Most times, hunters are with us for a week. The High Trails folks, the outfitter my dad and me work with, bring us the food the clients have ordered, and we get the ice. My dad's been doing this for a bunch of years. He has it pretty much figured out. Sometimes a picky client wants something off the menu, and it's usually my job to go get it. It doesn't happen much. We're not plugged in out here. The clients like it. They want to escape from civilization."

"What about showers or baths?"

"It's back here." Kenny showed Maybell the shower tent. "We were able to tap a spring, so we don't have to haul water. It's a frigging cold shower. You know, the clients seem to like it. It makes them feel like they're tough."

After he showed her the shower, he pointed and said, "There's a latrine back there. I bet it'll be fine with you to skip it."

"Definitely. Which one of these tent's yours?"

"Come on, I'll show you. The other tents, the ones for the clients, sleep two and sometimes three. Me and my dad have singles."

"I bet we can get two of us on the cot." Maybell started unzipping her jeans.

"I bet we can." Kenny made the same move.

Later Kenny went to the Jeep to get the six-pack. He extracted two of the folding chairs from one of the client tents, and he and Maybell sat down with their beers. Maybell asked, "You said your dad has wacky politics. What does that mean?"

"I don't know. I guess it goes back a ways. I think he inherited it from his father. I don't know where my granddad got it from. Anyway, he's an anarchist. He doesn't believe in government. He thinks the world would be a better place if there were no governments at all. The funny thing about him though is, if we didn't have any government, we'd have to do lots of negotiating, and he hates people. He never wants to negotiate."

"What do you mean? I don't get it."

"Okay, yeah, so what side of the road do you drive on?"

"The right, of course."

"With no government, if some guy wanted to drive on the left, who'd stop him?"

Maybell looked at Kenny and smiled. "Oh, I see, no cops."

"Yeah, so the only way I think it'd work would be for everyone to have a big meeting and decide which side of the road to drive on, but my dad would never go to the meeting. Also, even if the meeting decided on the right, what if some ornery guy still wanted to drive on the left?"

"Yeah."

"And it's not only the side of the road. Where'd you put the bridges, who'd own the roads, and who'd settle fights with no courts? It'd be a big mess."

"So, if it doesn't make sense, why's he believe in it?"

"He thinks he can live on his thirty acres and not bother anyone. He can't see why other people can't do the same. He's got no need for government."

"Doesn't he have to pay taxes?"

"No, he's proud of the fact he's never paid any taxes. He doesn't have a social security number, and as far as I know the county doesn't bother us. The High Trails people pay him in cash, completely off the books. It's how he pays me, too."

"Do you have a Social Security number?"

"Yeah, I do. My mom got one for me when I started school. That was probably one of the things that started my folk's divorce. It happened before they really started fighting, but I remember it being something they yelled about when they were arguing. She left us when I was eight or nine. I don't remember. I never see her."

"Must hurt."

"Naw, it's no big deal. She made her choice. Me and dad get along okay."

Maybell finished her beer, stood up, and threw the empty can into the woods behind Kenny's tent.

"Whoa there." Kenny got up to retrieve the can. "You can't do that. My dad would skin me alive if he found a beer can anywhere near the camp. Shit, I'm not even supposed to bring anyone out here. We have to be sure we left everything the way we found it."

"Sorry." Maybell shrugged. "I should have thought more."

Kenny came back with the can. "It's okay."

"Sorry again."

"Let's change the subject. I've told you about my father's weird politics. I can tell it's way different from your folks and all the confederate flags. What's that all about?"

"Yeah, we're a little different. Like I said before, my family's always been hung up on the Civil War. My dad calls it the War of Northern Aggression. He thinks it should never have happened. The people in the South should have been able to form their own country if they wanted to. It was wrong for the northern states to force them to stay in this country."

"That happened a long time ago."

"It doesn't make it right. And remember what happened. They set the slaves free, and what did you get? Racial mixing. It's what gets us riled up. The government is forcing racial mixing. The stupid supreme courts forced us to go to school with the black kids. Even the supreme court said states can't have laws banning mixed marriage. Everywhere you turn, there's an attack on the white race."

"I've been thinking about what you said the other day. Your parents think if the South had won the war, things would be different?"

"Yeah, different." Maybell smiled. "Different and better. Unlike your dad, my folks and now me too, we're real active in politics. We have to do all we can to protect the purity of the white race. If people don't want to mix, and I don't see why they'd want to, the government shouldn't force them."

"Actually, you sound like my dad. He's forever saying the government should get off people's backs."

"If I heard you right, he's running away. We don't. We keep fighting for what we believe in. My dad was real active in the George Wallace campaign. His getting shot was terrible. He understood the importance of keeping the white race on top."

Kenny could tell Maybell was really into this. He checked his watch and said, "We'd better clean up and get out of here. It's getting late, and the mosquitos will be out soon."

"My politics bother you, Kenny?"

"No, in fact, I think I probably agree with you. It sure makes more sense than what I hear from my dad all the time."

Chapter Ten
Ho Narwhal, October 1, 1971

Walking away from the factory, Ho opened his paycheck. He couldn't believe the note in the envelope. He'd received another raise. For some reason the raise, his third in the two years he'd worked at the brass-bed factory, wouldn't take effect for another month. Since he could do most of the jobs in the factory, he guessed he deserved it. He'd been able to fill in for maybe half of the people when they were out sick or on vacation.

On his way to his new apartment in Tyndall, Ho thought about his life. Things were going well but not everything. His father was still a mess, and lately he'd been hinting Ho ought to fork over some money. Linda also still struggled. She had no judgement when it came to men. There seemed to be a revolving door letting in bums. Ho had helped her with money, because with his sister, money seemed to go over better than advice.

His apartment had a small living room with a kitchen, a bathroom, and a bedroom. The rent was affordable, and with his new raise, maybe he could start saving. It was Friday night, and Ho had arranged to meet Rich and Janet at Joey's at nine-thirty. He'd met them in an art class at the community college. Mr. Cunningham had forced him to get a GED, and he had. Truth be told, it wasn't tough to pass the test. He was doing the community college course on his own. He figured he liked art class in high school, so why not try one in college?

After he changed out of his work clothes, Ho showered, dressed in khakis and a blue striped shirt, and fixed himself a simple supper. While he'd started getting a newspaper, he never had time to read it in the morning, so he sat down now to read it. The headlines were about the wage-price controls the Nixon administration was cooking up. Thinking about it, Ho figured out it was why his raise didn't go into effect for a month. The wage-price freeze started in August and would last for ninety days, an effort the administration was making to counter rising inflation. Horace had timed his raise for after the freeze. Ho wondered if his raise would violate the controls the administration was going to impose. He figured there was nothing he could do about it, so it shouldn't bother him.

One of the things Ho had been working on was not getting bothered by things he couldn't control. He'd started a personal campaign to rid himself of the leftover effects of his father's teachings. His experiences in Viet Nam and now here at the factory showed Ho that his father was wrong. People weren't out to get him. He and his fellow soldiers had worked together to make sure they all survived. At the factory, they were working together to fill the orders. Horace Cunningham turned out to be a great boss. There had been Christmas bonuses for all the workers. Ho even received one his first year, despite having only worked for a few months before Christmas. Now Ho was clearly part of the team.

The more he got to know him, the more Ho liked Horace Cunningham. Horace made no bones about it. He went to church, and the factory and store closed on Sunday. Horace was a great believer in the golden rule. It was painted on one of the walls in the factory. *Do Unto Others as You Would Have Them Do Unto You.* Horace lived it, too. He treated people right. Heck, he gave Ho a chance when he didn't have to. He was so different from Ho's dad.

Ray's golden rule would maybe be, do unto others before they do it unto you.

Rich and Janet were already at the bar when Ho walked in. Rich was big, maybe six-foot-four with red hair. Janet was more normal sized, about five-five or five-six, and a blonde. Their story started out a bit hokey and then had its ups and downs. In high school, Rich played football and made all-state, and Janet led the cheerleaders. Rich accepted a football scholarship to college, and Janet followed. Things were going fine until a serious knee injury ended Rich's football dreams. He'd had to drop out of college. To her credit, Janet stuck with him. They married and settled down back home in Tyndall.

"Good to see you, Ho," Rich said as Ho slid into the booth across from them. "We've already ordered our first round. The waitress should be back soon to get your order. We told her we were expecting someone."

"I'm simple," Ho said. "I'll take whatever dark beer they have on tap."

"You seem to be smiling a lot. What's making you so happy?" Janet asked.

"A note in my paycheck said I'm getting a raise starting next month."

"I get it," Rich said. "They couldn't give you a raise now because of Nixon's freeze."

"I guess so. Whatever. I'll take it."

The waitress returned in her pretend western outfit and took Ho's order.

After a lull, Janet said, "Ho, Rich and I have been talking about the trouble you're having in class. You're funny. You never seem to agree with the professor's analysis of the artist's motivation."

"Yeah, explain yourself," Rich added.

Ho nodded. "I think most of the time, the artist's only motivation is to make something he thinks looks good—something he likes. I think most of the 'analysis of the artist's motivation' is a bunch of bull."

"Even when the artist writes something as an explanation?" Janet asked.

"Yes, it's all pretentious bullshit. The artist says something because he knows the so-called art experts want to hear it."

"I don't see it," Rich commented.

"Let me give you an example. Suppose the artist says his painting represents his fight with convention. His painting is a bunch of straight colored lines going all different directions. My point is he could have done a lot of oblong shapes in different colors going in different directions. Both could represent defying convention. He drew the lines because he liked lines. He didn't want to draw oblong shapes."

"And you say the part about defying convention is crap he says to make people think his paintings have deep meaning?" Janet asked.

"You got it. I think the guy likes different colored lines, but he has to pretend to have a reason. I bet the painter didn't try to show emotion or some abstract idea. He tries to paint something he likes. Saying it's about emotion or an idea happens later to please the art world."

"Okay, now I understand you," Rich said. "Basically, you're a cynic. Still, you'd better be quiet about it in class. Clearly, the prof doesn't agree with you. In case you haven't heard, the secret to success in college classes is figuring out what the professor believes and spitting it back on the exam."

"Now you're the cynic?" Janet commented.

"Tell me I'm wrong."

"I can't. I think it's too bad."

Rich continued, "Some of the professors are better than others. Some of them want open discussion and encourage different opinions. I don't know about this guy. Take the painting in Ho's example. The lines could be about defying convention, or about confusion in the world, or about too much linear thinking, or whatever. If, according to the professor, the artist said it's about defying convention, that had better be what's on your test."

"I see," Ho responded. "Maybe I'd better tone down what I say in class. Don't misunderstand me. I can see how artists who do representational paintings are intending to make a particular point. Sometimes it's obvious, but the abstracts are hard for me."

The discussion turned to different subjects, Ho's lack of female companionship for one. While Ho would have liked to have a girlfriend, he told them he didn't have enough money to really take a girl out and show her a good time. Also, he had to go home to Viceroy a lot of weekends. His sister needed help. She was still living with their father most of the time. Ho had to keep the peace between them, and it was hard.

Rich and Janet's quandary about when to start a family also came up. Since Ho didn't think he had any expertise on the topic, he simply acted as a sounding board. Sometimes people needed a listener, and Ho could do that. Rich and Janet weren't too far apart on the basic issue. The difficulty was the timing. Janet wanted to get a little more established in her career as a dental hygienist, but Rich wanted to start immediately. They were only talking about a year's difference. Ho stayed out of it for the most part.

As Ho walked back to his apartment, he felt good. He enjoyed being with Rich and Janet. He'd also met some of their friends who came over to the booth to talk. The one beer he nursed most of the night didn't help him remember any names. He'd have to try harder the next time he met them. One of the advantages with his odd nickname was people almost always remembered it—or was that actually a disadvantage?

Chapter Eleven

Kenny Sturgis, September 13, 1980

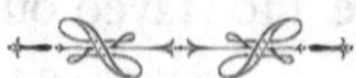

Kenny and Maybell couldn't get together until the next weekend. Kenny had been busy with the bow hunters all week. When he arrived at the Wilcox place, he didn't see Maybell. He'd expected to meet her by the van. He walked over to the van to look around and spotted a sign on the door. It said, "Come in Kenny." He opened the door and found Maybell with an orange ribbon in her hair and nothing else.

"Come here, stud. I've missed you," Maybell said, opening her arms.

About a half hour later when they retrieved their clothes, Maybell said, "Let's go into the house; my folks want to meet you."

Kenny was taken aback. *Shouldn't meeting the parents happen later in a relationship?* Still, he said, "Sure. Do I look okay?"

"You're fine. Did you take a shower before coming over? You don't smell like the camp."

Kenny walked alongside Maybell to the house. When he entered the front room, the lights were dim. The curtains were closed, and the walls had dark wood paneling. If the window hadn't been curtained, it might have reminded

Kenny of the log cabin where he lived.

Maybell's dad, a short, bald man, rose from his chair and came over to shake Kenny's hand. "Kenny, is it?"

"Yeah, Kenny Sturgis."

"I'm Jack, Jack Wilcox."

Kenny went over to the chair where Maybell's mom sat. Her looks were an unusual combination of her two daughters. Except for being closer to Maybell's size, at one time she was probably a good-looking girl like Joan. She had the same blonde hair and fair skin. Kenny found it odd. She was quite a bit taller than her husband. "Don't get up, ma'am," Kenny said as he reached out his hand.

"I'm Ruth. Pleased to meet you, Kenny."

"Sit over there." Jack pointed to the couch. "You too, Maybell."

Kenny took a quick look around. At first, he could see little resemblance between Maybell and her father. Then he noticed they both had the same big ears and a sort of off-center face. The more he looked, the more he became convinced Maybell's mom had been a real babe in her youth. A confederate flag covered in glass in a frame hung on the wall behind Maybell's father. *Jack. I've gotta remember to call him Jack*, Kenny thought.

"I see you've spotted the flag," Jack said.

"Yes. It looks old. Is there a story behind it?"

"Yes, there is. It's the battle flag for the regiment my kin, Lemuel Wilcox, led in the war. Even though Lem didn't survive, the flag got passed down to his wife. It's been in the family ever since. We're all real proud of Lemuel."

A silence followed, and Kenny figured he'd better fill it. "I don't have anything like that in my family. My dad never talks about our family history. As far as I know, we started from scratch with my grandfather. I've never heard of anyone before him."

Maybell asked, "So you don't even know where you're from? I mean, before your family came to this country."

"No, not for sure. I guess I heard my dad say something about being Scotch.

Then again it might just mean he's tight with money. He sure is."

They all laughed, pleasing Kenny.

Maybell's mom shifted in her seat. "Given your appearance, the blond hair, blue eyes, and fair complexion, you might be Scotch, or English, or even German or something up north."

"I'm most likely a mutt," Kenny said, trying to keep the humor going.

"Lots of us are," Jack said with a laugh. "Maybell said your dad has some interesting political ideas. I'm curious about that."

"Ummm… okay. Sure. He's basically a full-on anarchist. He doesn't think there should be any government at all. I don't get it. I don't see how it would work."

"I'll be damned! I didn't think there was anyone more in favor of limited government than me. It appears your dad may have me topped. No government at all, you say?"

"Yep, he thinks he can do fine on his thirty acres, and he doesn't see how everyone else can't do exactly the same."

"Does he use money?"

"Yeah, and it burns him up. He hates that the money he's forced to use is made by the government. He has a stash of gold too. I think he'd use it all the time if it weren't so cumbersome."

"I can't totally agree with your father. Government can be useful. What I don't like is the federal government. I don't see how people in Washington and New York, or California for that matter, should be telling us in Missouri what to do. It's none of their business."

"I can see that," Kenny responded.

Jack continued, "I'm a Jeffersonian. The government that governs least governs best. That's what Thomas Jefferson said. Jefferson's a Southerner, from Virginia. It's where my folks came from. Anyway, the federal government has been stretching its hands out and taking more and more power from the states where the power ought to be. It's all about giving things to the blacks. The taxes are high on white folks so they can give more money to the blacks.

I mean, what is welfare, anyway? Also, there's lots of things states can't do. States can't run separate schools for the races. They have to be integrated. States can't decide who can vote. Ignorant blacks are supposed to vote too. The whole so-called civil rights movement is a way for blacks to take more from whites. There's even more to it. The federal government's run by Jews, because most of the politicians are financed by Jews."

While Jack spoke, Kenny glanced over at Maybell. She stared at her father with big eyes. She clearly adored the guy and liked what he had to say.

When Jack stopped speaking, Kenny said, "You know sir, I agree with you. There's no way people in New York and Washington know what it's like to live here. If we want to separate the races in schools, or anywhere else, we ought to be allowed to do it. We're supposed to be a democracy. If the people vote for something, they should get it."

"You're right, boy. And you know where the problem is. A big part of it is the Supreme Court. Nine guys in Washington, DC can strike down a law passed in a state, no matter how much people in the state wanted the law."

Maybell jumped in at this point. "Congressmen from New York, hell they have so many people in New York they get a lot of votes in Congress, and they can pass laws we have to follow even though we'd never have voted for them. I tell you I don't feel like I live in a democracy. I feel like I'm being dictated to."

"You know the kinds of laws Maybell's talking about," Jack said. "She's talking about the kinds of laws forcing racial mixing. We're getting more and more of those. All races have to be served at restaurants. Blacks have to be allowed to use the same barbers as whites. You can't even keep them out of cemeteries. There's lots of those kinds of laws."

"You know, I never thought about that before. There aren't many blacks living around here."

"Why do you think we moved out here boy? Unfortunately, it's coming. If a colored family wanted to buy the Johnson place right next to us, do you think we could stop 'em? No, no we couldn't. It would be against the law—a federal law."

Ruth shifted in her seat and spoke up, "Enough politics, you two. Can't we talk about something else?"

"Okay, darling, but I don't think Kenny minds."

"No, it's interesting."

Maybell filled the short silence. "Why don't you tell them what you and your dad do? It's interesting too."

A half hour later, Maybell and Kenny excused themselves and the senior Wilcoxes knew all about the way Kenny and his father led groups of hunters. They were particularly interested in the regular hunters, not the bow hunters. He surprised Jack when he mentioned the shooting range on their property. Kenny bragged a little about his marksmanship and told them he was in charge of getting all the rifles the clients brought ready for a successful hunt.

As they were walking away from the house, Kenny asked. "What's next? I think I passed the test with your parents."

"Oh, you passed all right. I think they liked you. They don't usually like the boys I bring home."

"So, there've been a bunch of guys you've brought home before?"

"Not many, and none of them as nice as you," Maybell said as she bumped into Kenny and grabbed at his crotch.

Kenny smiled. "Okay, so what's next?"

"Let's take a drive. There's a place I want to show you."

After a short drive on the main road, Maybell told Kenny to turn right on a dirt road. The road made several switchbacks as it climbed a small mountain. At the crest stood a lookout tower with a few parking places. The stairs were in good shape, and they started climbing. When she got to the platform on the top, Maybell went to the railing.

"Come on over. The view's great."

"No, I'm not so good with heights. I'll stay here in the middle if you don't mind. I can see out all the sides. I just don't like the edge."

"Don't be a sissy."

"No, it's not that. It's something I can't control," Kenny responded with an edge in his voice.

"Oh now I've hurt your feelings. I didn't mean to."

"Isn't there something you get freaked out by—small places, spiders, snakes, big windstorms, or anything?"

"I'm not so hot on small tight places, claustrophobia I think they call it."

"Okay, so heights do it to me."

Maybell came over and hugged Kenny. "I shouldn't have called you a sissy. Let's go back down."

At the bottom, Maybell led Kenny over to a tree, turned toward him, and took off her blouse and bra and started kissing him.

When Kenny came up for air, he said, "I thought you didn't like the bugs and dirt."

"Shut up," Maybell said as she pulled him in again.

Chapter Twelve

Ho Narwhal, March 16, 1977

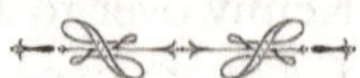

Ho sat in his new spacious apartment pondering his life. Things had changed dramatically in the last few years. He'd started work at Cunningham Brass Beds almost eight years ago and his role had changed considerably during that time. He wasn't even technically an employee anymore. The big change started by accident, but now it had turned into a whole new job.

It all started the fifth year he worked at the factory. One of his assignments then had been to gather the brass scraps. He swept the floors, sifted what he'd swept to remove the brass, and picked up the larger pieces of scrap. As much as Horace Cunningham tried to order precisely what they needed, the production process always generated scrap and various shavings to be sent to the foundry. By the end of each week, he had a substantial pile of brass to be recycled. About six months after Ho had been assigned this task, he started amusing himself by arranging the larger pieces of scrap into elaborate towers. The other workers noticed and began to look forward to what he created each Thursday before the scrap truck came by.

One Wednesday, the foreman Joseph McNulty, who'd worked for Mr.

Cunningham since the factory opened, asked Horace if Ho could keep his tower and use it to learn how to solder. Horace had come to the factory floor early on Thursday and he was fascinated by what Ho had created. He readily agreed to let Ho keep one week's worth of scrap for his soldering lessons.

With the help of Joe and some of the others, Ho picked up soldering quickly. He had been able to assemble and solder his big tower and another smaller one. After the soldering process they were solid pieces, not the rickety towers he'd made in the past. Ho worked hard on his construction both during his soldering lessons and after hours. After the two towers were together, he polished them. It was tricky because the towers were made of lots of little pieces. When Ho had both of the towers all shined up, he lacquered them to preserve their shine. Finally, he mounted them on an oak plank. The whole construction measured twenty inches long, and the taller tower was a little over a foot tall.

He'd taken his towers home to add the wooden base. When he brought the finished construction into work, all his coworkers gathered around, slapping him on the back and telling him it looked great.

"What are you going to do with it?" asked the foreman, Joseph.

"We should give it to Horace. It's his brass."

"Great idea," Joseph responded. "I think he'll really like it."

"Why don't we all go to his office right before lunch, and we can give it to him?" Ho suggested. "Please, everyone come. You all have been a big help."

At quarter to twelve, the workmen all trooped into the front office. Ho trailed the group, carrying his new creation now covered with a sheet. Joseph spoke for all of them. "Boss, we have a present for you."

"What the heck?"

The workers parted, and Ho stepped forward with the towers and put them on Horace's desk. "Go ahead and do the unveiling," Joseph said.

Horace removed the sheet and stepped back to look at the creation on his desk. After a considerable pause, he said, "Oh my God, it's beautiful." Turning to Ho, he asked, "Did you do this?"

"Yes. But everyone helped. You remember my soldering project. We wanted you to have it."

Horace surveyed his office, and then he pointed to some bowling trophies a long-ago Cunningham Brass Bed team had won. "Take those down. I want to have Ho's sculpture in my office. The trophies can go in the outer office."

Ho remembered wondering if "sculpture" was too grand a word for what he'd done. In any event, Horace's reaction thrilled him. Everyone patted him on the back as they walked out. Ho had mixed feelings. While he loved the fact that Horace liked his towers, he thought his art projects had ended. He couldn't keep using the brass scraps. Horace made money recycling it.

Everything changed two weeks later when Horace called him into the office. Being called into the boss's office made Ho apprehensive. He hadn't completely rid himself of his father's notions. He figured nothing good would come from the boss wanting to see an employee. He'd been wrong. When he entered Horace's office, Horace pointed to his two towers and asked, "Do you think you could do something similar again?"

"Sure, it took some time, but I kind of liked it. Another one wouldn't turn out the same, the shapes you can make depend on the set of scraps. They're different depending on exactly what we're making any week. If we make a lot of single beds, it's different than if we're making a lot of kings or queens."

"What if you weren't working with scraps?"

"I don't understand."

"I'd better start at the beginning. Yesterday after the factory closed, I stayed for a meeting with Phillip Montgomery. He owns a bunch of boutique hotels, and he buys lots of beds from us. He loved your little sculpture, and he asked me where it came from. I explained the origins of the piece, and he found it really interesting."

"Wow," Ho stammered.

"Let me cut to the chase, Ho. He wants to buy sculptures for his hotels. I think he has twenty-one of them."

"Holy cow! I don't know how long it would take me to do that many. This one took a lot of time."

"He wants them bigger… maybe six feet long and two or three feet high. I think the width, actually the exact size, would depend on the particular hotel. He wants them for the lobbies. I think his idea is to have it be a trademark, something to set his hotels apart."

Ho didn't know what to say, so he simply stood there.

Horace filled the silence. "Ho, I know this comes completely out of the blue for you. I think it's a great opportunity. You have real talent. It would be a shame for you to be toiling away on the factory floor. While I can replace you there, I don't think anyone else can make sculptures like you can. I told Montgomery I thought we could get him what he wanted."

"How would it work?" Ho didn't quite know what to think.

"I haven't worked out the details yet. First, you'll have to tell me what you need. I'll get the brass. You can pay for it out of what he pays you for the finished product. You'd need some space. Maybe we could clear the shed out back. Right now, it's full of junk but if it were cleaned out, it would make a good studio to work in."

Art studio. He didn't quite understand what Horace was talking about. "I don't know. You're talking about a big change."

"I know it's a lot to take in. I've had my eye on you for a long time. I'm sorry I couldn't move you up faster, but I have a lot of good employees. This is a whole new deal, and I think it's exciting."

Horace asked Ho to take a seat beside his desk as he outlined the finances of his proposal. He only had rough estimates; precise figures would come later. What he outlined sounded great to Ho. Horace figured Ho would get $30,000 for each of the twenty-one sculptures. When Ho stopped him, Horace said a guy like Montgomery would consider $30,000 chicken feed. Horace figured the brass would cost him less than $1,000, and he would charge Ho fifteen percent of his gross as rent and a finder's fee. While Horace said there would probably be some other expenses, he figured Ho could clear about $20,000 for each sculpture.

That kind of money was almost five times what Ho made each month, and he'd get that for one sculpture. He didn't know how long it would take to make the twenty-one sculptures Montgomery wanted. He thought it couldn't take much more than a month for each one. He could be making well over $100,000 a year, maybe $200,000! Ho couldn't believe it.

When they'd hashed it all out, Ho's last question made Horace laugh out loud. Ho had asked, "When this is all over, can I have my regular job back?"

"Sure Ho, you can have your regular job back. That is, if you haven't made enough money to buy the factory."

Horace's response made Ho laugh.

Things happened fast after that. Ho went with Horace to St. Louis to meet Mr. Montgomery at his hotel. As Horace had predicted, the $30,000 price tag didn't bother Montgomery. They decided the St. Louis hotel would get the first sculpture, and they went out to the lobby to measure the space. Ho, Horace, and Montgomery had a fabulous meal in the hotel restaurant, the best Ho had ever had. Ho was glad Horace told him to get a new outfit for the trip.

After he started on Montgomery's towers, life changed dramatically for Ho. At Horace's urging he'd received a $10,000 advance on the first sculpture. With the seed money, Ho bought the tools he thought he'd need. The first sculpture took a month and a half to finish. As it neared completion, Ho had an idea. He thought the sculptures would be more professional if they were on a brass base. He decided to buy a furnace so he could melt brass to pour as a base. Even though the furnace cost quite a bit, he still cleared $10,000 on the first sculpture. As a final touch, Ho labeled the sculpture with an H, followed by a little sketch of a Narwhal whale, an odd-looking creature with a tusk sticking out front.

Though Ho worried, he shouldn't have. Mr. Montgomery was thrilled with the sculpture for the St. Louis hotel. Ho had been able to rent a pickup truck to transport the sculpture to the hotel. After his first success, Montgomery picked out the next hotel and sent Ho there to do the measurements. As a result, Ho traveled across the country and stayed in nice hotels, all expenses paid.

Ho finished five sculptures the first year. While the dimensions varied, the basic theme was the same. He even hired an assistant by the time he started the third one. His assistant, Martin Lopez, was a guy he'd met at the community college. Ho only needed him part time, which worked for Martin. It turned out to be good for Ho to have a helper, and Martin proved to be adept at the polishing.

When Ho totaled things for the year, he'd cleared a $120,000 for the nine months he'd been working under the new arrangement. He worked so hard he didn't have time to spend much of the money, so he had a sizeable savings account. Toward the end of the year, when Horace found out Ho put his money in a savings account, he had a long talk with Ho and introduced him to his stockbroker.

The second year, Ho had the routine down and he finished the remaining sixteen of the twenty-one sculptures Mr. Montgomery wanted. Truth be told, Ho was thoroughly tired of making very similar sculptures. He'd become proficient with all the tools and the furnace. While he wanted to make more interesting pieces, he stayed focused on Montgomery's work, and the money rolled in. He finished up Montgomery's work and thought about making other pieces.

To be a better artist, Ho decided he'd better learn more about art. He enrolled in another art history course at the community college and bought a few art books. On his trips to Mr. Montgomery's hotels to do the measurements, he'd gone to art galleries and museums whenever he had a chance. For reasons he couldn't quite understand, he really liked certain artists. A big sculpture at the foot of the escalator in the Hirshorn Gallery in Washington, DC appealed to Ho. It was done by an artist named Joan Miro and called the Lunar Bird. It was an unusual piece and for some reason it appealed to Ho. He also discovered he liked Salvador Dali and a few other surrealists. Their work often made him laugh. Ho decided he wanted to make art that would make people laugh.

While Ho thrived, all was not well with the rest of his family. Linda continued to pick date losers. One time, Ho came home and found Linda had a bruised face. Her most recent boyfriend had apparently beaten her when she'd done something annoying. Linda begged Ho not to retaliate. After a long discussion, the story came out. The boyfriend provided the pills that eased the pain in her leg. She didn't think she could live without the pills. Even though Ho had worried about this before, she'd never admitted it. Ho begged her to let him pay for a trip to a rehab. Finally, she relented, and she spent six months in treatment.

While Ho's father probably should have been committed somewhere too, he wouldn't allow it. Jack couldn't keep a job or stop his drinking. Ho knew his father would never stop asking him for money, so he decided to give him six hundred dollars a month and be done with it. Unfortunately, his father's attitude and the drinking always led to the same place—failure. Ho didn't like this option. Still, it worked. He was careful around his father to never say anything about how much money he actually made.

The final change in Ho's life was his love life. Ho had never been good at attracting women. Money and a little fame went a long way. Ho had several dates with women from the community college. Nothing came of them. Most of the women were too young for him. He had one success, Beverley Ortiz, Mr. Montgomery's assistant. She even accompanied him on a couple of his trips to make measurements. Their relationship fizzled after a while. Beverly was a college graduate and she seemed to look down her nose at Ho's GED and ten community college credits. While Ho was the one who broke it off, it didn't seem to bother Beverly.

Chapter Thirteen

Kenny Sturgis, September 21, 1980

At six on the dot, Maybell's van rolled up to his house and parked beside his Jeep. Surprisingly, Kenny's father had taken the hint and gone into town for dinner. He told Kenny he'd be in town until nine or nine-thirty.

Kenny had just approached the van when Maybell opened the door. She had on a tight purple top partway unbuttoned and jeans. They stopped for a kiss. When they broke apart, Maybell said, "I can tell you're happy to see me."

Kenny blushed. "Is it obvious?"

Maybell stroked the front of his jeans. "Yep. I think you'd better show me your bedroom fast."

"Right this way. My dad went to town tonight, so we are totally alone."

Maybell stopped when they entered the house. "Nice place. It's really neat for a place where two guys live."

"You saw the camp. My dad likes things just so. I think it's rubbed off on me. My bedroom is over here."

"Wow, you're eager," Maybell said as she unbuttoned her blouse while following Kenny.

After they finished in the bedroom, Kenny grabbed his rifle, scope, and a box of ammo from the storeroom. As they exited the house, Kenny turned toward the shooting range, but Maybell headed back to her van.

"It's this way!"

"Hold your horses, boy. I have something to show you. I'll be right back."

Kenny stared at Maybell as she came out of her van carrying a rifle case. "I brought you a gun to try out. I'll watch you shoot your gun, then you can try mine."

"Here, let me carry it," Kenny offered as he approached Maybell.

"No, silly, I've got it," Maybell turned away from Kenny.

"Okay, fine. I only wanted to help."

Kenny led Maybell to the shooting range. They went down to the target area and set up a few beer cans. Before Maybell came, Kenny had made sure fresh cans were ready and removed the mangled ones.

First, Kenny went over some basic safety rules. "Always point your rifle downrange, never at the house. And be sure it isn't loaded when we're up here setting up the targets."

"Makes sense."

"I'll let you shoot from close up first." Kenny walked back to the fifty-foot marker. "We usually use this for practice with pistols. In your case, it will be a good place to start."

Maybell put down the rifle case she'd been carrying and came up beside him. When she grabbed at Kenny's rifle, he jerked it away. "Wait! I'll give you the rifle. It's another safety thing. Never grab a rifle. Always wait for someone to give it to you."

"Okay." She'd never seen Kenny like this—clearly in charge.

"Now let me show you how to load the gun." Maybell came closer to watch. When they had the clip loaded and seated in the rifle. Kenny showed Maybell how the bolt action worked. Before he gave her the rifle, he had her put in ear plugs.

"This thing's heavy," Maybell said, hefting the rifle.

"You get used to it, and it's going to kick some when you shoot."

"I think I can handle it. I've shot a shotgun before."

"Let's see what you can do."

Maybell's first shot was nowhere near the target. She laughed and turned toward Kenny, pivoting the gun in his direction. "Rifle down range!" Kenny shouted, waving his hands.

"Sorry." Maybell shifted the position of the rifle.

Kenny came up to Maybell. "The rifle's going to want to go up with the shot, so hold it steadier. Also, I think you jerked the trigger. Try to squeeze it; don't jerk it. To tell the truth, no one hits the target on their first try. Relax and try again."

Even though Maybell's next shot missed too, Kenny could tell she'd gotten closer. "Try again. You were a lot closer."

Maybell shot again, and this time she sent a beer can spinning. She jumped up and spun around in celebration.

Kenny ducked and yelled, "Rifle down range!"

Maybell stopped spinning and looked a little embarrassed. "It's okay, silly. I'm not going to shoot you."

"Lots of accidents happen with guns. Some of the guys I work with on this range aren't as sober as they should be. I guess I've developed some reflexes."

Maybell came up to him, careful to keep the rifle pointed toward the targets, and gave Kenny a kiss. "It's okay. I'll try to be more careful."

"Let's move you farther down to make it more interesting." They moved back to fifty yards. Maybell hit a beer can on her fourth try. After she managed the hit, she came up to Kenny and handed him the rifle. "I think my shoulder's starting to hurt. I'm going to call it a day. We're about fifty or sixty yards away, right? When we met, you said you could hit targets from three hundred yards?"

"That's what I said."

"Show me," Maybell said, picking up the rifle case she'd brought.

"You gonna show me what you brought in the case?"

"In time. First, I want to see what you can do with your rifle."

"We'd better set up more targets." After replacing the two beer cans Maybell hit, Kenny and Maybell walked back to the far end of the shooting range. "See this marker here," Kenny said, pointing to a line in the dirt. "It's three hundred yards, as close as we could measure."

Maybell peered at the targets. "I can barely see the targets. There's no way you can hit them from here."

"You're right, the sun is pretty low, but I think I can still hit one or two. First, I have to put the scope on."

After Kenny attached the scope, he lay down in the prone position and said, "Get behind me now. I'm going to show you how it's done."

He sighted in on the left-most beer can, calmed his heartbeat, held his breath, and squeezed the trigger. A puff of dust on the berm told him he hit the dirt off to the left a little. He adjusted, and his next three shots sent beer cans flying.

Maybell jumped up and down excitedly. "You really can shoot. I could barely see the targets. Once you had it straight, they were jumping off the shelf. Now let's see what you can do with this," Maybell turned and opened the case she'd brought.

Kenny stood up, dusted himself off, and asked, "What's in the box? And why're you acting all surprised at my shooting? I told you I could do it."

"Yeah, you did. The thing is, I don't think I had a real idea of how far three hundred yards really is. I know it's three football fields, but who has ever been able to see three football fields stacked together? It's impressive. Come see what I brought you."

Kenny stepped closer and peered into the rifle case. "It's a real sniper rifle! Where'd you get it?"

"It belongs to one of my friends. He said you could try it out if you wanted to. Here, you take it out of the case."

Kenny pulled the gun out of the case and admired it. "It's a Walther WA 2000," Kenny said, reading off the gun. It had a wooden stock, a big scope, and a funny-looking bipod mounted on the top of the barrel.

"I think it came from West Germany."

"I'd sure like to try it. You have bullets for this?"

Maybell reached into her pocket and pulled out three bullets. "My buddy only gave me three. It should be enough for you to get the hang of it."

"Wow, this is awesome," Kenny said as he continued inspecting the rifle.

"You'd better get down and shoot the thing," urged Maybell. "It's starting to get dark."

Kenny lay back down and settled the gun. He loaded one of the bullets in the chamber. While he'd heard about these single-shot sniper rifles, he'd never seen one before. He aimed at one of the three remaining beer cans. He could see it clearly through the powerful scope. The bipod made it easy to keep the rifle steady. He held his breath and squeezed the trigger. The beer can went flying.

"Wow! First shot!" Maybell clapped her hands and jumped up and down.

Kenny loaded another bullet and nailed another beer can. *This gun's amazing*, thought Kenny as he stood up. "I'm going to go back another fifty yards. This thing makes it so easy; three hundred yards is nothing."

"Okay, champ." Maybell picked up the case and Kenny's rifle.

Fifty yards back made it the far end of the rifle range, so Kenny laid down in some old weeds. He calmed his breathing, sighted through the scope, and took his last shot. The final beer can went flying.

"You can't miss." Maybell came up and kissed Kenny. After the kiss, she opened the case and said, "Here, you put it away."

As they walked back toward the house, Kenny said, "Be sure to thank your friend. It was a real privilege to shoot that gun. With the scope and bipod, I think I might be able to hit a target five hundred yards away."

"You think?"

"Yeah. It's a sniper rifle, and snipers take shots from farther away than five-hundred yards."

After Kenny and Maybell put the two rifles away, they decided to go eat at the McDonald's next to the highway. Having two vehicles made it awkward. Kenny parked at the edge of the parking lot and hopped into the van with Maybell. They used the drive through and ate in the back of the van parked beside Kenny's Jeep.

As they were eating their burgers and fries, Maybell said, "My dad's having one of his group meetings on Thursday night. Do you want to come?"

"Group? I don't understand."

"It's people with the same politics as my dad. It's called the Charleston Group—folks who think the federal government's being too pushy. Folks who think all this forced racial mixing is a real bad idea. You know, like my dad and me."

"So, they have meetings?"

"Yeah, it's good to know the people who share your views. Want to come?"

"Sure."

"Good, you can come over to our house for dinner at five-thirty. Then we'll go to the meeting."

They finished and Kenny had put all the wrappings in the can Maybell had for dog fur. "Now for dessert," she said and gave Kenny a smile.

"Right here in the McDonald's parking lot?"

"Right here beside McDonald's." Maybell started unbuttoning her blouse.

Chapter Fourteen

Ho Narwhal, July 23, 1979

Ho supervised the loading of his ten brass sculptures. When loaded, the truck would head to the gallery in St. Louis. The transport of the pieces didn't concern him, but what would happen to them after they arrived had him uptight. In two days, they would be for sale at the New Age Gallery, and he would be the guest of honor at the reception opening the show.

Before agreeing to put Ho's works on sale, the gallery owner, MacElroy Jenkins, toured Ho's shop. With his ascot and loud checked sport coat, Jenkins looked like the kind of arty person Ho wasn't inclined to like. He wondered where a gallery owner in St. Louis acquired an English accent. Ho didn't think he came from England. Anyway, Jenkins liked the sculptures. Ho had a very clear memory of his first encounter with Jenkins.

The first sculpture Jenkins inspected was a sort of turtle with feathers and five legs. It stood two feet tall and was four feet long. Jenkins asked, "What do you call this one? It's surreal."

"I don't like to title my work. I number them. It's simply called five."

To his credit, Jenkins knelt to study the sculpture closely. "The workmanship is superb. That is important to me. If you have unique pieces like this, it can't be sloppy. You're a real craftsman."

Ho mumbled, "Thank you."

Jenkins continued inspecting the works in silence. At times, he looked very closely at the workmanship, and at other times he stepped back against the wall for a different view.

After what seemed like too long, Jenkins turned away from the sculptures and came up to Ho. "I love your stuff. I'd like to host a show in my gallery. I'm so glad Phillip Montgomery convinced me to come down here."

"Thank you." Ho could only come up with a short response.

"I think these pieces will create a big stir. There aren't many people who can carry off surrealism like you can. The combination of the superb workmanship and the whimsical subject matter really works. Let's go somewhere to work out the details."

Ho turned to Horace Cunningham who'd been observing the encounter, and said, "Horace has agreed to advise me, so we can we use his office."

When they settled the contract, Ho felt dazed. He couldn't believe the prices Jenkins wanted to charge. Ho understood when he got a look at the cut the gallery extracted. Jenkins set the high prices to maximize his take. Ho would rather have had lower prices, so he'd be able to sell some sculptures. He didn't think they'd find many buyers at the prices Jenkins charged. In the end Jenkins got his way, and Horace assured Ho everything was on the up and up.

When the truck was fully loaded, Ho followed it to St. Louis. He'd packed his suitcase before coming to his workshop. He didn't think he'd enjoy the grand opening party where he'd be the center of attention. He wasn't sure if he'd have to speak. He'd asked his friends Rich and Janet if they'd ever been to a gallery opening, but they hadn't. They suggested asking the community college professor about this kind of event. Unfortunately, he'd been so busy finishing his last sculpture that he hadn't found time to ask.

Two nights later, decked out in his new blue suit, Ho paced through the gallery space. The lighting looked good, and the brass contrasted nicely with the light blue walls. As hard as it was for Ho to admit it, MacElroy Jenkins knew how to display his work. Ho wished he'd fought harder to change the name Jenkins had put on the collection. He'd called it the Brass Menagerie. Even though Ho wasn't a fan of puns, in the end, he let it go.

Ho had seen the guest list for the opening party. He only recognized five names: Phillip Montgomery, his wife Joanne, Horace Cunningham, his wife Ellen, and Beverly Ortiz. The rest were a complete mystery to him. Jenkins gleefully pointed out that representatives of two museums were coming, and he showed Ho the names of two newspaper reporters. Knowing the press would be there didn't do anything to alleviate Ho's nervousness.

At the appointed hour, people started to drift in. Ho stood on the sidelines to see how the first few arrivals reacted to his sculptures. Many of the reactions pleased him. Some people smiled, and he even heard one person laugh. Of course, others were more serious, and he saw some people shake their heads, making him think they didn't approve.

As the gallery filled, Jenkins brought people over to meet Ho. He shook hands with a great number of people and said, "Thank you very much" to all of them who expressed that they liked his sculptures. Most of the people he met were holding glasses of wine in one hand. Ho had decided not to drink. He wanted to keep his wits about him. He had been able to make small talk with the people. He'd attempted to turn questions back on people. Lots of people asked him why he didn't name his pieces. He told them he hadn't been clever enough to think of the right names. Besides, the person who purchased the piece should have the honor of naming it. Then he asked them what they'd name a piece. They seemed to like being asked.

About a half hour into the opening, the first sold sign went up on a sculpture, number two, sort of a giraffe, but with a dorsal fin like a shark and only three legs. Ho met the couple who bought it and had a nice chat with them. He repeated his offer to let them name the sculpture, and they seemed very pleased.

Ho felt better after the first sale. He continued to mingle among the strangers. He was relieved to see Horace and his wife Ellen heading his way. He knew he could talk to them. When Horace came closer, Ho could tell Horace was bringing someone to meet him. While the guy looked familiar, Ho couldn't place him. But he noticed him when he came in. MacElroy had run over to greet him, and everyone seemed to know him. Lots of other people had crowded around him. Ho liked it. The pressure came off for a moment.

When Horace and his group reached Ho, he said, "Ho, this is my brother Walter. Walt, this is Ho Narwhal. He's the artist."

Ho reached over to shake Walter's hand. As he looked at the smiling face, Ho could tell why everyone had flocked to him when he came in. He was magnetic.

"It's nice to meet you, Ho," Walter said. "This is my wife, Mary Jean."

Ho thought Mary Jean might be one of the most attractive women he'd ever met. She had auburn hair, strong cheekbones, and a slim figure. As she shook Ho's hand, she said, "I love your delightful sculptures. How do you ever decide on your subjects?"

"The evidence suggests I have a wild imagination," Ho replied, and everyone laughed.

"I have to agree," Walter commented. "Horace has been telling me your story. He says you're completely self-taught."

"You're right, this all started at Horace's factory. I'm still getting used to it."

"Well, your sculptures are amazing. I wish I could afford one."

Right then, Ho recognized Walter Cunningham. He was a state senator on everyone's short list to run for governor next year. Ho hadn't known he was Horace's brother. They didn't look anything alike. Horace was bald and not very tall. In contrast, Walter stood well over six feet and had a full head of wavy light brown hair.

Ho responded, "Don't tell him I said this, but I think MacElroy, the gallery owner, has priced them out of most people's reach."

"I don't think so. I know a lot of people in this room, and a bunch of them won't be bothered by the prices. You've already sold one. I bet Jenkins knows what he's doing. It's nice to meet you, and good luck with the show. It appears to be a big success."

"It's nice to meet you, and thanks for coming," Ho said. Then he leaned over to Walter and continued. "It looks like lots of other people want to talk to you. That's great. I'm not sure I like being the center of attention. I can tell you're used to it."

"I don't want to take your spotlight, Ho."

"No, please do."

Walter winked at Ho and turned to mingle with the crowd. Ho liked the guy. As he walked away, the crowd seemed to follow him. While it would drive Ho crazy, Walter seemed to thrive on the attention. Ho guessed a politician had to like the crush of the crowd. *I sure don't.*

After another half hour of greeting people, he didn't know, and selling four more sculptures, Ho noticed an odd group enter the gallery: a distinguished-looking older couple and a little girl maybe nine or ten years old. They were unusual for this crowd. For one thing, there hadn't been any other children. Maybe there were some teenagers, but certainly no one as young as this kid. Ho watched as the little girl wandered away from the older couple, probably her grandparents, and ran up to Five, the turtle with feathers. He loved it when the girl broke out into a big smile. She returned to her grandparents and pulled them toward the sculpture.

The child's grandparents didn't seem to be as enthralled as the youngster. Soon they were in a conversation with some other guests, and the little girl started to wander. Ho saw her smile at another sculpture and even laugh out loud once. He decided to talk with her. Even though he didn't have much experience with little kids, he wanted to try his luck. This little girl seemed to be his biggest fan.

Ho walked up to the girl and said, "You seem to like these sculptures."

Not the least bit startled, she looked up at him and said, "Yes, I do. They are so silly. They make me laugh. I guess the artist wouldn't like me laughing at them. But they're silly."

"I don't think the artist would mind at all. In fact, I am very sure he'd be happy you liked his work."

"You think so?"

"I'm positive."

"He's supposed to be here. He has a funny name, Horace Narwhal. A narwhal is a whale like a unicorn. Maybe it's why he makes all the funny animals."

"Would you like to meet the artist?"

"Yes, do you know him?"

"Yes, I do. I'm him. Horace Narwhal at your service." Ho reached out his hand to the little girl.

She grasped his hand and shook it. "Linda Daniels. Pleased to meet you, Mr. Narwhal."

"Linda's a pretty name. My sister's named Linda. Do you live in St. Louis, Linda?"

"We used to, but we recently moved to Springfield for my mom's job."

An attractive young woman hurried up to the two of them. When she saw the woman, Linda ran to her and gave her a hug. "Mom, I'm talking to the artist. Don't you love his silly animals?"

"She's not bothering you, is she?" the woman asked as her daughter pulled her toward Ho.

"No, Linda's my favorite art critic," Ho said with a smile. He reached out his hand. "I'm Horace Narwhal. I guess I'm the one all this fuss is about."

"Karen Daniels," said the woman as she shook Ho's outstretched hand. Ho thought she was stunning. Her dark brown hair was tied in a small bun, and she had a bright smile, dimples when she smiled, and the most beautiful warm brown eyes. She wore a severe business suit, so she didn't quite fit in with the rest of the crowd.

Linda, who had the same brown eyes, said, "He liked it that I thought his animals were funny."

"Yes, I loved it when I saw Linda laughing at the sculptures. While I probably shouldn't be saying this, most people in this crowd are too uptight for my tastes. When I made these pieces, I wanted to make people smile. I don't know if this art crowd smiles very often."

"I think I know what you mean. I only just arrived. Linda came with her grandparents. Why don't you let Linda give me a tour of your work, then I'll come back and tell you what I think."

"I'm sure Linda will be a great tour guide. She's one of my biggest fans."

Ho watched the mother and daughter walk away together, hand-in-hand. Karen looked as good from the back as she had from the front.

Ten minutes later, as the gallery started to empty, Karen and Linda walked up to Ho. They had the older couple in tow. Karen said, "Horace, I'd like you to meet my parents, Geoffrey and Susan Daniels."

"Please call me Ho," he said as he shook the Daniels' hands. "I talked to your granddaughter Linda earlier. She's a very astute art critic."

"You're only saying that because I laughed at your sculptures."

"You liked them."

"Yes, I did."

"And what about your mother?" Ho asked, recognizing he very much wanted Karen Daniels to like his work.

"They are very unusual pieces. Also, I can see what you were saying about being too uptight. I didn't want to laugh out loud. Maybe I should have. Some of those animals are so preposterous. Also, you are quite a craftsman. The sculptures are well done. I liked them. They're fun."

"It's the reaction I wanted."

"I bet that's not all," Geoffrey Daniels said. "I bet you wanted some people to like them enough to part with some of their dough. It looks like that's worked out too. I think you've sold five of them tonight. It's a smashing opening. Congratulations."

"Thank you. I didn't know what to expect."

"It was nice to meet you, Ho," Karen said. "And Dad's right. Congratulations. This is an amazing show."

As the group turned to leave, Ho spoke up. "If you guys want to come see where I work, it's in Tyndall, not too far from Springfield. You'd be welcome any time."

Linda hopped up and down, and almost yelled, "Could we go? I want to see how he makes them!"

"Thanks for the invite," Karen said with a smile. "You never know. We just might show up."

When the last guests departed twenty minutes later, only Ho, Jenkins, and his assistants remained. Ho decided to help gather up wine glasses.

"Don't bother with the glasses," Jenkins said. "I want to talk to you about next steps. Come into my office."

In the office, Jenkins told Ho about all the people who'd bought his sculptures. He also told Ho one of the big museums in town put a reserve on one. The people from the museum were going to bring the entire acquisitions committee to the gallery later in the week. "It's only a formality," Jenkins said. "Also, there are several other people who will likely come back. It's been the most successful opening we've ever had. Ho, you're on your way to becoming a major artist."

Being incredibly tired, Ho didn't know what to say, so he only said, "Thanks."

Chapter Fifteen

Kenny Sturgis September 27, 1980

Kenny had felt honored when Maybell told him her dad suggested he should go to the meeting. Looking around the room, he wondered about the name, the Charleston Group. Maybell explained how Charleston, South Carolina, was the site of the first battle of the Civil War. He figured he might be the youngest guy there. There were about eighteen or twenty people, mostly men. Maybell was one of only six women. When the actual meeting started, he didn't know what to expect. Kenny figured he'd best be quiet.

The leader, Jim Lewis, according to Maybell, went to the little stage set up in the living room. A confederate flag hung on a pole beside the stage and chairs were arranged in front of the stage. When Lewis walked up to the small podium, he said something Kenny couldn't understand, and everyone stood. Then they did a sort of stiff-arm salute and repeated a pledge of some kind. While Kenny followed along with the hand gesture, he didn't know the pledge. He tried to catch Maybell's eye. No luck. She stared at the leader and repeated the pledge. When he finished, everyone sat down.

After people settled back in their chairs, Lewis started his speech. Even though Kenny usually didn't like speeches, he found Lewis easy to listen to. He talked about things Kenny didn't know much about, so he couldn't follow much of it. He talked about the evils of so-called affirmative action. Kenny had a faint idea about affirmative action, but he didn't know any details. Lewis said it amounted to discrimination against whites. According to Lewis, affirmative action was going to send the United States down the tubes. Lewis explained how nations led by whites thrived and nations led by nonwhites did not. Kenny didn't know much about the countries Lewis mentioned. Still, he got the point. If you let blacks and browns take over your country, it wouldn't end well. According to Lewis, it was one of the clearest lessons of history.

Next, Lewis traced how affirmative action first affected hiring on federal jobs and how it spread. Colleges created quotas for blacks, shutting out white college applicants with better records. Banks were being forced to give mortgages to blacks who didn't qualify for the loans. Affirmative action had crept into society at all levels. Kenny couldn't help being stirred when Lewis ended this section of his speech by saying, "It is evil, evil, evil. Affirmative action is the work of the devil!"

The final part of Lewis' speech centered on politics. He didn't like Carter. While he was from Georgia, part of the South, Carter had completely abandoned his Southern heritage. And Reagan was no better. He was a movie actor. While he was could say his lines, you didn't know what he really thought. In the end, Lewis said it didn't really matter who got elected president. The federal government was a monster, and it couldn't be controlled. Local politics contained the only hope for the entirety of the country.

For local politics, Lewis turned the meeting over to one of the women, his wife Sally Anne. Kenny didn't find her as riveting as her husband. She had a list of local elections, and she went into great detail about the candidates and where they stood on issues like affirmative action. Toward the end of the talk, she focused on some guy who was running for governor, Cunning something. Kenny didn't catch it. Clearly, Sally Anne didn't like the guy. By the end, the speech had become mind numbing, too many details. Kenny scanned the room. While Maybell seemed to be getting a little restless, she still focused on the speaker. Everyone else was the same. Kenny remembered his time in school. Many of the other students could concentrate on the teacher, but Kenny couldn't.

When the speeches finished, Maybell and her father introduced Kenny to lots of people. He caught some of the names, but he wasn't good with names until he saw them written out. Most of the guys were adults, some of them pretty old. Later, Kenny thought he should have been better with the name of the guy who had been introduced as some big-wig in the state police— Hop something. Kenny didn't catch the whole name. Everyone seemed to be happy he'd been able to make the meeting.

At work, he made a special effort to try to memorize his father's client's names, and he usually did well. A situation like this was hopeless. He did remember Lewis, so when he was introduced to him, Kenny said, "You gave a great talk, Mister Lewis."

"Thank you, son. Are you the boy who's such a good shot? Maybell mentioned you were coming."

Kenny blushed a little and replied, "I reckon I am. I shoot real good. I showed Maybell some. We have a shooting range out back of our house."

"Well, it's great to have more young people coming to our meetings. I hope you come again."

"I sure will."

On the way out of the house, Maybell took Kenny over to meet the younger set of the group. Again, Kenny didn't catch all the names. There was a guy with a double name starting with Billy, but Kenny didn't get the last part. Another one was called Duncan, he thought, but he wasn't sure if it was a first or last name. Kenny was sure about one of the names—Swindle, the name of a tall guy in his mid-twenties. Maybell explained his name was William Swindler, but everyone called him Swindle. Swindle and his buddies, Billy whatever and Duncan, were chewing tobacco. Kenny thought it was weird walking around with a Dixie cup so you could spit in it all the time. His father didn't allow any tobacco, and it didn't bother Kenny.

When they returned to the Wilcox's house, Maybell and Kenny lingered by Kenny's Jeep while Maybell's father said his goodbyes and went into the house. As the door closed, Maybell grabbed Kenny's hand and led him toward her van.

"Won't your father figure out what we're doing?" Kenny asked as he followed along.

"I don't care. And I don't think he'd care either. I think he really likes you, Kenny. You made a good impression on Jim Lewis, and that counts a lot with my family. Come on, I have plans for you."

Kenny went willingly.

Chapter Sixteen

Ho Narwhal, August 8, 1979

Ho had been thrilled when he received a phone call from Karen Daniels a few days after the show. Linda wanted to bring a friend to see Ho's workshop. They made the arrangements to come down on Saturday.

On Friday, Ho cleaned up and prepared his project for Linda and her friend. Stopping at the door and looking back, he realized his shop hadn't looked this good for quite some time. As he walked home, he thought about Karen, who he really wanted to get to know. In their brief encounter at the art gallery, Ho thought he detected a little spark. He shook his head. What an idiot. He'd been nice to Linda. Any mother would approve. In any event, he was excited about seeing them both.

The next morning, he took extra time primping and wore his best work clothes. He made it to his workshop at nine-thirty, a half hour before his guests were to arrive. At quarter past ten, Karen knocked on the edge of the open door.

"Come on in," Ho yelled as he moved away from his most recent creation. Karen and two ten-year-olds came in. Karen looked good. She wore her shoulder-length hair loose this time, and it softened her face. He tried not to stare. *I'd better focus on the little ones*, he thought.

Ho smiled and turned to the little girl he didn't know. "While I know Karen and Linda, we haven't met. I'm Horace Narwhal. I work here."

The little blonde girl, an inch or so taller than Linda, took Ho's outstretched hand and shook it shyly. Linda announced, "Ho, this is my friend Cathy Townsend."

"Nice to meet you, Cathy, and good to see you again, Linda… and you too, Karen." Ho shook the two outstretched hands. He stepped back and said, "This is my workshop. I'll show you around, and then I have a project you can help me with."

"Can we really help?" Linda asked excitedly.

"Yes, if you are very careful."

Linda looked at Cathy. "We can be careful, can't we Cathy?"

Cathy nodded. "Sure."

"Okay, first let me show you around." Ho then showed them the brass rods and sheets he started with, the furnace where he melted the brass, the tools he used to shape the brass, and the polishing tools. Next, he showed them the steel skeleton for the next animal. He explained how he welded the skeleton together, covered it with copper mesh and then brass. Finally, he showed them the plaster table where he made models for his sculptures.

His audience had been quiet and attentive. Finally, Linda couldn't help herself when she saw the plaster model of a funny-looking horse. "What is it?"

"It's number twelve," Ho answered.

"Don't tease them, Ho," Karen said. "I think number twelve is a horse, don't you girls?"

"Can I pick it up?" Linda asked.

"Sure."

Linda picked up the model and turned it over. "It has eight legs," she exclaimed as she showed the model to Cathy.

"So it's a spider, not a horse," Cathy said. "Wait, it's more like a spider who's wearing shoes."

Turning the model back over, Linda said, "At the top, it looks like a horse, but a horse with a sort of flat body."

"Linda, remember the art show last weekend?" Karen said with a smile. "He doesn't sculpt normal animals. A flat horse with eight legs and shoes is just the kind of thing Ho would make."

While the girls were still inspecting the model, Ho went over to a large bench in the middle of the workroom and removed a sheet covering the brass version of the model they were looking at. "Come over here. This is the full-sized piece. It's the one I need help with."

When the others gathered around Ho said, "I think this, whatever it is, needs some hair, so I've drilled holes where I want the hair to go. Then I added little holders for the hair."

He held up some pieces of brass wire. "These short wires are going to be the hair on the back of the horse, or whatever, and these longer ones are going to be the tail."

"The wires are all straight," Cathy said. "Won't it be funny with its hair sticking straight up?"

"I think it already looks funny," Linda commented. "I'm not sure it makes much difference what its hair is like."

"No, Cathy's right. I think the hair shouldn't be sticking straight up. My plan is to bend the wire after they are soldered into the holders. Even though I guess I want it to look funny, I don't want it to be too funny."

Karen spoke up. "You have a strange objective—funny, but not too funny."

"It's sort of what I aim for. You guys want to help?"

The two girls nodded and crowded around the horse.

"Okay, I'm going to put a little solder into the holders, and then after I've heated the end of the wire a little, I'm going to ask you to insert the wires and hold it still for a couple of minutes until the solder cools. Hold the wire from the end I didn't heat." He demonstrated how to hold the wire. "If you're at the end, it won't be too hot to hold. Karen, why don't you go first."

"Okay."

First, he put the tip of the soldering iron into the holder. "It has to be hot, or the solder won't stick. I'll start on the back of the horse."

After he held the tip of the soldering iron in the holder for a minute, he heated a drop of solder and inserted it. Then he moved away and put his soldering iron on the wire Karen held. After ten seconds, he said, "Okay, you can put the wire into the hole."

She inserted the wire. "Do I stick it down all the way?"

"Yes, all the way, and try to keep it still once it's in there."

Ho then moved to the left side of the horse and prepared a holder for Linda. By the time he'd moved to the other side of the horse and had Cathy's wire inserted, he said, "Karen, see what happens if you let go of your wire."

"It's standing up on its own."

"Great, you ready for another one?"

"Sure, there are a lot of holders to fill."

Ho repeated the process moving from one holder to the next. With three people holding the wires, the solder would be set on the first wire when he completed the third one. As a result, he could repeat the process without having to wait. After about half an hour of continuous work, he asked, "Want to take a break?"

"No!" they all chorused. "There are lots of empty holders."

Ho and the girls worked for another half an hour and finished all the hair on the back of the horse. "Now are we going to work on the tail?" Linda asked.

Ho gave Karen a look, and she shrugged. "If you want to, Linda."

"Yes."

"Me too!" Cathy added.

"Let's get a drink first," suggested Ho as he went over to a plastic cooler he filled with Coke and 7-Up.

After their drinks, they went back to work. They found the tail a little more difficult. The wires were longer, they had to tip the animal on its nose, and the holders were closer together. There was only room for two wire holders, so Karen stepped back and let the girls do the work. It didn't take long for the twelve tail wires to be soldered in place.

When they completed the last wire, Karen clapped. "It looks magnificent."

Linda and Cathy stepped back to admire their work. "I think Ho's right, it's going to be better if the wires are bent, especially the tail," Cathy said.

"I think you're right, Cathy," Karen said.

"I'll have to wait a while before I can bend the wires," Ho said. "I have to melt some brass to disguise the holders and fill any holes. After I'm sure it's set up well, I can bend the wires, and after a little more polishing the sculpture will be finished.

"Where is number twelve going?" Karen asked.

"It's going to a museum in Chicago. It's my first commissioned work. In fact, I had it partly finished when I received the commission. While it wasn't ready for the show, it didn't turn out to be a problem. Now, I have a couple of other commissions, so I have lots of work to do."

"Do you know what animals you're going to do for the other commissions?" Karen asked.

"Unfortunately, I don't. I guess I'll have to come up with something."

"It must be great to have everyone so enthusiastic about your work."

"It is, and it's a little scary too."

"I love your animals," broke in Linda.

"Me too," Cathy added.

"Thanks girls. I like it when people approve of my work. It makes me really happy. Now, since you were so much help, I want to take you to lunch. I think the child labor laws say I can't pay you. But I can take you to lunch."

"You don't have to do that Ho," Karen said.

"I insist."

Ho took Karen and the girls to one of the nicest restaurants in Tyndall. It was on the banks of the river. After they finished lunch and asked permission, the girls removed their shoes, rolled up their jeans, and went wading in the river. Karen and Ho moved to one of the outside tables so they could keep track of the girls.

When they were seated, Ho asked, "What do you do? You've seen what I do. I don't have any idea what you do."

"I'm a cop. Actually, I work for the state troopers. I'm part of the special detective force. We're a small unit covering crimes too tough for local police forces to handle, and we do some security for the governor."

"I never would have guessed." Ho was curious. "How does it work with Linda? Doesn't a detective have irregular hours?"

"Yeah, it's been tough. There are times I have to dedicate a lot of hours to a case. Linda used to stay with my parents when I worked. Since we moved to Springfield it's been harder. I've found a family to take her after school and one of my neighbors is a grandmother who will sleep over if I am going to be gone all night. It's hard sometimes, but Linda understands."

"I would never have guessed detective. How'd it happen?"

Karen smiled at him and took a sip of her water before answering. "Here's the short version. I went off to college like all my friends. Then I goofed up. I got pregnant toward the end of my sophomore year. Don't ask me how it happened. I thought I had protection. Anyway, the guy wanted nothing to do with me or my baby. When he asked me to get an abortion, I couldn't do it."

Ho smiled at her. "Now I have an explanation for the ten-year-old with the same last name as your parents and no wedding ring."

"Yes, I moved in with my parents and had Linda in December. I played the role of a stay-at-home mom for Linda's first two years. Then I got restless. Finally, I went to St. Louis U as a part-time student. I had been aiming to be a history major at Virginia, where I first went to college, but it seemed impractical. I wanted something that would lead to a job. St. Louis has a criminal justice major, and it worked."

Ho leaned forward in his seat, arms resting on the table. "Isn't it tough for a woman detective? I mean, don't you have to put up with a lot? Police departments are full of macho guys."

"I've run into some. I made sure the guys learned early on that I won't put up with any of their bullshit. I'm good at what I do. I hope I've earned some respect."

"I'm sure you have."

"Your turn," Karen said with a smile. "How'd you end up making brass sculptures?"

"It started when I worked on the production floor of Horace Cunningham's factory—the one my workshop's behind. After a few years, I started making little towers out of pieces of scrap. One thing led to another, and I soldered together one of my towers for Horace. He really liked it. Horace showed my piece to Phillip Montgomery, who owns a bunch of hotels, and he liked it. He gave me a commission for more of them."

"So, the brass mountains at the Excelsior Hotel in St. Louis are yours?"

"Yes, it's the first one I did."

"It's not anything like the animals at the show or the horse we worked on today."

"I started on the weird animals after I finished the work for Montgomery. The sculptures at his hotels are very similar. I wanted to do something different."

"I'd say you succeeded."

Ho shook his head. "Frankly, I'm flabbergasted the animals have been such a big hit."

"What about before you worked for Mr. Cunningham?"

"I served in the Army then—Viet Nam."

"Were you drafted? What did you do?"

"It's complicated," Ho said, wondering how much of his story he really wanted to tell Karen, who was giving him a quizzical look. He decided to be honest. "Okay. I was a high school drop-out. The only job I could only get was as a clerk in a convenience store. Some of my buddies convinced me to help them rob the store, and we all were caught. I wound up in the army because the judge said he'd drop the charges if I volunteered for the draft. While the other two guys served some jail time, they both were out before I completed my hitch in the Army. It's a long time ago now, but I still don't think it was fair."

"I can see why. What did you do in the Army?"

"I was in the infantry."

"Wow. In Viet Nam?"

"Yes, it was a long year. Turns out it was good for me. I grew up a lot and learned a great deal."

"What?"

Again, he hesitated, but decided to give her the unvarnished truth. "To understand, you have to know about my father. He is a bitter man who thinks the world is out to get him. He turned a lot worse after my mother died. Unfortunately, his attitude rubbed off on me. For example, I didn't succeed in school because I thought the teachers had it in for me. I dropped out, which was one of the dumbest things I ever did. My company in Viet Nam was different. Everybody looked out for everyone else. No one was out to get anyone. We cooperated. I'd never seen anything like it."

"Did the officers and the enlisted men get along?"

"I guess they didn't always. In my company they did. The big thing I learned was—my father's attitude is no help. If you think everyone is out to get you, you act in ways that make it true. In my father's world, everything is someone else's fault. Mostly it's his fault. Being away made me see how his view is a trap."

Karen hesitated, then asked softly, "Being in the infantry in Viet Nam turned out all right?"

"Yes, and landing the job in the brass bed factory helped too. I found another group of workers who fit together well. Again, they cooperated. Horace Cunningham is a wonderful boss. He has the golden rule painted in big letters inside the factory, and he really lives by it. He's been a great help with the business side of my becoming a sculptor."

Linda and Cathy ran up to the table. Their legs and the bottom of their rolled-up jeans were soaked.

"You two had better sit down and dry off. We can't put your shoes on until your feet are dry. Ho and I are having an interesting discussion. Did you know he was in the Army before he started being a sculptor?"

Linda piped up, "I figured he went to sculptor school somewhere."

"Nope, no sculptor school. I learned by fooling around with bits of brass when I worked in the factory in front of my workshop. Basically, I taught myself. I should have stayed in school, but I didn't."

When the girls' feet were dry, they put on their shoes and were ready to leave. Linda asked Ho to send them a picture of the completed horse. He assured them he would if he could have their address. Karen extracted a pad of paper from her purse and wrote her address and phone number on it.

The little girls shook Ho's hand before they climbed into the back seat of the car. Karen got them buckled in their car seats. Then she came around to Ho and, much to his surprise, gave him a hug. "Thank you so much," she said. "You were wonderful with the girls, and I really liked getting to know you. Call sometime. You have my number." She smiled, climbed in the car, and drove away.

Chapter Seventeen

Kenny Sturgis, October 17, 1980

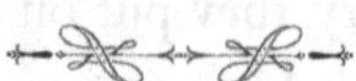

Kenny went to Maybell's house early on Friday morning. He'd told her he couldn't stay long, because a new group of hunters were scheduled to show up on Saturday and he and his dad had some preparation to do. She said she'd be okay with a short visit. They hadn't had many chances to meet since the start of hunting season. When he drove up, she stood waiting beside a car he didn't recognize. Kenny thought it might be twenty or even thirty years old, and it clearly needed a paint job. Kenny couldn't tell what color it had started out—something dark, blue maybe.

"Whose car is this?" Kenny asked, as he climbed out of his Jeep.

"It's my new one, a fifty-five Oldsmobile. Want to see how it drives?"

"Sure, but you know it's not what I came out here for."

Maybell opened the car door for Kenny and grabbed his butt as he entered. "I know what you want but you can take a few minutes to admire my new wheels. Drive to the end of the driveway and back."

When he returned at the end of the short drive, Kenny climbed out and said, "It runs pretty smooth for as old as it is." Honestly, the car didn't impress him at all. It steered hard and sounded louder than he thought it should. While his Jeep was loud, Maybell's old car was worse. Kenny didn't want to admit to Maybell he didn't like her new car. She could be moody, and he didn't want her in a bad mood. As it turned out, she was in a good mood. She grabbed his hand and almost dragged him to the van, eager to please him. Twenty-five minutes later, when they stepped out of the van, Maybell's dad opened the front door and shouted. Maybell had a phone call.

"Stay right here, Kenny. I'll see who this is and be right back."

While he waited, Kenny inspected Maybell's car. The more he looked at it, the more he saw flaws. The body showed quite a bit of rust, and the tires were almost bald. He couldn't believe how pleased Maybell seemed to be with the vehicle. It wasn't as nice as her van. The whole thing didn't make sense.

Maybell came out of the house with a disappointed look on her face. When she reached Kenny, she said, "One of my best clients called, Mrs. Stein. Something's come up, and she can't keep her appointment for her poodle on Monday. She wants me today. I can't turn her down. She offered to pay double because of the short notice, and she always gives me a big tip."

Even though Kenny was disappointed, he didn't want to say it. "It's okay. My dad will be glad to see me. He doesn't like me going off and not telling him where I'm going."

Maybell enveloped Kenny in her arms, pressed her breasts into his chest and gave him a big kiss. After they separated, she said, "Listen I'm busy all week but I'm going to be off next Saturday. Just you and me. Pick me up at eight in the morning, and we'll make a day of it. I'll bring my picnic basket with food."

"Sounds great. It's two weeks before my birthday. A day with you would be an early present. I guess you need to go now. I'll take off."

"Wow, you'll be eighteen. I'll bake a cake on your birthday, and maybe I'll have an early one next Saturday."

"Sounds good."

Kenny turned around in the parking area and drove down the long driveway.

As he made it around the last bend, he saw Joan Wilcox walking toward him. She waved for him to stop.

"Please, could you give me a ride into town?" Joan pleaded.

Kenny didn't know any reason not to be nice to Maybell's sister, so he leaned over and opened the door. "Sure, come on in."

Joan put a big folder, or something she'd been carrying, on the back seat. Responding to Kenny's inquisitive look, she said, "Art portfolio."

While Kenny tried not to stare, he couldn't help noticing how Joan's skirt hiked up as she climbed into the Jeep. She was really a stunning girl. With long legs, blonde hair, big blue eyes, and large breasts, Kenny had heard a bunch of guys saying they thought she'd make a great playmate of the month.

At the intersection on the main road, he asked, "What were you doing out here? You're still in school, aren't you?"

"Yes, and I need to get there. Joel Nixon said he'd pick me up twenty minutes ago. He didn't show. I'm gonna be late. I'm sure I can talk my way out of trouble. Drop me off at the main office. Principal Brown likes me."

"I guess Joel's in big trouble."

Joan smiled. "You're right. I don't know what excuse he's going to come up with. No matter what he says, I'm going to make him crawl."

As they picked up speed, the noise of the Jeep made further conversation impossible, so they drove the rest of the way in silence. When they pulled up in front of the office at the high school, Joan grabbed the portfolio, turned to Kenny, and flashed a big smile. "Thanks so much, Kenny."

"No problem."

Much to Kenny's surprise, Joan didn't climb out right away. She sat beside him, staring at him. After a pause he didn't understand, she said, "Kenny, I shouldn't be saying anything. But watch out for Maybell. I don't know what she's cooking up for you, leading you on the way she is. You know she has a boyfriend, don't you?"

Kenny didn't know what to say. After an uncomfortable silence, he got defensive. "Don't worry about me and Maybell. We have a good thing going."

Joan gave him a sideways look, opened the door, got out, and then leaned back in the window and said, "Don't say I didn't warn you."

Kenny watched Joan flounce her way into the main office. He wondered if any of his old high school friends saw him drop her off. They would wonder how they got together. While the idea cheered him up some, he wondered what Joan had been talking about. He'd have to tell Maybell about it. Then he thought, *What does Joan know? She sure doesn't know how fast Maybell hustled me into her van after I checked out the old car she bought.* Still, Joan's warning made him a little uneasy.

Kenny drove around town, wondering what to think about his morning. Maybell had been fantastic. She clearly liked him. At the same time, what about what Joan had said? Then he figured it out. The only explanation was jealousy. Joan was jealous because Maybell had found him. Joan usually attracted all the guys, and he thought she craved being the center of everything. She couldn't stand to have Maybell be the one getting attention. Their folks clearly liked Kenny, and they'd invited him to the Charleston thing. Kenny bet none of Joan's boyfriends had ever been invited to one of those meetings.

It made him feel much better to have figured things out. He had to be right. Joan was a manipulator. He was a little mad at himself for almost falling for her crap.

Kenny dropped by the A&W for a quick snack and then drove home, surprising his father with his early arrival.

"I thought you weren't going to be back until two o'clock or so. At least it's what you told me last night," his father said.

"Some of my plans fell through, so I came back early. I figured you might need help getting ready for the group this afternoon."

"Good for you son. Maybe you're finally getting to be more responsible."

Kenny went into the house, wondering what his dad would think next Saturday when he didn't show up 'til really late. Maybell said she'd make sure they could be together the whole day.

Chapter Eighteen

Ho Narwhal, September 10, 1979

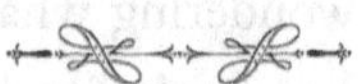

Ho didn't mind the thirty-minute drive to Springfield. He looked forward to seeing Karen and Linda again. He'd been on edge when he'd called Karen last Monday to invite the two of them to the installation party at the museum in St. Louis. While the party was a month away, he didn't want to wait to invite them. It was a long drive for them, almost three hours. Still, he knew they often made the trip to see Karen's parents on the weekends. He'd been surprised at how readily Karen had accepted and even more surprised when Karen asked him if he'd like to go to the theater. She'd said she had been about to call him. She had an extra ticket for *Fiddler on the Roof* on Saturday.

During the week, he spent quite a bit of time trying to prepare. He'd purchased the Broadway cast album at the record store. While he liked some of the music, he still felt unprepared. Though he studied up as much as he could, he didn't know much about Jews or Russia. Even though he knew he was a hick, he didn't want it to show. By the time he left for Springfield, he still feared the gaps in his education might reveal themselves. For one, he'd known his religious education was severely lacking, and he hoped he wouldn't have to get into any deep discussion with either Karen or Linda, maybe particularly Linda.

Ho heaved a big sigh when he pulled up to Karen's apartment. He checked his clothes, hoping the khakis and new blue sport coat were right for a play. He hadn't worn a tie. He found them uncomfortable, so he decided to take a chance. Karen greeted him at the door in a green pantsuit. She was stunning with her hair done up and gold earrings. Her dimples deepened as she smiled at him. Ho couldn't miss the perfume she wore. It smelled great. Ho didn't know what to say, so he blurted, "Where's Linda?"

"Oh, she's at a sleepover at a friend's house. She told me to say hi and to be nice to you."

"Well tell her hi back, and I'm sure you'll treat me fine." Ho was stunned. Was this a date? He'd assumed Linda would be there.

Karen directed him to a good place to park close to the theater. When they reached the entrance, she gave him the tickets to be punched. He liked having a lady who gave them programs and directed them to their seats. The theater was impressive. Their seats were on the main floor. While other people filled the balcony, Ho checked out the men. Most of them wore ties. He felt better when he saw some open collars. He even saw some guys without sports coats, so he figured he'd be fine.

Before investigating the program, Ho admitted to Karen that this was the first play he'd seen since high school, and even then, they'd been put on by the students.

"You're in for a big treat. This group is touring with the play. They're professional actors, not the top-of-the-line ones, but still professionals. Some of them are up-and-comers though, so you might hear more about them later. The program has a list of the performers and what they've done in the past. I like to see where they're from."

Ho opened the program and found the part Karen had mentioned. She was right. The actors were from all over the place. Ho took his time reading. He was startled when the musicians began warming up. He could see the top of some of their heads in front of him. While he knew *Fiddler on the Roof* was a musical, he'd figured they'd use recordings. *I have a lot to learn*, he thought.

During intermission, Karen led Ho toward a small bar where they were serving wine. She said, "I'm going to the restroom. Order me a white wine. I think they only have Chablis. I'll be right back! Thank you!"

Ho joined the line at the bar and eventually ordered two white wines. He thought they were a little expensive. Karen, who'd been looking for him, waved when she could see him searching for her. They clinked glasses and drank their wine.

"Are you enjoying the show?" Karen asked.

"Yes, very much. I've heard some of the music before, but it makes more sense in the flow of the story. It's funny, the play is a mix of happy and sad. The father wants to uphold tradition, but his kids don't."

"Yes, I think it's a universal problem. I can already see it happening with Linda in small ways. Still, it's there just the same."

"I'm surprised. I thought you and Linda got along all the time."

"Oh no!" she said with a laugh. "Definitely not all the time."

"I bet the conflicts aren't as deep as the ones in this play."

"You're right about that. We usually get along fine. She's a good kid."

As they finished their wine, the lights blinked, which startled Ho. Karen grabbed his hand. "It's the signal for us to get back to our seats for the second act."

They found a place to discard their glasses as they walked back. Ho was thrilled as Karen held his hand while they made their way to their seats. They continued holding each other's hands during the rest of the play.

After they joined the audience in a standing ovation and people started to file out, Karen asked Ho if he wanted to go out for a drink.

"Sure. I hope you know where we can go. I don't know much about Springfield."

Karen directed Ho as they drove to a little bar several blocks from the theater. They arrived with several other people who'd also been to the play.

Ho recognized a couple who'd been seated near them and a few others as well.

Ho had a beer and Karen ordered another Chablis. They started out talking about the play, but soon shifted to other topics. He found it easy to talk to Karen. Her work interested him. There were some parts of it she couldn't talk about. Also, she quizzed him about his latest projects. Ho was proud to say he'd attracted three new commissions, so he'd decided to put off the idea of another show in the St. Louis gallery.

On the way to Karen's apartment, Ho started to get nervous. He never knew what to do about the goodnight kiss. He wanted to kiss Karen, but he didn't want to be too forward. An awkward moment on her front porch could ruin what had been a wonderful evening. When they arrived, Karen took all the decision making out of his control. She held his hand as they walked up to her front door and pulled it behind her when they stopped. Their bodies were close together. She put her other arm around him and gave him a soft kiss that lingered.

When they broke apart, Karen said, "I had a wonderful night Ho, thanks for coming."

"I did too," Ho stammered. "Karen, I think you're wonderful. I'd love to call you again."

Karen gave him a little kiss and said, "I'm counting on it." Then she opened her apartment door and went in.

Ho was overjoyed as he drove home. He'd never been with a woman like Karen. He'd always thought girls like her would be out of his league. She was gorgeous and she had a big-time job. Since he'd met her parents, Ho knew her upbringing hadn't been anything like his. But she liked him. He could tell from the goodnight kiss. She definitely liked him.

Ho knew he'd broken away from most of his father's influence. Still, sometimes the effects lingered. In a way, this was one of the persistent things. If you're a loser, you'd think a great girl would never have anything to do with you. He'd been trying to break this kind of thinking. Over the years he had become more certain his father's attitude was a trap. If you thought you were a loser, you became one. Ho's current work made him anything but a loser. He'd become a near-famous sculptor. Maybe he'd even have a successful relationship with Karen.

Two days later, Ho called Karen and they arranged for a picnic the following Saturday. The picnic in a park on the outskirts of Springfield was another great success. Again, Linda brought along one of her friends. As a result, Karen and Ho had time alone. Linda had the good sense to go into the apartment ahead of Ho and Karen, so they shared several goodbye kisses before Ho drove home.

Karen called Ho the next Monday evening and told him she would be in Tyndall on Wednesday night and available for dinner. Things were moving fast. Given their ages, maybe Ho should have expected as much. As they had arranged, Karen came to Ho's studio at six o'clock. She was in her work clothes, a brown suit with a tight skirt. Ho had quit early and run home, so he had showered and dressed in newly pressed clothes.

After dinner, Karen asked, "Where do you live? I'd like to see your place."

Ho had hoped, but he hadn't thought much of his chances. It was probably too soon. "Sure, I even cleaned it up a little."

When they reached the apartment, Ho and Karen quickly embraced, and Karen said, "I've been wanting to kiss you since before they brought our food."

"Me too."

After a long and intense kiss, Ho asked, "Would you like to see the bedroom?"

Karen smiled. "Lead the way."

Chapter Nineteen

Kenny Sturgis, October 25, 1980

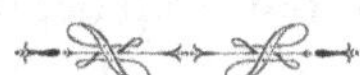

Kenny woke early on Saturday, eager for his day with Maybell. Nothing could stop him from seeing her. It had been more than a week since they'd had a chance to be together. Last night, his dad was pissed when Kenny told him he couldn't be there for the arrival of the new batch of hunters. His dad shouted about how he'd dock Kenny's pay. Kenny shouted back that he didn't care and stormed off. He didn't return home until he knew his dad would be asleep, and he woke up before the old man in the morning. *It's best to let things calm down some.*

Kenny had some time to kill, and he hadn't eaten breakfast, so he drove to the McDonald's out by the highway and had a leisurely meal there. He wondered why so many people liked McDonald's. Except for breakfast, he didn't like the food. The place was surprisingly busy this early. He overheard people talking about some kind of political rally. Kenny guessed it had something to do with the elections the people at the meeting had been talking about.

He dawdled over his breakfast and then drove back to town through the business district. None of the stores were open. Kenny parked in the high school lot and wondered what Maybell had in store for him. She said it would be a special day.

He'd thought about it more, and he figured he had it right about the nonsense last week from Joan. She was jealous. Her older sister had someone—him and her own boyfriend had stood her up. She just wanted to throw a monkey wrench into what he and Maybell had going. Families were funny.

When he drove up at eight o'clock, Maybell appeared at the end of the Wilcox driveway. She'd stepped out from behind a bush, picnic basket in her right hand and a rolled-up blanket under her left arm. She tossed both in the back of the Jeep, jumped in, and slid over to give Kenny a kiss.

"Happy week before your birthday!" she shouted and then motioned for Kenny to take off. Kenny liked her outfit. It was surprisingly warm for October, so she had on summer clothes—short-shorts and a skimpy red top.

"Where are we headed?" Kenny shouted over the roar of the Jeep.

"Keep going, hon. I'll tell you when to turn."

After twenty minutes, Maybell had him turn left down a gravel road. After she directed him to make several more turns, Kenny didn't have any idea where he was. They were on unfamiliar country roads.

"We're almost there!" Maybell shouted as they started up a steep road.

The road eventually dead ended in a wide spot near the top of the small hill.

"We can park over by the fence. I know the people who own this property. No one will bother your Jeep here. Help me get the picnic basket."

Kenny grabbed the basket and jumped out. He went around to Maybell's side as she turned to reach for the rolled-up blanket. Kenny moved close and grabbed her rear end. Maybell wiggled provocatively and said, "Hold up boy. There'll be plenty of time later."

Out of the Jeep, Maybell directed him to climb over the fence with the picnic basket and then help her over.

"Our spot is right up here," Maybell said, pointing to a slight rise.

When they arrived, Kenny could tell why Maybell had picked this spot. It was breathtaking and completely private. They'd stepped through a break in the trees, into a little meadow with a grass floor. She spread out the blanket and knelt on it.

Kenny put down the picnic basket and stared as she started unbuttoning her blouse.

"Don't just stand there. Come down here and help me." Kenny didn't need to be told twice. In a flash, he kneeled on the blanket and unhooked Maybell's bra.

After they'd made love, Kenny felt tired. "I'm pooped," he said. "I didn't get much sleep last night. My dad didn't take it well when I told him I wasn't going to work today, so I went to town and didn't come back till after he was asleep. This morning, I left before he woke up."

"Why don't we take a nap? It's real nice out here, and it's going to be a warm day. We don't have anything planned. Let's snuggle. I think a nap is a good idea."

As Kenny woke from the nap, he rolled over on the blanket and saw Maybell, fully clothed, sitting there staring at him. "Wow, did I sleep too long?"

"No, I only woke up a few minutes ago myself. Get dressed. I want to show you around."

Kenny dressed quickly and followed Maybell out of the little meadow. "Do you think it's okay to leave the picnic stuff here?"

"No problem. We won't be gone long."

As Kenny followed her, it became clear Maybell knew where she was headed. They crossed several fences and finally came to a little pond. "Let's go skinny dipping," Maybell said, starting to take off her clothes.

"We don't have any towels."

"The sun's out and it's warm. We'll dry off. What's wrong? Can't you swim?"

"Sure, I can swim. You surprised me. That's all."

Kenny could tell Maybell was a good swimmer, and it made him feel inadequate. He'd never had any swimming lessons. He'd been to the pool in town a few times before his mother left. While he could keep his head above water and get where he wanted to go, he wasn't comfortable in the water. When they finally crawled out, Kenny was tired, while Maybell seemed invigorated.

"Not much of a swimmer there Kenny, are you?"

"No, I guess not. My mom took me swimming before she left, and I guess she taught me. Then she was gone, and my dad never followed up. The story of my life."

"Poor baby." Maybell came up to him and kissed him. After the kiss, she led him over to a patch of grass in the direct sunlight.

"Lay down here beside me and dry off then we can head back to the picnic basket."

After they finished their lunch, ham and cheese sandwiches and a couple of pieces of the cake Maybell brought, she stood up and shifted the picnic basket to the side and started folding up the blanket. "Come on, I have other places to show you."

Back in the Jeep, Maybell directed Kenny where to turn. After a few turns, Kenny, who'd been completely confused when he started, stopped trying to figure out where they were going. Twenty minutes after they started, Maybell directed Kenny to park on the side of a dirt road they'd been driving on for the last mile.

"Here, climb over this fence. There's a great view from the top of this hill."

Kenny followed her across the fence and had no trouble keeping up with her as she followed a narrow trail up a hill. They were both breathing hard when they made it to the top. "Look around. Isn't this an amazing view?"

Kenny had to admit the view was spectacular. He could see for a long way, but he didn't recognize anything. Mostly he could see trees with leaves starting to change color.

The rest of the day followed the same pattern. Maybell led Kenny on several more drives, followed by short hikes. Kenny had given up trying to keep track of where they were, so he was quite surprised when they wound up at the place where they'd first parked. Maybell grabbed the blanket from the backseat and yelled at Kenny, "Come on, let's go back to our room."

"You don't have to ask twice."

Maybell almost tackled Kenny after she'd spread out the blanket on the grass. After, she laughed. "Look at our clothes. They're everywhere!"

Kenny laughed too. "I guess we were kind of in a hurry."

"Put on your clothes and go back and get the picnic basket. There's more cake, and there are a couple more Cokes."

Kenny finally dropped Maybell off at the top of her driveway in the dark. He had no idea where they'd been. He wasn't even sure Maybell hadn't taken him back the same way they'd come. After climbing out of the Jeep, Maybell came around to Kenny's window, kissed him, and said, "Call me later in the week, and we'll figure out when we can get together again."

Chapter Twenty

Ho Narwhal, October 25, 1980

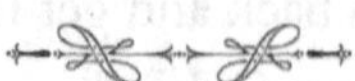

Ho finally summoned the courage to propose to Karen in June. She'd told him the answer would be yes if Linda approved. Driving toward the Walter Cunningham rally, he smiled as he remembered the moment. He'd had an answer ready for Karen.

"I already asked Linda, and you know what she said?"

Surprised, Karen said, "No, what did she say?"

"She said, 'Of course, what's taken you so long?'"

They planned a December wedding, and Ho marveled at how his life had turned out. His family was still a mess. He didn't think there was much possibility of change. Despite his misgivings, the meeting between Karen's parents and his father and sister went off without a hitch. His father had been surprisingly well behaved, and the two Lindas had gotten along well.

Ho had no difficulty finding a place in Springfield for his studio. The second place he looked at only needed a few modifications before it would be perfect. Its owner had built it to be a warehouse, so Ho had to remove the shelving and install a few more electric outlets. The windows were high, but they let in plenty of light. Best of all, the new studio had much more floor space than his old place in Tyndall. Moving all his equipment and the two commissions he had underway would be a big job, but Ho figured he could get it done.

He looked forward to the Cunningham rally mostly because Karen would be there. She'd snagged the reserve duty in case something went wrong. She wasn't part of the protection detail, only a backup. After the rally, she and Ho were going to Tyndall. He didn't like being away from her so much, but they both had busy lives.

Ho arrived at the rally, arranged his blanket, and sat. His car was in a makeshift parking lot in a farmer's field, so he had a bit of a walk to get to the natural amphitheater behind a fruit stand. He found a place in the tenth row. He enjoyed watching the crowd arrive. The warm weather boosted the turnout, and the colorful crowd seemed to be in a party mood. Ho saw several people with picnics and others with beer and wine.

Walter Cunningham, Horace Cunningham's brother, was incredibly popular, a shoo-in to be elected governor. The person elected governor wouldn't matter too much to Ho. On the other hand, it would matter a great deal to Karen. Because of her job, she couldn't let it be known how much she wanted Walter Cunningham to win. Ho had stepped up and proudly worn his Cunningham button. He'd also donated a couple of miniature sculptures to a Cunningham fund raiser. They'd sold for outrageous prices, and Ho had been pleased when Walter personally thanked him after the event.

Ho spotted Karen getting out of the black station wagon following Cunningham's. Separating herself from the guys on protection duty, she went to a reserved seat in the second row and scanned the crowd. Ho waved both hands over his head, and they exchanged smiles when Karen waved back.

Ho settled back onto his blanket and waited as the final members of the crowd filed in behind him while the VIPs greeted the candidate in front of the fruit stand. Finally, the VIP group was escorted to their seats in the front row. Ho checked his watch. They were only running ten minutes late—

pretty good for one of these rallies. While the crowd had been nice to the people who spoke first, Ho sensed people were reserving their enthusiasm for Cunningham.

Cunningham seemed surprised at the loud, prolonged standing ovation he received after his introduction. He finally put his hands up to settle the crowd and Ho sat down, hoping the people in front of him would do the same. Cunningham walked back to the podium from the front of the stage and reached into his coat pocket. At the same time, Ho heard a snap and then a muffled boom off to the right. Suddenly Cunningham crumbled to the ground and a dark stain spread over his white shirt.

Ho's army training kicked in. The snap came from the bullet breaking the sound barrier and the boom came from the rifle firing. *When you hear the crack first, the bullet is coming in your direction*, he thought. Frantically, he looked for Karen. She alone stood up on the stage and stared off at where the shot had come from. He followed her gaze to the hilltop. Others either ran to the stage to try to help the candidate or dove under their chairs in case there were more shots. Suddenly, Karen started running toward where Ho had seen a little puff of smoke on the hill. He struggled to work his way through the stunned crowd so he could follow Karen.

By the time Ho made it through the crowd, Karen was about a hundred yards up the hill. He ran after her as fast as he could and made up some of the distance between them when she slowed. She bent down and started searching the ground as Ho caught up to her.

She looked surprised to see him. "This must have been where the shot came from. You can tell because of where the bipod left marks in the dirt. Do me a favor, keep people away from this area. It's going to be crucial in the investigation."

"Wow, it's an incredibly long shot." He scanned the area and turned back toward the stage behind the fruit stand.

"Yes, whoever did it was a very good shot. Stay here and protect this crime scene. I'm going to see what else I can find."

Ho didn't like the idea of letting Karen go off by herself, but she'd been clear about what she wanted. He watched her disappear over the crest of the hill.

Several uniformed policemen arrived, and a helicopter landed near the stage. Ho guessed they were going to rush Cunningham to a hospital. When the first officer reached him, Ho said, "Keep people away from this area. The guy shot from here. See? Here are the marks his bipod made. He must have been a sniper. Guard this spot. It could contain evidence. I'm going to follow Karen Daniels with the state police. She went over the hill."

Ho headed up the hill after Karen. He liked the way the uniformed guy had obeyed him. While the guy didn't know him from Adam, Ho had been very definite. People listen to someone who sounds like he knows what he's talking about.

When Ho crested the hill, he saw Karen closing the door of an old rattletrap car. It seemed to have crashed into some bushes to the right side of the dirt road twenty feet or so from the top of the hill. She was removing a pair of latex gloves. When he came up to her, she turned to him with a stern look on her face. "I thought I told you to guard those marks."

"I handed off the duty to a uniformed officer who came up. More of them are on their way. What's up with this car?"

"The gun's in the back seat—an exotic sniper rifle. I opened the doors to get a closer look. I didn't touch anything. But I learned a few things. First, the gun had been shot recently. You could smell it. Second, the guy chews tobacco. He slobbered on the stock where he put his cheek. I could smell that too. Apparently, the guy was in such a hurry, he ran his getaway vehicle off the road. I figure he panicked and took off on foot. I have to go back to call this in. If we set up a perimeter, we might be able to catch him. He can't have gone far on foot."

Karen paused as she stared into the trees. "I hate to ask you the same thing again, Ho. But can you stand guard on this car? Don't let anyone touch it. I don't want anyone near it until the techs get a chance to process it."

"I'll keep people away from the car. You do what you have to do."

Karen ran back toward where Ho had come from. Five minutes later she appeared, leading a group of officers. One of them had bright yellow crime tape and Ho helped him string it up around the car while Karen and the others headed down the hill.

Ho guessed he was relieved of duty when the one officer stayed in front of the yellow crime tape guarding the car. He didn't know what to do. Part of him wanted to try to follow Karen and the others, but he knew he shouldn't. Karen would blow her stack if he followed her. He decided to go down the hill and check things out. At his first guard post, he saw more crime tape and another uniformed guard. When he checked the stage and the amphitheater, he didn't see any action. Most people seemed to be leaving. As he turned around to climb back up the hill, he heard a helicopter landing. A swarm of police exited the copter and headed toward him. Ho recognized the rotund shape of Bill Hooper, Karen's boss, who led the group.

When he got close, Hooper recognized Ho. He was red-faced and puffing hard. Addressing Ho, he asked, "What are you doing here?"

"I was at the event, and I ran after Karen when she headed in this direction. We think the shot came from inside the crime tape over there. Karen found marks from a bipod the shooter used."

"Check it out, Charlie," Hooper said briskly.

An older man in a police uniform veered toward the tape.

"Anything else, Narwhal? That's your name, right?"

"Yes, Horace Narwhal. There's a car up the hill. Karen thinks the guy used it. He crashed it into some bushes, so she thinks he took off on foot."

Ho followed the rest of the group up the hill. When they reached the car, Hooper motioned the guard out of the way and ducked under the crime tape. After peering in the windows, he put on latex gloves and opened the back door. Careful not to touch anything, he lowered himself onto his knees and sniffed the barrel of the rifle.

"This rifle's been fired recently, and it's a sniper rifle for sure. I've never seen anything like it before," Hooper reported. "Sal, make sure when he's finished down there to have Charlie get up here. Things are breaking fast."

Turning to Ho, he continued, "You seem to know more than anyone around here. What else happened?"

"Karen and some other guys, I think local police, went down the hill to search for the guy. They've been gone about five minutes."

"Okay, we'll see what they can find. I heard Karen call in to have a perimeter set up. I hope we can snag this bastard."

After five minutes, while the police milled around looking at the car from different angles, Charlie, Ho figured he had to be the tech, came up to the group.

Hooper spoke up. "Charlie, I put on gloves and opened the back door. The gun in there was fired recently. I didn't touch anything. I think the guy panicked and ran his get-away vehicle into those bushes. Karen Daniels and some locals are trying to track him down on foot."

"Daniels was right," Charlie said. "The place down there is where the shot came from. The marks from the bipod are there and you can see where the guy was on the ground. There are clear marks where his elbow and shoes were. When the rest of my team gets here, we'll look for fiber evidence. I think I'll wait to examine the car until they arrive. You've already made the most important determination. The rest of the evidence is the kind of thing we'll be able to gather with more equipment. This car's not going anywhere."

"Good. I think this guy is a good shot, but otherwise, he's not too bright. A guy with any sense wouldn't leave his weapon in the car."

"Maybe he didn't want to be running away with such a big rifle," another officer commented. "If someone saw him, it would be a dead giveaway."

"Maybe. I guess. If it were me, I'd at least toss the thing in the woods somewhere. I mean, I think this is the fastest anyone has ever found the weapon involved in a big crime. It's weird."

Fifteen minutes later, more police arrived. Ho figured they were the crime scene techs because they reported to Charlie. He directed a couple of them to where they thought the shot came from and explained to the rest of them about the car. The techs ducked under the crime tape and started to work.

Ho felt like a fifth wheel. Still, he couldn't leave. He had to drive Karen. He paced, a little worried about what she was doing. He hadn't thought much about Karen's work being hazardous. He guessed police work involved some dangerous situations, but Karen was a special investigator, not a cop who had to respond to domestic abuse cases or hostile traffic stops, and she hadn't been on any swat teams that he knew of. What she was doing now bothered him.

About a half hour after the crime scene techs arrived, Karen trudged up the hill looking a little bedraggled. While Ho wanted to rush up and hug her, he held back. She was on duty, and he expected she would have to report to her boss.

"We didn't find a thing," she told Hooper. "There were lots of footprints in the dirt and a whole bunch of motorcycle tracks. We spread out and I followed a hiking trail. It's not easy with all the leaves already down. I didn't see much. The other guys are still searching. I don't think they'll find anything."

Charlie, who'd overheard Karen's report, said, "I think we can find out who this guy is. We've been able to lift prints from the gun and the steering wheel. While I can't be sure, they might be identical prints."

"Great, Charlie. We should know who we're after in a few hours," Hooper said.

Next, Hooper turned on Karen angrily and shouted, "And Daniels, you're in big trouble. Your advance team should have covered this hill. There's no way we should have had a candidate for governor getting shot. There's going to be hell to pay."

Karen reacted swiftly. "I wasn't on protective duty. You put Jerry Watson in charge, remember? I only came here in case there was an incident."

"I apologize. I forgot."

Karen's anger was evident as she continued. "Yeah, I guess you did. After the shot, I ran up here, found the place where the shot came from, discovered the car, and organized a search. What more did you want me to do?"

Hooper didn't respond. He simply walked away.

On the return drive, Ho and Karen were mostly silent until Ho said, "I hope they find the shooter quickly."

"You'd be surprised at how dumb some of these guys are. This guy was one hell of a shot, but not so smart. He couldn't drive straight, and then he left fingerprints all over the car and the rifle."

"I agree, I'm surprised he left the rifle in the car."

"It's a good break for us. Let's turn on the radio and see if they have any more information on Cunningham's condition. It's about to be five o'clock, they should have some news now."

After another song, the station broke for news. The announcer only gave a cryptic report. All the hospital spokesman would say was Walter Cunningham was in critical condition. They had lots of details on the shooting, but Karen and Ho knew this information already.

After a five-minute silence, Ho said, "I can see what you've been saying about Hooper. I couldn't believe it. He tried to blame the shooting on you when you weren't even part of the guard detail."

"Bill Hooper's never really accepted women in his unit. No, I'm not right. He's okay with the women crime techs. It's women detectives he doesn't like. He'd love to find some way to get rid of me. I have to live with it all the time. He couldn't help himself back there. He hoped he could pin the shooting on me, but he couldn't. It's his buddy Jerry Watson who should be in trouble."

Chapter Twenty-One
Kenny Sturgis, October 26, 2020

Kenny's father had barked at him some when he'd pulled into the camp the previous evening. It hadn't been as bad as Kenny had thought it would be. He guessed his dad knew better than to have a family fight in front of the customers. They left early for the morning hunt and settled into their normal routine. As the group made its way back to camp for lunch, Kenny carried a deer one of the customers had bagged, so he straggled behind the group by about twenty yards.

When he reached the campsite, two police officers were talking to his dad. His dad pointed to him. As Kenny went to put the deer on the rack, one of the policemen followed him. After he'd unloaded the deer, the policeman came up and asked, "Are you Kenneth Sturgis?"

Kenny turned to the policeman and replied, "Yeah, what of it?"

The other policeman had come over, hovering nearby. The first policeman said, "It's over son. You are under arrest for attempted murder. Turn your back, we're going to cuff you."

"What the hell?"

The policeman grabbed Kenny's shoulders and spun him around, and the other policeman snapped handcuffs on him.

The move dumbfounded Kenny. "What's this about?"

"Come on kid, we know it's going to be your fingerprints all over the rifle found at the Walter Cunningham scene. There's no denying it. And your dad said you were gone all day yesterday. We're taking you in now. At the station they'll read you your rights, and you can have a lawyer if you want. You probably know the drill. We're only doing our job."

"Who the hell is Walter Cunningham?" Kenny blurted.

"Come on kid. Don't try to act dumb."

The policeman shoved Kenny toward the police car.

"Dad," Kenny pleaded, looking at his father. Kenny's dad simply shook his head and turned away. The customers didn't know what to do. Then one of them asked, "What did you say about Walter Cunningham?"

"A sniper shot him at his rally yesterday. I think Cunningham's in bad shape. I don't know if he'll make it."

"I never shot nobody!" Kenny yelled.

"Be quiet son," the policeman who'd cuffed Kenny said. "If you can prove you didn't do it, you'll have your chance.

Kenny knew enough to obey the policeman, so he didn't give them any trouble when they loaded him in the back of the patrol car. As they drove, he started to find the whole experience funny. He knew where he'd been yesterday, and he knew he had a witness. He'd been with Maybell all day. She'd provide his alibi. When he had a chance to talk to someone in charge, he'd be set free as soon as they talked to Maybell. At the police station, several flashbulbs surprised Kenny as the police escorted him into the building.

Inside, Kenny went through the routine. Somebody read him his rights, next came fingerprints and photographs before they deposited him in a cell. As things progressed, he thought of it as a game. With Maybell's help he'd be out, and he'd have a great story to tell. After about half an hour, some guy in plain clothes opened his cell and led Kenny to a room down the hallway.

They sat down facing each other across a small table.

"Kenneth, I'm Detective Johnson, and I have some questions for you. First, the officers read you your rights. Did you understand what they said?"

"Yeah, what I say can be used against me, and I can have a lawyer if I want one. It's no problem, because I didn't do nothing, and I can prove it."

"Okay, no lawyer. Now Kenny, we've been checking up on you. You turn eighteen next Saturday, right?"

"Yeah."

"It means we can't charge you as an adult, a big break for you. I know it's only by a week, but you were a juvenile when the shooting happened."

"So what? It don't matter. I didn't do nothing."

"So you say. You're wrong though. Anyway, when we checked up on you, we found you're known to be a real good shot with a rifle, right?"

"What of it?"

"Where were you yesterday from about ten in the morning till three? We already know your father said you weren't at work where he thought you should be."

"Finally, we're going to finish this. I went out all day with my girlfriend, Maybell Wilcox. She can tell you where we went. I don't actually know. She led the way. Anyway, we were together all day from eight in the morning until after dark. I have an ironclad alibi, so there's no reason for any more questions."

"Maybell Wilcox, you say. Where does she live?"

Kenny gave Maybell's address and phone number to the detective.

"Sit tight right here while I go get someone to call this girl."

The detective came back in a couple of minutes and gave Kenny a funny look. "While we're waiting to hear from your girlfriend, I have some more questions."

Kenny smiled. "I don't know why you're bothering. Like I said, I didn't do nothing."

"We'll see. Try this. Someone called earlier with a tip about you, and we compared the prints we just took to what we found at the scene. How do you explain that we found your fingerprints on the gun used to shoot Senator Cunningham?"

"I don't know what you're talking about."

"And we found your fingerprints on the car the shooter tried to use as a getaway vehicle. Care to tell me about it?"

"I repeat. I don't know what you're talking about." Kenny kept the smile on his face.

"I'll tell you what we're talking about. We're talking about the evidence we can use to convict you. We have you dead to rights. You'd be better off admitting what you did. It's likely Cunningham will die. Then it will be murder, not attempted murder, and then the death penalty would be involved if you were an adult. You should wipe the smile off your seventeen-year-old face."

"I have an iron-clad alibi like I told you. You shouldn't waste your time or mine, officer. The guy who shot whoever you're talking about is still out there."

"We'll see," Johnson said as he leaned back in his chair, staring at Kenny.

After a few minutes of silence, Johnson started asking questions again. "Who helped you with this? I mean, you had to have help. I don't think you could have pulled this off by yourself."

Kenny smirked at Johnson. "I don't know why you're bothering with your questions. I told you I didn't do nothing. You're checking on my alibi right now. Let's see how it goes from there."

Silence descended as Johnson stared, and Kenny continued to smirk at him.

After fifteen minutes of silence, someone knocked on the door, and Johnson pushed his chair back and went out the door.

He popped back into the room two minutes later with a smile on his face. "We were able to talk to Maybell Wilcox, and she said she doesn't know what you're talking about. She was doing dog grooming yesterday. It's her business.

She said she's not your girlfriend. She barely knows who you are."

This pronouncement shocked Kenny. After a moment, he said, "Are you sure you were talking to the right Maybell Wilcox?"

"Quit it son. We called the number you gave us, and the person who answered the phone identified herself as Maybell Wilcox. Your story doesn't hold up. Care to tell me now how your fingerprints were on the gun and the car?"

Kenny sat stunned. His mind raced. *What is going on? Why did Maybell say she barely knew me?*

"Listen. We have everything we need to book you. Your fingerprints were on the gun and the getaway car, and you can't tell us where you were. You can make it a lot easier on all of us if you tell us why you did it. Who put you up to it? Who helped you?"

Kenny didn't respond, his mind numb.

The policeman waved his hands in front of Kenny's face. "Kenneth, you in there?"

Finally, Kenny mumbled, "I want a lawyer."

Chapter Twenty-Two

Ho Narwhal November 3, 1980

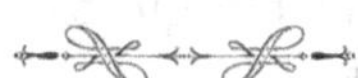

Karen and Ho attended the funeral for Walter Cunningham at a big Episcopal church in Springfield. While the doctors tried valiantly, they were only able to keep Cunningham alive for three days after the shooting. Everyone in the political world in Springfield was in shock. Dick Watson, the candidate for Lieutenant Governor, stepped up on the ballot to take Walter's place, and the party quickly nominated someone for Watson's slot on the ticket. The funeral was by invitation only. Since Karen's parents knew the Cunningham family, and Ho had been a donor to the campaign, they were invited.

Ho thought he looked okay in his new black suit and purple tie. Glancing around, he didn't feel as out of place as he thought he might. They were sitting in the middle of the large church, which had filled to capacity by the time the organ music started. A choir sang a solemn song, the pastor or priest gave a sermon, and three people from the Cunningham family spoke. Ho paid particular attention to Horace's talk. Clearly, Horace was having a hard time holding it together. Still, he gave a moving eulogy of his younger brother.

After the service ended, they filed out somberly. Ho still felt a little uncomfortable at gatherings like this. He recognized a few people but didn't speak to anyone. He didn't know what he could say. Karen, though, seemed more comfortable. She greeted several people as they exited the church. Ho had never been to a funeral before. He realized it hadn't been a typical funeral, not with the TV station vans parked outside. He hadn't noticed them when they'd arrived, but he suspected they were filming then, too. He hadn't seen any cameras in the church, so the people coming and leaving might be the only video the TV people could shoot.

After the funeral, Karen and Ho greeted the Cunningham family at a reception in the church hall. Walter's wife stood straight and reserved in the receiving line. Horace surprised Ho by giving him a brief hug and thanking him for coming. After the reception, Ho and Karen went to a restaurant by themselves. Karen had been busy with the investigation, so Ho hadn't seen much of her since the night after the shooting.

"How's the investigation going? The papers make it seem like this guy Sturgis did it for sure."

"Most of the evidence points to him. Remember I said that it wasn't too bright to leave the sniper rifle behind? Carl Riggs, he's the head of our crime techs, found fingerprints on the rifle and the car. The prints matched Sturgis. People are treating it like an open and shut case."

"People are? It doesn't sound like you're convinced."

"I've been checking out Sturgis and his story. I've become skeptical about the obvious conclusion everyone is rushing to. The whole thing seems too convenient. He leaves the expensive sniper rifle behind and he doesn't wear gloves."

"You think somebody set up this guy?"

"It's his story. I interviewed his father, who he works for. Mr. Sturgis is a hunting guide. He's not interested in talking to law enforcement so I didn't get much out of him. Still, he didn't think his son had any interest in politics at all, and he couldn't believe his son was mixed up in Cunningham's murder."

"Who else did you interview?"

"A bunch of the kid's friends in Sheffield. Sturgis dropped out of high school before graduating. But I tracked down some of his old friends. His ex-girlfriend verified he wasn't political at all and she also said he was a really good shot with a rifle. She told me about a shooting range out behind the Sturgis house. I went out to the house and sure enough they have a rifle range. Mr. Sturgis told me they used it to sight in the rifles hunters bring to their hunting camp. Anyway, it checked out. Kenneth Sturgis is a good shot, good enough to have made the Cunningham shot. His other friends were also surprised he'd been mixed up in something political. He came across as a typical teenage high school drop out."

"His shooting ability and the fingerprints should be enough. Is there more?"

"I went to check out Sturgis's alibi. He says he spent the whole day with his girlfriend. Her name's Maybell Wilcox. She told the police she barely knew Sturgis, and she certainly wasn't his girlfriend. She runs a dog grooming business out of a van, and she goes to peoples' houses to groom their dogs. She told me she was doing dog grooming on the Saturday of the Cunningham shooting. She gave me the names of the clients she visited that morning, and they backed up her story."

"Wow, I don't see how it could be a set up like Sturgis claims. His alibi doesn't check out, he's a good enough shot, and his fingerprints were there. What makes you think otherwise?"

"It started as only a feeling. First, it was too easy. The guy crashes his car with his fingerprints all over it and leaves the gun there, again with his fingerprints all over it. It's like he wanted to be found. Anyone smart enough to do all the planning involved wouldn't be so stupid. He would have worn gloves, for one thing.

"Second, Sturgis is very convincing. His story about being out all day with the girl, Wilcox, is full of details. You can tell he believes it happened. Third, Maybell Wilcox's story lacked the same level of detail. She said she groomed the dogs. I wanted more details than she gave. I went away from talking to her feeling less than satisfied."

"You said her clients backed up her story."

"Yeah, I know. Again, none of them had many details. And there's one more big thing. Remember when you came up to me after I'd inspected the car? I smelled two things. The gun had been fired recently, and the guy who shot it chewed tobacco."

"Right, I remember."

"Kenny Sturgis says he's never chewed tobacco in his life. I think his exact words were: 'It's a disgusting habit.' I'm going to check with his father and his friends. If what he says checks out, it's going to make me wonder even more about a possible set up."

"I suspect a dental exam would tell you if he ever chewed tobacco."

"Good idea. I have a meeting with Bill Hooper tomorrow. I'll make some calls to see if anyone knows anything about Sturgis chewing tobacco."

"No offense honey, except for the tobacco chewing, you mostly have a hunch. I bet Hooper won't have much time for anything other than strict evidence."

"You're right. I won't be basing my report to Bill on my impressions. I'm going to stick with the chewing tobacco. I clearly smelled the remnants of chewing tobacco, and I'm sure Charlie Riggs would have smelled it and maybe even other officers there smelled it too. Chewing tobacco is easy to spot."

"Did Sturgis have an explanation of how his fingerprints were found on the gun and the car?"

"No, he doesn't. It's weird. He clammed up when I asked him about it. It's like he knows something he doesn't want to tell anyone."

"If he was set up, it had to be part of the job. Is it easy to transfer someone's fingerprints from one location to another?"

"Yes, you can transfer prints, but it's not easy. I don't think it happened. Charlie said the fingerprints were right where you'd expect them to be if

Sturgis shot the rifle. If someone transferred fingerprints, they'd have a hard time getting it past Charlie."

The next day Karen had her meeting with Bill Hooper at two in the afternoon. Karen knew he didn't like her so she always tried to keep their meetings professional. Bill started the meeting. "I read your summary, Karen. I find your hesitation about this case hard to understand. The guy's fingerprints were all over the rifle and the car. His alibi doesn't work. The girl denies what he's saying and there are people who back up her story. What more do you want?"

Karen expected this response. "I was the first one to see the rifle. I very clearly smelled the residue of chewing tobacco on it. As I said in my report, there is no evidence Kenneth Sturgis ever chewed tobacco. I can't believe he started the habit on the day he decided to assassinate Cunningham. It doesn't fit."

"I didn't smell any chewing tobacco and I think I was the second person to open the car door."

"Did you only smell the barrel to see if the rifle had been fired?"

"Yes, I guess I did."

"The chewing tobacco was on the stock. If you only sniffed the barrel, you could have missed it."

"Listen Karen, nobody else said anything about chewing tobacco and the evidence is overwhelming. This guy Sturgis did it. There's hard evidence no one is disputing and his alibi doesn't stand up. Later this afternoon I'm sending our report to the district attorney who's going to prosecute the case. Our work is done. You're off the case now."

Karen knew enough to leave things alone at this point. Hooper had made up his mind. She rose from her chair and left his office without saying another word.

Chapter Twenty-Three

Kenny Sturgis, December 10, 1980

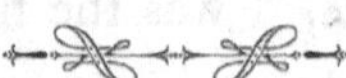

Kenny met his lawyer the day after his first encounter with the police. Since his father wouldn't help, and he didn't have any money in a bank, the court appointed a lawyer, Doyle Bernard. His lawyer told him he graduated from law school two years ago, and he didn't seem very sure of himself. Doyle was a big guy and said he'd been a football player in college. Kenny thought he had to be about fifty pounds over his playing weight. As a result, his clothes didn't fit. He looked like somebody had tried to put too much toothpaste in the tube. He leaked out in several places.

Besides a sloppy appearance, Doyle didn't impress Kenny as being a towering intellect. He asked some stupid questions and he repeated himself too often for Kenny's liking. After their first couple of meetings, Kenny became thoroughly convinced Doyle was a doofus. Clearly, they weren't getting along.

Doyle had been with him at his bail hearing and didn't put up much of a fight when the judge set bail at five hundred thousand dollars. Kenny knew his father could have probably afforded it. He also knew his father would never voluntarily show up in any courthouse. Maybe because he was a juvenile, they kept Kenny in a single cell. Kenny was fine with the arrangement. He didn't want any roommates.

Kenny hated jail, particularly because it forced him to be inside all the time. The food wasn't good either. Early in his confinement, he'd spoken to the police often. He'd told them the truth. He'd spent the day with Maybell. He gave them lots of details. The only one of the police who seemed to believe him had been the good-looking lady from the state police, Karen Daniels. Kenny got tired of answering the same questions over and over. He kept his answers the same, no matter how the various police and lawyers phrased the questions.

He had another appointment with Doyle later that day. He didn't think it would be much use—none of the previous ones had been. After lunch, the guards took him to the little room where he met with Doyle. An older guy was with Doyle. *Who's this tiny gray-haired guy?* Then he reconsidered. *Maybe he isn't that little. He just seems small compared to Doyle.*

Doyle introduced the guy. "Kenny, this is Garland Rice. He's an attorney who volunteered to help with your case."

"Nice to meet you, Mr. Rice," Kenny said as they shook hands. *Maybe this Rice guy will be sharper than Doyle. At least he's older and probably more experienced.*

Garland initiated the discussion. "Kenny, I work with Lawyers Against the Death Penalty. It's a nonprofit organization interested in abolishing the death penalty. We come in and consult on cases in which the state is likely to ask for it. We do everything we can to stop the use of the death penalty."

"Death penalty? Didn't someone tell me they can't use it on a juvenile?" Kenny started to sweat.

"It's complicated," Doyle responded. "I've been researching your case, and it doesn't look good. It comes down to your word against Maybell Wilcox's. Unfortunately, she has people who back her up. The Lewises and the Swindlers will testify she groomed their dogs on the day of the murder.

You don't have anyone to corroborate your story. And the victim was an incredibly popular politician, who was likely going to be elected governor. You have a rough road ahead of you, Mr. Sturgis. I thought maybe Garland could help. He has a lot more experience in these kinds of cases than I do."

"The death penalty doesn't make sense," Kenny countered. "I was seventeen when this killing occurred. I didn't do it, but if I'm convicted somehow, they wouldn't use the death penalty on a juvenile, right?"

Garland responded, "I wish it were that simple, son. I think the district attorney is going to move to try you as an adult. I expect Doyle will get a notice about the motion any day now."

"But I was only seventeen."

"Like Doyle said, this is a big case. Walter Cunningham wasn't a nobody. His killing is a big deal, and it was clearly premeditated murder. I don't think much of our chances of defeating the motion. We have to prepare to defend you as an adult facing the death penalty."

"Holy shit!"

After an uncomfortable silence, Garland continued. "If I'm going to be any help to you, I need to know the facts in the case—all of them. You must be completely honest with me. Can you do it?"

For the first time in all this, Kenny started to panic. Somehow, he didn't know how, he'd thought since he didn't have anything to do with the shooting, he'd be able to get off. Now he wasn't so sure. The death penalty option scared him. "Sure," he replied, tilting his chair back a bit and staring at Garland.

"Good. Explain what you did on Saturday, October twenty-fifth."

Kenny didn't think repeating his story would do any good, but he figured he'd have to play along with Garland. He'd kind of thought Doyle was a joke. The older guy seemed more serious somehow, so he told the story.

When Kenny finished, Garland asked, "So you picked her up just at dawn and dropped her off after the sun had set?"

"Yes."

"Did you think it was odd she wanted to be picked up and dropped off at the end of her driveway?"

"The pickup wasn't odd. She said she didn't want to wake anyone at her house. Now that you ask about it, I guess the drop off was weird. I didn't think anything of it at the time."

"And you said you didn't know where you guys were that day?"

"Yeah, like I said, she directed me on all the turns. I don't think I could find the places we went even if I had a chance."

Garland looked at Doyle and said, "It appears this girl had Kenny here in the palm of her hand."

"He was thinking with his crotch."

"He's a teenage boy."

"I think that's what I said," Doyle replied, and the two men laughed.

Doyle's remark offended Kenny. He didn't like being laughed at. Even though he wanted to say something, he decided not to. *Maybe they're right.*

Garland resumed his interrogation. "I understand Maybell has denied your version of events. According to the police report, she says she barely knows you."

"She's lying!"

"Like Doyle said before, she has folks who back her up."

"Those folks are lying too."

"I know it's what you think. Most times it's tough to deal with people who are lying. Then there's the fingerprint evidence. You've never been able to explain it."

"I know, and I've been thinking about it since the day they arrested me. The only thing I can think points back to Maybell."

"How?"

"One day she brought over a sniper rifle for me to shoot. It might have been the rifle used in the shooting. I'm sure my fingerprints are all over it. I didn't think anything about it when the police first asked. I thought Maybell would be on my side then. Heck, I thought she loved me."

"Do you remember what kind of rifle she brought that day?" Garland asked.

"I don't know. Some kind of West German thing with a bipod on the front and a great big scope."

Doyle searched through his notes. "A Walther WA 2000, right?"

"Yeah, maybe. I'd never seen anything like it."

"What about the car?" Garland pressed.

"Same thing. Maybell had me get into a piece of crap car she'd bought recently. I guess my fingerprints were all over it too. I think she told me it was a fifty-five Oldsmobile."

"Checks out," Doyle said. "When did it happen?"

Kenny scratched his head and thought. "I guess about a week before this all started. It was an old beater car. I remember Maybell was so happy about it. I got in and drove it up and down the Wilcox's driveway. It had to be the last time I saw Maybell at her house."

"Kenny," Garland offered. "I know Doyle's been searching for a defense for you. While what you're telling us now gives us a strategy, I don't like it. It boils down to a claim you were framed by Maybell with the cooperation of some people who lied about her grooming their dogs."

"Yeah, it has to be right. Why don't you like it, Mr. Rice?"

"I don't like it because we don't have a shred of evidence to support our claim. All the things you talked about happened when you were alone with Maybell, right?"

"Yeah, I guess so."

"And you couldn't come up with anyone who ever saw you and Maybell together."

"Her parents knew we were seeing each other. Maybell told me they were happy we were dating. They should back me up."

Doyle spoke up at this point. "Kenny, the police told me they talked to the Wilcox's, and they said they didn't know who you were."

After a pause, Garland broke the silence. "If this girl is trying to frame you, she sure as hell has done a good job. Going back to the Saturday you were out with her; didn't you think it was strange that you didn't see anyone else the whole day?"

"No, we didn't hang out with other people. She always took me to private spots where we could be alone. I guess I acted the same way. We went out to my house when my dad was gone and to the hunting camp when it was empty."

Doyle looked at Garland. "It's an amazing story. If it is true, this girl must have planned it from the get-go. Tell me Kenny. How did you meet Maybell? She's older than you, right?"

Kenny told the two lawyers about meeting Maybell at the A&W. As he listened to his own story, he could tell the two men thought it seemed farfetched. An older hot girl came up to him and came on to him big time. The only thing he remembered was Maybell asking him about his shooting. When he added more details, the attorneys seemed interested.

Garland asked, "This is the first time you ever interacted with Maybell?

"I think so. We live in a small town, so I guess I'd seen her around. Like Doyle said, she's older than me."

"Didn't you think it was a little weird? You know, older girl, younger guy…"

"I guess I should have. Telling it now makes it sound dumb. At the time, mostly I thought for some reason I'd gotten lucky. She's hot and she wanted me. Maybe I should have wondered more about it, but I didn't."

Garland rose and walked toward the door. "You've given us a lot to think about Kenny. I suspect the next step is the hearing about trying you as an adult. I don't think much of our chances but we'll fight as hard as we can."

Doyle joined Garland standing and reached out to shake Kenny's hand. "We'll be in touch."

Kenny felt like a complete fool as the policeman escorted him back to his cell. *Maybell set a trap for me, and I fell into it big time.*

Doyle and Garland went to a diner down the street from the jail. After they'd ordered their drinks, Doyle asked, "What do you think?"

"I don't know what to think. The young man tells quite the story. I thought you had trouble getting him to talk."

"Yeah, I don't think he likes me. I think we started off on the wrong foot. When we first met, he would hardly talk, and I guess my frustration showed through in some of our interactions. You're only the second person he's opened up to at all."

"Who else?"

"An investigator for the state police, Karen Daniels. I guess Kenny has a soft spot for good-looking women. He talked to her fairly easily."

"I know Karen. What kind of things did he talk about with her?"

"She found out a lot more details about his alibi and his relationship with Maybell than he ever gave me."

"Did she seem to believe him?" Garland asked.

"Yeah, she did, but it could be good technique on her part."

"Probably."

Back at the jail, Kenny lay on his bunk, completely lost. For some reason, he thought about his mother. He remembered seeing her putting her kid on the school bus. He wanted to confront her, but he hadn't had the guts. She'd abandoned him when he was just a kid. The way things were now, he would probably never see her again. Somehow the thought made him even sadder.

Chapter Twenty-Four

Ho Narwhal, December 20, 1980

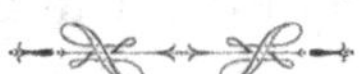

$\mathcal{S}$itting in the first-class cabin on their flight to the Cayman Islands, Ho held Karen's hand as she slept beside him. He marveled at the wedding band on his left hand. He was the luckiest guy in the world. He'd married a wonderful woman. The wedding had gone off without a hitch and yet he hadn't been surprised when Karen fell asleep during this flight. The whole thing had been exhausting for her.

Karen had worked right up until the day before the wedding. Despite the fact she'd delegated most of the wedding preparations to her mother, she still had decisions to make. Also, she had to purchase Christmas presents. She and Ho would be on their honeymoon for the actual day. While Linda had been disappointed they'd be missing Christmas, she understood why things had to work the way they did. His new daughter amazed Ho. She had been thrilled to be her mother's maid of honor and performed the role flawlessly. She could be so grown up, but when it came to Christmas, her age showed.

When the pilot announced they'd be landing in fifteen minutes, Ho nudged Karen and she opened her eyes.

"We're about to land, sweetheart."

Karen stretched and yawned. "I didn't think I'd sleep through the entire flight. I guess I was exhausted."

"You've been going hard for the last two weeks. I think it's good we didn't plan much for our week on the island."

Karen smiled. "Yes, time on the beach and time in the bedroom."

"Look at the island—you can see it out your window."

Ho had never been to the Caribbean but Karen had been to Martinique once before. They were ready for it to be warmer than Missouri. Still, they were amazed at how nice it turned out to be. Ho nudged Karen as they checked into the hotel. "The people checking in are all pale. They're a real contrast with some of the people out there by the pool."

"You mean the pink ones?"

"Actually, I meant the tan ones. I guess the pink ones are good to see, too. We brought lots of sunblock, didn't we?"

"Yes, my maid of honor made sure we were prepared for the sun."

"She's amazing. You're a great mother."

"And you're going to be a great dad, too. She really likes you."

Karen and Ho enjoyed themselves on Grand Cayman. They did all the tourist things. They went on an evening cruise and ate in some spectacular restaurants. Also, like all the other tourists, they went out on a boat and played around with the stingrays. They spent every morning on the beach. Since they lathered on the sunblock and avoided the heat of the day, they avoided sunburns. By the end of the week, they were tanning.

The interesting thing about the honeymoon was they learned even more about each other. Karen learned the full story about Ho's time in the Army and how he became interested in polishing brass. She had lots of questions about his time in Viet Nam. Ho learned more about Karen's decision to go into law enforcement and heard about her frustrations with her current boss, Bill Hooper. Karen told Ho she knew lots of the guys in her unit resented her rapid rise through the ranks while others had no problem with it. When she first started working for the state police, Bill Hooper had been, at best, neutral. After her last promotion, the neutrality turned into open hostility. The situation obviously made Karen tense, and it bothered Ho.

Karen received a phone message the night before they left Grand Cayman. After pacing around the hotel room for a while, she turned to Ho. "Garland Rice sent a message. He's an attorney for an anti-death penalty group. He's working on the Sturgis case."

"The guy who shot Walter Cunningham?"

"Yeah. In a court hearing two weeks ago, the judge granted the state's request to try Sturgis as an adult. Garland thinks the district attorney is going to ask for the death penalty."

"Seems sensible. It was cold-blooded murder."

"Ho, when we talked about it earlier I told you it didn't seem right to me. I'm sure I smelled chewing tobacco on the rifle, and Kenny Sturgis didn't chew tobacco."

"I remember and after you told him about your doubts, Bill stopped your role in the investigation."

"Actually, he stopped the whole investigation."

"So, what does this guy want?"

"Garland, Garland Rice. He wants to talk to me about my investigation and my impression of the case."

"Is it something you can do?"

"I could, but Hooper wouldn't like it. If Rice starts asking questions about chewing tobacco at the trial, I could get in big trouble. Hooper will know I was the source. He'd blow a gasket."

"Wait, didn't you tell me the head tech—was it Charlie? He must have smelled the chewing tobacco too? Wouldn't it be in his report? The report would be something available to the defense attorneys, wouldn't it?"

Karen came over and kissed Ho. "You're amazing! Of course Charlie's report would mention the chewing tobacco smell. He probably sampled the moisture on the rifle stock. It should be the evidence Rice needs to plant doubts in a jury. He doesn't need to talk to me. I couldn't add anything he won't find out in due course."

"Right, and it would be better not to talk to him. Springfield is a small place. Even if you try to keep it secret, a meeting between you and a defense attorney might not stay secret. There would be no faster way to sink your career. I think you should call back and tell this guy you're off the case and insist that everything he needs should be in the reports."

"I agree. Ho, it's so good to have you here. I mean, while Linda's great, I need to talk to an adult sometimes, and now I have you. It's wonderful."

At the St. Louis airport, Ho hung back when he saw Linda in the group of people waiting to greet the deplaning passengers. He wanted Karen and Linda to have their mother-daughter moment. Karen would have nothing to do with it. She grabbed Ho and dragged him beside her as she walked toward Linda. Linda tackled them both shouting, "Welcome home, Mom and Dad!"

Ho immediately teared up. No one had ever called him Dad before. Karen understood, and she kept the group hug going long enough for Ho to compose himself. When the three of them separated, the newlyweds greeted Karen's mother, who'd driven Linda to the airport.

On the drive home, Linda thanked them for the two postcards they'd sent. She asked, "Are the Cayman Islands as pretty as the postcards look? Are there pink flamingos there? Tell me all about it."

Karen responded, "The postcards use really good pictures. I bet we have some good ones too. It will take a few days to get them developed. You'll be the first to see them. As for telling you all about it, I'm not sure a young lady your age should hear all about a honeymoon."

Chapter Twenty-Five
Ho Narwhal, February 3, 1981

Ho arrived early at the Sturgis trial and grabbed a back-row seat. He was attending as a favor to Karen. Bill Hooper's removal of her from the case and calling off the investigation so abruptly a couple of months ago still bothered her. She'd been completely shut out. In preparation for attending the trial, he'd read the newspaper stories. Not surprisingly, the trial turned out to be a big deal. Still, everything he read indicated it should be short. Kenny Sturgis didn't appear to have much of a chance. Just before things were about to start, Horace Cunningham came in with several members of the Cunningham family. He'd wondered if they'd be there. It couldn't be easy for them.

After the courtroom filled, Kenneth Sturgis was led in a side door. The kid stopped in his tracks two steps into the courtroom, transfixed like a deer in the headlights. Eventually someone behind him prodded him and he walked to the defense table. He wore a dark blue suit with a green tie. The suit was new, and it didn't seem to fit very well. Ho thought he was a good-looking young man—tall and blond with a recent haircut. Sturgis looked around the courtroom. *I guess he's wondering who would show up at his trial,* Ho thought.

Sturgis finally sat beside his two defense lawyers. One of them was a big young guy who oozed out of his suit a little. The other lawyer, the older one, had to be Garland Rice, who had contacted Karen wanting to talk about the case.

The trial started with the district attorney presenting the state's case. According to the district attorney, a gray-haired veteran of many trials, the case was open and shut. He showed the television footage everyone had seen over and over, and then he told the jury about the fingerprint evidence on the rifle and the getaway car. He followed up by saying they would present evidence indicating Kenneth Sturgis was an excellent marksman fully capable of making the shot that killed Walter Cunningham. Finally, he said Kenny Sturgis tried to present an alibi. Unfortunately for him, the alibi didn't hold up. The person he'd used as his alibi told the police Sturgis was not telling the truth.

For such a high-profile case, the district attorney's opening remarks were short. Ho had expected the guy would grandstand more. A glance at the jury suggested the guy knew his business. The jury, seven men and five women, all seemed to nod along with him. He had their attention throughout, and he might have lost some of them if he had gone on much longer.

Sturgis's lawyer, the big guy, gave the opening remarks for the defense. It turned out his name was Doyle Bernard. Not as polished as the district attorney, he came across as young and nervous. He only made one simple argument. The state didn't present any evidence of a motive. Bernard painted his client as completely apolitical. The defense would present his friends' impressions of Kenny. They would testify he was outgoing and friendly and never expressed any radical ideas. The killing of Walter Cunningham was clearly a political act, but Kenneth Sturgis wasn't a political person at all. After those brief remarks, Bernard sat down.

The state started its case with witnesses who attested to Kenny Sturgis's marksmanship. They used two St. Louis businessmen who had been on hunting expeditions with Sturgis and his father. Both men testified they were very impressed with Kenneth's shooting ability. They described a shooting range behind the Sturgis cabin and shots the younger Sturgis had made from long distances. In both instances, in cross examination the defense asked if either of the men had heard Kenneth Sturgis say anything political. Both witnesses answered, "No."

Ho had been primed to pay particular attention to Charlie Riggs's testimony. Karen had told him this should be the defense's biggest chance. She expected Riggs would have to testify about the chewing tobacco found on the rifle, and it would give Sturgis's lawyers their chance to cast doubt on the prosecution's otherwise very strong case. Ho was shocked when the prosecutor called Bill Hooper to testify instead of Charlie. Hooper presented the evidence collected by the state investigators and only mentioned the fingerprint evidence, nothing about chewing tobacco residue. The only cross examination covered a few inconsequential details about fingerprinting, including a question about whether Hooper could tell whether the fingerprints were fresh. Hooper seemed confused and then admitted it was difficult to tell the age of fingerprints.

At the lunch recess, Ho called Karen from a pay phone across from the courthouse. "Charlie Riggs didn't testify. Bill Hooper did."

"Bill?"

"Yes, he was the only witness who discussed the state's evidence. Charlie Riggs is on vacation, so Bill testified about the state's evidence. He only talked about the fingerprints, very cut and dried. The defense didn't really question him on cross examination."

"I'm surprised—I didn't know Charlie was gone. Then again, I'm sure Bill liked testifying. He always likes to hog all the attention. I bet the courtroom was packed, and press were all over the place. They don't allow TV cameras in the courtroom, but they're probably outside."

"Yes, I saw the trucks when I arrived. Will this mean the evidence about the chewing tobacco won't get admitted?"

"No, I don't think so. It should have been in Charlie's report, so the defense will know about it. They will probably call Bill back when they get their chance. The prosecution has already put the report in the record, haven't they?"

"You're right. It was the first thing they did with Bill."

"It's odd, the defendant's lawyers should have brought up the contradictory evidence during cross examination. Anything in evidence is fair game after it's been admitted."

Karen paused. Finally, Ho broke the silence. "Is something fishy going on?"

"Yes, I think there is. I don't know what to do about it. I'm sorry to ask this. Can you stay for the whole trial, honey? While I need to know what goes on, I don't want to show up. Bill wouldn't like it."

"Sure, no problem. I don't think it's going to take long."

Ho found the afternoon of the trial uneventful. The prosecution rested early, and the defense didn't really present anything rebutting the prosecution's case. They hinted that the fingerprint evidence might have been planted, but they could only hint. Ho thought their whole plan was to present Kenneth Sturgis as a very unlikely political assassin. Their only witnesses were character witnesses, some of Sturgis's high school friends, and a couple of his father's clients.

The final arguments mirrored the opening remarks. The prosecutor hammered away at the evidence—Sturgis was a good shot, and his fingerprints were found on the rifle and the car. The defense emphasized the lack of motive—Sturgis was a nonpolitical teenager who didn't have any reason to commit the crime. As the defense always does, they tried to plant doubt in the jury. From what he could see of the jury's reaction, Ho didn't think they succeeded.

Chapter Twenty-Six

Kenny Sturgis, February 3, 1981

Kenny sat despondently while the judge gave instructions to the jury. He'd pleaded with Doyle and Garland to testify. They wouldn't let him. They argued his testimony would only allow the district attorney to put Maybell and the people who backed her story on the stand. It would be Kenny's word against several others. He really didn't have any evidence of his innocence, only his word. In the end, Doyle and Garland told him it wouldn't work. Kenny finally backed down. During the trial, he could tell things weren't going well. The whole thing made him sick.

After the jury left to deliberate, the bailiff led him to a room where his attorneys joined him. After about ten minutes of silence, Doyle finally spoke up. "Garland, do you have an estimate of how long this is going to take?"

"I haven't been involved in many cases this early. Most of my work has been done in the penalty phase so I'm no expert. I shouldn't think it would take too long. Frankly, I don't think much of our chances. We couldn't suggest any holes in their case."

"Yeah," Kenny blurted. "Because you wouldn't let me testify! I could have told them I wasn't anywhere near the shooting, and I could have told them I didn't even know Walter Cunningham. I couldn't have picked him out of a lineup."

Doyle looked a little annoyed. "We've been through it before, Kenny."

Garland stood up and started pacing. "Yes Kenny, we have. Did anything surprise you? Anything at the trial?"

Kenny thought for a few minutes. "I don't know. Not much. I think I've seen the guy who testified about the fingerprints somewhere before."

"Bill Hooper."

"Yeah, you're right. I remember it now. The meeting I went to with the Wilcox's."

"What meeting?" Garland asked, sitting down.

"It was something called the Charleston Group, I think. The Wilcox's are hung up on the Civil War. Seriously, the meeting was boring. Lots of talk about black people moving in and taking over, and then some stuff about who to vote for. I tuned most of it out. I did like the talk by the guy Lewis. We were at his house."

"Lewis? Did you say Lewis?" Doyle said, grabbing his notes and paging through them.

"Don't bother searching for it, Doyle. The Lewis's are one of the couples who said Maybell Wilcox had groomed their dogs on Saturday. Kenny, you say Bill Hooper was at the meeting?"

"Yes, I remember him being introduced as some bigwig in the state police."

They were interrupted by a knock on the door. The bailiff stuck his head in and told them the jury was ready with a verdict.

When they returned to the courtroom, the jury read their verdict—guilty of first-degree murder.

Kenny gasped, trying hard to hold himself together.

In the few minutes they had with Kenny before the guards led him away, Garland and Doyle consoled him and told him they would be preparing for the penalty phase of the trial. The district attorney had already made it clear the state would be pressing for the death penalty. Garland assured him that they would fight the prosecution tooth and nail.

Back in his cell, Kenny finally broke down and cried. He felt completely alone, and he was probably going to be sentenced to death. The last few weeks had been the most miserable of his life, and the trial hadn't been any better, maybe even worse. He hated the way the people in the audience and the jury stared at him. He'd wanted to scream out loud that he didn't do it. Doyle and Garland had told him to stay quiet. Now he felt completely helpless and hopeless.

As Ho exited the courtroom, he wondered about Karen's reaction to the verdict. He knew she thought something shady was going on. It looked like her boss had suppressed evidence. Going against Bill Hooper wasn't going to be easy. He'd been the head of Karen's agency since well before she arrived, and he had lots of support all over the state. Ho had heard rumors he had some interest in going into politics. Bill would fight Karen at every turn.

As well as thinking about Karen's predicament, Ho wondered what Kenneth Sturgis must be thinking now. If Karen was right, he probably was innocent. Now he was a convicted felon who was probably going to be sentenced to die. Ho guessed the guy must be freaking out. Ho was glad he'd gone to the trial for Karen. Maybe he could be part of straightening things out.

Chapter Twenty-Seven

Karen Daniels, February 7, 1981

After talking things over with Ho during the weekend, Karen devised a plan. She'd call Charlie Riggs and explain what she thought had happened. If Charlie was willing to give her a copy of his report on the Sturgis case, she'd call Garland Rice. He would have a copy of what Bill Hooper had provided the court. If, as she suspected, the two documents weren't identical, Garland would want to petition for a mistrial because the state had withheld important evidence. It would create an incredible stir.

She didn't understand why Bill Hooper wanted to railroad Kenny Sturgis. Whatever the reason, she had to tread carefully. At least until everything was resolved, Bill was her boss. If things turned out the way she suspected, the whole thing would probably to blow up big time and Bill would be in big trouble. People in policing didn't like it when another member of the force accused one of their colleagues of wrongdoing, so she could be in hot water.

Karen's first call to Charlie went to his answering machine. According to the message, Charlie and Margaret were on vacation until next Sunday.

After a nervous week, Karen finally reached Charlie. He seemed surprised to receive Karen's call. "What's up?"

"I'm worried, Charlie. I need you to keep this call confidential."

"I will if I can. What's got you so worried? We just pulled in from a two-week vacation. I don't know what's been going on."

"It's about the Sturgis trial. I think something very wrong is happening."

"I saw a story about it in the newspaper on vacation. They found Sturgis guilty. The trial was quick. The fingerprint evidence couldn't have been clearer."

"Did the report you sent to Bill before your vacation mention chewing tobacco residue on the rifle stock?"

"Yes, of course it did. It's a strong smell and the rifle stock was still damp with the saliva."

"Yes, I smelled it too. I found the rifle."

"Why do you ask?"

"My husband attended the trial and Bill didn't say anything about the chewing tobacco evidence. He only testified about the fingerprints. I understand why the prosecutors didn't want to bring up evidence that doesn't fit their case. What I can't understand is why the defense didn't hammer them on it. Kenny Sturgis has never chewed tobacco. I asked him about it."

"Wow, and the defense would have had a copy of my report. I can't understand how they missed it. The attorney was a public defender, I think."

"Yes, you're right, but I know the other attorney involved, Garland Rice, and he's sharp. Before the trial he called me and wanted to talk about the case, but I turned him down. I told him everything he needed to know would be in your report."

"You think Bill didn't give them the full report?"

"I don't know what to think, but it sure seems like a strong possibility. So, would you be willing to give me a copy of your report?"

"What are you going to do with it?"

"I'm thinking of taking it to Garland. I want to compare your report with what the D.A. entered into evidence."

"Holy shit, Karen! You're talking serious stuff."

Karen nodded, solemn. "I know I am. It's about someone's life. People are convicted when they are guilty beyond a reasonable doubt. The chewing tobacco evidence might be enough to make someone doubt the whole thing. If for some reason Bill decided to hide evidence, he shouldn't be allowed to get away with it. It's criminal."

"I don't know. What if Bill finds out I gave you a copy of my report? There would be hell to pay. Bill can really carry a grudge."

"If we can show he hid critical evidence, he won't be our boss for long. I wouldn't worry about him coming after you."

"I guess you might be right. Still, I'm nervous about this. Let's meet somewhere for lunch tomorrow. I'll bring a copy of my report. I don't want to be seen giving it to you in the office. All things considered, I'd still like to stay out of this if I can."

"I understand your concern, and I share some of it. Why don't we meet at Sal's on Twenty-Third Street tomorrow? Is noon okay with you?"

"Sure. I'll see you then."

After her lunch with Charlie, Karen called and arranged a meeting with Garland Rice. He'd been surprised when she called and a little annoyed when she wouldn't tell him what was going on. She asked him to bring his files on the Sturgis case and told him she would explain more at the meeting. They agreed to meet at eight o'clock in Karen's apartment.

When Garland arrived, Karen introduced him to Ho and Linda and then led Garland to her study and closed the door. "I'm sorry to be mysterious about this meeting, Garland. Remember when I told you to pay attention to the evidence coming from our office?"

"Yes, it was all about the fingerprints."

"Do you have it with you?"

"I do." He reached into his briefcase, extracted a folder, and handed Karen a piece of paper.

Karen quickly read the report, and then handed Garland the copy of

Charlie's report, which she had on her desk. "This is a copy of the report Charlie Riggs gave Bill Hooper in preparation for the trial."

Garland read the report and then stared at the ceiling for a few minutes. "This is a bombshell, Karen. Bill Hooper suppressed evidence. If we'd known about the chewing tobacco residue on the rifle stock, our case would have been much stronger. I have to prepare a motion for a mistrial."

"I'm sorry I couldn't get this to you any faster. Charlie Riggs has been on vacation for the last two weeks. I only got a copy of his report at lunch today. My husband attended the trial, and he told me the chewing tobacco residue evidence never came up. I've been waiting for Charlie to get back from vacation."

"Kenny's sentencing hearing is tomorrow. I can't bring up my mistrial motion then. I guess we'll have to let him get sentenced and then start the process." Garland paused and then continued, "This is going to be an incredible mess. We're going to out-and-out accuse Bill Hooper of suppressing evidence. I'm probably going to have to rely on testimony from Charlie Riggs. Are you sure he wants to buck his boss?"

"While he's nervous about it for sure, I think you can count on Charlie, and since the whole thing turns on the chewing tobacco residue, I can testify too. I was the first one to find the rifle, and I definitely smelled the chewing tobacco."

The next day proceeded as Garland and Doyle had feared. The judge sentenced Kenny to death. While the lawyers had told Kenny to expect this outcome, he had a hard time sitting there and listening to the legal mumbo jumbo. It meant they were going to kill him. Right before the guards led him away, he listened while Garland told him they were working on a way to get the verdict overturned. He didn't believe him. *The trial is over and they're going to kill me.*

As they led him away, Kenny scanned the half-empty courtroom and wondered if it would be the last time he'd ever be out of jail. All hope was gone.

Chapter Twenty-Eight

Ho Narwhal, February 15, 1981

At ten-thirty in the morning, Ho answered the phone in his studio. Karen was on the line. "Ho darling, I have a favor to ask of you."

"Your wish is my command."

"Wow, how long will that last?"

Ho smiled. "What is it?"

"Garland and his lawyer wanted to get a message to Kenny Sturgis. Unfortunately, they were too late. The process of transferring him to the state penitentiary had already started and they weren't allowed to see him. They are really worried about the boy. While they are almost certain they are going to be able to get his trial declared a mistrial, it's going to take a while. They want him to know he shouldn't worry. The state pen is a horrible place, particularly death row, and they want him to know they'll be able to get him out soon."

"What do you need from me?"

"Garland and Doyle are tied up with the depositions for the mistrial motion, so they want someone to go down to the pen and tell Kenny not to worry. He needs to know about the motion for a mistrial."

"Wouldn't it be better if you went? At least he's met you, and you're an official somebody. I'm a nobody."

"I can't go. I'm one of the people being deposed, and you know all the details. Garland is going to be by your studio in a half hour with an affidavit you can use to show you're a representative of the legal team. With the affidavit you'll be able to visit Kenny. It's a big rigmarole to get permission to visit someone on death row, so it's best if you travel down there tonight and start the process tomorrow morning. I think they're transporting Kenny to the prison this afternoon, so tomorrow will be his first full day in the state pen. We think he'll be really freaked out. Having an update on what's going on up here will be good for him."

"What did I say? Your wish is my command. Sure, I'll go. I can interrupt my work for a day. After I get the papers from Garland, I'll go home, grab lunch, and pack a bag. I hope you and Linda have a good night. I'll call from a motel or something."

While Ho prepared his lunch, Kenny and four other guys were put in chains and herded into the back of a van headed for the state pen. It was cold even in the jackets they wore over their prison outfits. Kenny had been lucky to have his own cell before. Now he was treated like everyone else. His hands and feet were chained, and the chains around his ankles were attached to the floor of the van. A guard rode in the back with the prisoners. *He must have drawn the short straw*, Kenny thought. *It stinks in here.* Kenny didn't know why they had all the security. No one was coming to save him.

He sat back and watched the world go by through the windows. He didn't know how long the ride to the penitentiary would take. All he knew was that he was uncomfortable and incredibly depressed.

As Ho filled his gas tank on the way out of town, a green state prison van drove by. *It's probably the van carrying Kenny*, he thought. *It's headed out on the highway I'm about to take.*

Thirty minutes after he left the gas station, Ho entered a mountainous stretch in the road. He saw the prison van a couple of hundred yards ahead of him. The drive was slow and despite the scenery, Ho was focused on watching the van in the lead. As he approached a steep part of the road ending in a little curve, he heard a burst of what sounded like gunshots and the unmistakable sound of a vehicle crashing. Ho instinctively slowed and pulled over to the side of the road. He climbed out and ran up to the curve to see what was happening. The prison van lay off the road, turned on its side and a man in a big coat carrying a rifle approached it. He wore a ski mask over his head and what Ho thought might be overalls under the coat. Ho ducked down behind a tree and watched. The man dodged behind the front of the van and evaded a shot coming from the back. Then he went around the van and fired a shot at where the guard must have been.

When he didn't hear an answering shot, the guy peered into the van. Ho could see him relax and walk back to the side of the road ahead of the van. He put down his rifle and picked something off the ground. When he reached the van, he yanked open one of the back doors. Next, he threw in the thing he'd picked up into the back of the van. Ho thought it looked like it could be a large pair of bolt cutters. After looking around, the guy ran, picked up his rifle, and waited on the side of the road.

Ho glanced behind him. There were no cars. Ahead of him the prisoners slowly crawled out of the over-turned van. They had been able to use the bolt cutters to sever the chains, but they still had the metal bands on their wrists and ankles. Soon there were four prisoners assembled. The escaped prisoners embraced the man who'd freed them and headed away with him, running as fast as they could. Kenny Sturgis hadn't been one of the four who'd run away. Ho waited, and nothing more happened. He checked behind him. A truck approached in the distance.

Ho decided to see if Kenny was in the van. He ran up to the van and peered in. Kenny slumped in the back of the van. His chest was moving, so he had to still be alive, just unconscious. Thinking fast, Ho crawled in the van, grabbed the bolt cutters, and snapped the chains holding Kenny's arms and legs. He was also able to cut off the handcuffs, but the straps on his legs were too thick. Next, he dragged Kenny out of the van, lifted him on his back, and ran as fast as he could back to his car. Ho checked and the truck had come closer, but it slowed as it labored up the hill. Ho lay Kenny in the back seat, with his legs folding his leg so he would fit, closed the door, and ran back to wipe his fingerprints from the bolt cutters and anywhere else he might have touched. Back at the car, he jumped in and drove off. He didn't know where he would go, but he didn't want to stay anywhere near the van.

Twenty minutes later, Ho came to an intersection and turned away from the road to the prison. When he heard groans coming from the back seat, he said, "You're with a friend, Kenny. I'll explain everything when I find a place to stop." He didn't hear any response from the backseat. He'd been racking his brain trying to figure out what he should do. Two minutes later, he pulled into a roadside rest area. Ho found a parking space far from the other parked cars. He glanced behind him at Kenny and saw him move a little. Ho realized Kenny couldn't be comfortable crammed into the small back seat.

After a few minutes, Kenny seemed to come around. Ho repeated, "Lie still Kenny, you're with a friend." Kenny groaned and opened one eye. "I think you were knocked in the head when the van you were in turned over."

"Who are you…? Where am I…?"

"I'm Horace Narwhal. You can call me Ho. We're in a roadside rest area. I stopped here because I thought you were about to come to."

Kenny kept his eyes closed while he spoke. "I remember being in the prison van. I heard some shots and then the van started swerving, and I think it turned over. I don't remember anything after that."

"My car was behind the van. I heard the shots and saw the van roll over. A guy with a rifle must have shot the driver and the other guy in the front. He killed the guard in the back. The other prisoners got out and ran away with the guy who did the shooting. I dragged you out and put you in my car."

"Are you part of the team who ambushed the van?"

"No, I don't know anything about any ambush. I was on my way to the prison so I could set up a meeting with you tomorrow."

Kenny finally opened his eyes. After a moment, he slowly swung his legs around so he could sit up. Halfway through the maneuver, he grabbed his head. "I have a monster lump on the back of my head."

Ho could tell Kenny was still woozy, and his eyes weren't focusing well. "I'm sure you had a serious blow to your head. You've been unconscious for quite a while."

Finally sitting up in the back seat, Kenny said, "Tell me again. I don't understand what you said about setting up a meeting."

"I'm doing a favor for Garland Rice—your lawyer. He wanted me to tell you he and Doyle are going to enter a motion for a mistrial in your case. The head of the state police, Bill Hooper, altered the evidence in your case. Garland said to tell you he's very confident his motion will be granted, and you will be taken off death row."

"I… I don't understand."

"Okay, here's what I know. When the state police detective found the rifle in the getaway car, she smelled chewing tobacco residue on the stock. The guy who leads the forensic team smelled it too, and he took some samples. The report he sent to Hooper mentioned the chewing tobacco evidence. The report Hooper entered as evidence at the trial didn't mention it. Since you've never chewed tobacco, the omitted evidence would have put a big hole in the prosecution's case. It could have created reasonable doubt in the minds of the jurors. This kind of cheating by the prosecutors is serious stuff. Heads are going to roll—most particularly, I think Bill Hooper is going to lose his job."

Kenny didn't seem to understand. "So, where's Garland?"

"Garland's tied up preparing the mistrial motion. He is taking depositions and doing legal research. I don't know everything he has to do. I'm not a lawyer."

Suddenly, Kenny held his head and stopped talking. Ho thought maybe he'd pass out again. Finally, Kenny spoke. "Who are you?"

"Like I said, I'm Horace Narwhal. I became involved because my wife, Karen Daniels, is the state police detective who found the gun. She remembered the chewing tobacco smell, and when I told her it hadn't been mentioned in the trial, she started the whole process leading to the mistrial motion. She couldn't come to the prison, so she asked me."

Kenny seemed to lose focus, then he sat up straighter. "What are you going to do?"

"We have to figure out our next move. The attack on the prison van and the prisoners' escape will be all over the news, and the police are going to be searching for you and the other escapees everywhere. I think our best bet is to go to the nearest police station and have you turn yourself in."

"No way. I'm not going back to any jail."

"I told you Garland's going to get your conviction thrown out. You won't be in jail long."

"No, I'm not going back to jail at all. Thank you for your help, goodbye."

Kenny jerked open the door, leapt out, and started running toward the woods at the back of the rest area. His stride was wobbly, and he only made about ten steps before he stumbled and fell face first on the pavement.

Ho climbed out of the car and went to help Kenny up. One look into his eyes told Ho Kenny had a serious concussion. His most recent fall hadn't helped the situation. "Kenny," he said, pulling him to his feet. "You need to get to a hospital. You have a concussion at least. You need to be checked out by a doctor. No one's going to put you in jail."

Kenny tried to struggle out of Ho's grasp, to no avail. He didn't have any strength and didn't try to sit up when Ho put him in the back seat. Ho turned on the overhead light and unfolded the map. He figured they were about ten miles from Morris, which would be big enough to have a hospital.

Kenny didn't say anything during the drive to Morris. Ho couldn't tell if he was conscious or not. He pulled into the hospital's emergency entrance, and after a minute a medic came out to see what he wanted. After Ho gave a quick explanation, the medic rushed back in and returned with a couple of other people. They put Kenny on a stretcher and wheeled him into the hospital. Ho gave a brief explanation to the emergency room doctor, telling him about his suspicions about a concussion.

Five minutes later, the doctor reappeared. "You were the guy who brought in the head injury victim, weren't you?"

"Yes, I'm Horace Narwhal, Doctor McNulty." Ho felt proud of remembering to read the doctor's name tag.

"You were right, your friend has a severe concussion. He seems to have taken a major blow to the back of his head and a smaller, but still substantial, one on his forehead. We're taking him to x-ray now to see if there's a skull fracture involved. No telling what's going on. Who he is? He's clearly in a prison uniform, and he has shackles on his ankles."

"Yes, you're right. It's a prison uniform. His name is Kenny Sturgis. He's the guy convicted of killing Walter Cunningham. Someone ambushed the van taking him to prison and it rolled over. It's where he got the blows to his head. I found him beside the road, clearly in distress."

"I should call the police. This guy is an escaped prisoner. I heard about the ambush of the van on the radio on my way to work."

"Yes, you should. I was going to do it after I heard he was okay."

"While I wouldn't say he's okay yet, I know what you mean."

"I sort of feel responsible for him. How long do you think he'll be hospitalized?"

"People with serious concussions need quite a bit of bed rest. If it's a skull fracture, it's more serious. He'll be in the hospital for a while. Given who he is, the police may want to move him to the prison infirmary, but I'll refuse. He shouldn't be moved anywhere for a couple of days at least."

The doctor went to call the police, and Ho went in search of a pay phone. Karen listened carefully as Ho recounted the events of his afternoon.

"You did the right thing," Karen said. "Find a motel. Don't try to drive back today. I'll call Garland. We'll probably want you to go to the hospital tomorrow morning to check on Kenny. Garland or Doyle will hopefully be able to get there tomorrow afternoon."

Chapter Twenty-Nine

Kenny Sturgis, February 16, 1981

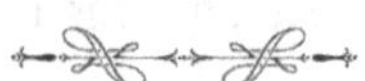

Kenny woke up and tried to roll over, but he couldn't. Somehow he'd been strapped to a strange bed and some kind of device held his head in place. He wasn't sure he could move at all. He made some noise as he struggled, and a policeman come into view.

"Those straps are for your own good son. The hospital doesn't want you making any movements. You have a skull fracture."

Right then a young nurse walked in. "I'll take over, officer," she said. Kenny thought she might be attractive. As much as he wanted to, he couldn't turn his head to get a good look at her.

Kenny didn't know what was going on, but a skull fracture didn't sound good. The nurse flitted in and out of his view. She took his pulse, temperature, and blood pressure. Kenny had never been in a hospital before, even when he was born. The nurse wrote on a clipboard from the foot of Kenny's bed. After she finished, she came to the side of the bed where Kenny could see her clearly. "Okay Mr. Sturgis, here's the deal. You fractured your skull, which is serious business. You are to be confined to bed for several days. The restraints are there to keep you from moving. It's critical that you keep your head still. It's why we have the apparatus on your head. If we think you'll behave, it can come off in a couple of days. I don't know what you did to warrant the police outside your door. Whatever, there's going to be a policeman there twenty-four hours a day. The doctor should be by when he does his rounds. He can give you more information."

"What if I've got to pee?"

"Good question," the nurse said. She came around to the other side of Kenny's bed and put something in his hand. "You've been catheterized, so you don't have to worry about peeing. This is a nurse call button. Press the button and we'll come to help you if you need to do anything else. I don't know what kind of diet they'll have you on. Right now, we have you on fluids. We'll feed you too if necessary. Your job is to lie still." The nurse left, closing Kenny's door.

Kenny's head throbbed, and a few other places in his body didn't feel so good either. He guessed he'd been banged up when the prison van turned over. He sighed and decided to try to go back to sleep.

After a fitful night's sleep at a local motel, Ho headed to the hospital early the next morning. Before leaving the motel room, he'd turned on the morning news. The attack on the prison van led the program. The news reported Kenny had been "recaptured." The other four prisoners were still at large. They had pictures of police roadblocks and flocks of police scouring the area around the overturned van. Authorities didn't seem to have any idea what had taken place or who had been responsible. All they knew was three guards had been killed and four of the five prisoners were still at large.

As he drove to the hospital, Ho wondered if he should stick with his story. He'd lied and told the doctor he'd picked Kenny up on the side of the road. He didn't say anything about witnessing the attack on the van. He actually hadn't seen much. The guy had on a ski mask and a big coat, and he'd cleared out with the four prisoners soon after Ho started watching.

At the hospital, Ho faced unexpected barriers. He wasn't related to Kenny in any way, and only relatives could see someone in Kenny's position. After being rebuffed, Ho remembered he had Garland's letter authorizing him to speak to Kenny at the state pen. He went back to his car and returned with the letter. The hospital receptionist appeared to be skeptical, but she carried the letter to the office to confer with her supervisor. Five minutes later, she came back, returned the letter, and told Ho he had permission to visit Kenny.

When Ho approached the police guard at the door, he could see a doctor in the room. He showed the letter to the guard and went into the room. Ho introduced himself and started to explain his presence. Surprisingly, the doctor interrupted him. "You're the sculptor, aren't you? I love your stuff. I saw it in the gallery in St. Louis."

Ho was a little embarrassed. It had happened to him a few times before. Still, he was not used to being recognized. "Yes I am, and I'm glad you like my stuff. I'm here to see Kenny. How's he doing? I picked him up yesterday and brought him in last night."

"Mr. Sturgis has a fractured skull. We have him immobilized."

"I can see. Can he move his head at all?"

"No, we want his head completely stable for a few days. He's young and healthy, so he should heal rapidly. A skull fracture is nothing to play games with. When the concussion symptoms dissipate, we'll take the head restraint off. If he keeps his head completely still, he should be okay. If he moves too much, he'll experience severe headaches. It usually keeps people with skull fractures in line."

"When will the police want to move him?"

"I don't know. I'll object if they want him moved in the next couple of days. If I have my way, he's not going anywhere. We need to keep him restrained."

"Good, his lawyers have moves afoot to arrange for his release. One of them will be down to see him this afternoon. Can I have a few words with him now?"

"Sure, I'm finished. Nice to meet you. As I said, I really like your sculptures."

When the doctor left, Ho moved into Kenny's line of sight. "Hi there,

Kenny. How are you doing?"

"Not so great. The nurses and the doctor say I cracked my skull and being all bound up like this is so uncomfortable. You told the doctor one of my lawyers was coming. Who are you anyway?"

"You don't remember?"

"Sorry."

"Like I said, I picked you up beside the road and brought you here. You don't remember any of it?"

"No, I came to for a little when they were wheeling me around last night. Then I conked out again. I only really came around this morning. I don't remember anything after I heard some shots and the van started to roll over."

"Let me fill you in. My name's Horace Narwhal, but people call me Ho. I'm helping your lawyers. I was supposed to talk with you at the state pen this morning to tell you Garland thinks he'll get a mistrial in your case. If everything works out, you won't have to be in the state pen for long. If your trial is declared a mistrial, they can't keep you on death row, and it's possible you won't have to stay in any kind of jail."

Ho could tell Kenny was tiring. His eyes weren't quite focused. "Listen," Ho continued, "I'll let you rest now. Garland should be here this afternoon. He'll fill you in on the details. They're filing their motion for a mistrial this morning."

"Thanks."

"And I guess the police will want to question you. They are going to be interested in what you know about the ambush of the prison van."

"Like I told you, I don't know nothing. I conked my head and passed out right when it started."

"Lie back and relax. There's nothing else you can do. I want you to know the legal proceedings are under way. Also, I'll tell the police your lawyer wants to be there when you're questioned. It should stall them for a while."

"Thanks again."

Ho went to call Karen and then found a place for breakfast.

In the middle of the afternoon Garland Rice showed up at the hospital. Ho helped him with the people at the front. They met a detective when they arrived at Kenny's room.

"Hello, Mitch," Garland said as he shook hands with the detective. "Thank you for waiting. I wanted to be there when you questioned my client."

"He has a right to have you there. Who's with you?"

"Let me introduce my associate, Horace Narwhal. By an incredible stroke of luck, he's the one who picked up Mr. Sturgis after the attack on the prison van. Ho, this is Mitch Andrews."

Ho shook hands with the detective. "I was on my way to do a favor for Garland by getting a message to Kenny at the prison. Like Garland said, luckily I came across Kenny lying beside the road. I picked him up and took him to the hospital last night."

Ho thought the detective looked skeptical, but he finally spoke up. "Why don't you wait outside, Mr. Narwhal. Garland is the only one who's supposed to be here when I question Mr. Sturgis. Stick around though, I might have some questions for you."

"Okay," Ho said as he backed away from the room.

Twenty-five minutes later, Garland and the detective found Ho in the hospital's main waiting room. The detective spoke up. "Sturgis doesn't know anything about what happened yesterday. The last thing he remembers is hearing some shots and then the van starting to swerve. We found large bolt cutters in the van. I guess the other prisoners must have cut him loose and dragged him away. When he didn't come to, they probably left him where you found him."

"I guess so. I bet he's not a good witness right now. Sometimes things come back to people. Maybe he'll remember more later."

"We'll have more information when we catch the other guys. I don't think they'll get far. To the best of our knowledge, they only have prison clothes, and even though they cut the chains, like Sturgis, they still have shackles on their ankles. Unless they have some outside help, they should turn up soon."

"I suspect you're right."

"Here, write down your name, address, and telephone number," Detective Andrews said, giving Ho a notebook and pen. "We may want to talk to you later. For now, just let me say, you did the right thing bringing Sturgis to the hospital."

"Thanks," Ho replied, passing the notebook back to the detective.

Garland and Ho agreed to go to a breakfast place Ho had found. After they ordered, Garland said, "I have a good feeling about the mistrial motion. Bill Hooper clearly suppressed evidence. The difference between Charlie Riggs' original report and the one Hooper put into evidence is clear. I think we'll get a mistrial declared, and I think Hooper's in deep shit."

"What's Karen's role in all this? Will the fact she set the whole thing in motion come out?"

"I don't think so, but it might. I submitted her deposition with my motion. It's only there because she's corroborating what's in Charlie's report. The difference between what's in the two reports is the critical evidence. The big question I have is—what is the judge going to do with what he knows now? Judge Thurston is well connected politically. My bet is he'll contact the governor about Hooper's misconduct. The governor would want to get out in front of all this and fire Bill Hooper soon. At the very least, he needs to be warned about the brewing storm. It will be interesting to see how quickly things happen."

"Hooper is Karen's boss. I hope none of this hurts her."

"I've advised Karen to keep her head down. Some of her coworkers were tight with Hooper, and they might try to make things unpleasant for her. She's a big girl though, and I think she'll be fine."

"I hope you're right. Let's change the subject. The detective didn't learn anything from Kenny, right?"

"Yes. The poor kid's head injury is serious. He couldn't remember anything about yesterday."

"He and I had a bit of a conversation after he briefly came to yesterday afternoon. When I heard him starting to regain consciousness, I parked in a corner of a rest stop so we could talk. I told him my name and why I was on my way to the state pen. When I told him he needed to turn himself in, he jumped out of the car and started to run. After a few steps, he fell flat on his face. I picked him up and drove him to the hospital. I don't think he remembers any of our conversation."

"Maybe he hurt his head again when he fell running away from you. Anyway, he says he can't remember anything after the van turned over."

Ho took a long drink of coffee. "So, what happens after a mistrial is declared?"

"It's up to the prosecution. They can try the case again if they want to. I don't know in this case. The fingerprint evidence is strong, and they don't have any other suspects. My guess is we'll have another trial."

"Is there any way you can strengthen your case?"

"While the chewing tobacco evidence surely helps, it would be better if we could figure out who did the shooting."

"It doesn't sound easy. Is there anything Kenny can tell you?"

"Kenny's story amounts to a claim his girlfriend and some other people framed him in a very complex conspiracy. It starts with the girl, Maybell Wilcox. She came on to him completely out of the blue. Kenny claims they started a hot and heavy affair. One day she brought a sniper rifle for him to shoot. Another day she had him do a short drive in the vehicle used as the getaway car. Those two episodes account for the fingerprints. Also, Kenny claims she took him on an all-day road trip in the hills the day of the shooting."

"Sounds plausible. Well, at least not completely farfetched."

"It's not only Maybell Wilcox who he claims was involved. She denied being with Kenny on the day of the shooting. In fact, she says she barely knows who Kenny Sturgis is. She has an alibi for the day of the shooting, and people back her up. We didn't think it sensible to even try to present Kenny's story at the trial."

"If Kenny's telling the truth, there must be a way of finding out. Don't conspiracies like this eventually unravel? It's hard to keep everything secret. Bill Hooper pulled Karen off the case and shut down the investigation before she could follow up on Kenny's claims. Do you think he's part of the plot to frame Kenny?"

"It sure looks like it."

"When I get home, I'll talk to Karen. If Hooper is out of the way, maybe she'll be able to follow up on Kenny's story."

Chapter Thirty

Karen Daniels, February 19, 1981

Karen had been walking on eggshells the last three days at work. She knew eventually the story about Bill Hooper would drop, and at ten in the morning it happened. Bill's office was at the end of the hallway, only three doors down from Karen's. Through her half-opened door, she saw two uniformed state troopers head toward Bill's door. She stayed in her office not wanting anyone to think she knew anything about why the troopers had come. Five minutes later, the state troopers walked by, escorting Bill. Immediately, people popped out of their offices asking each other if they knew what was going on.

Soon they all congregated in front of Bill's secretary, Mary Beth, who had a little office in front of Bill's larger one. "What's going on Mary Beth?" John Selby, the most senior in the group, asked.

"Those troopers were from the governor's special detail," Mary Beth answered. "I didn't hear much of what they said. They gave Bill something to read. I don't know what. Then they escorted him out of his office. They didn't let him take anything, and he didn't say a word the whole time."

"I'm going to call the governor," John said as he hustled back toward his office. All the others stared at each other in stunned silence as they followed, hovering around John's closed door.

A few minutes later, John opened his door. "I just got off the phone with the governor. Bill Hooper is being held on suspicion of tampering with evidence. I'm the acting director now. The governor said they'd do a search for a replacement for Bill in a week or two. We're supposed to carry on and avoid talking to the press. If anyone asks you anything, refer them to the governor's office."

"Did the governor give you any details about why they are holding Bill?" Mary Beth asked.

"No. He didn't. I don't have the faintest idea what this is all about. Do any of you?"

Karen thought fast. *If I keep quiet now and my role eventually comes out, I'll be in big trouble. I'd better tell them what I know.* "I think it's about the Sturgis case—the guy convicted of shooting Walter Cunningham. Bill didn't present all the evidence in Charlie Riggs's report. I know his lawyer, and he thinks his motion for a mistrial has a good chance."

"How'd you know about this, Karen?" John asked.

"I saw the rifle the shooter left behind before anyone else. It reeked of chewing tobacco. Charlie reported that he found traces of it, but Bill didn't mention chewing tobacco at the trial. When the lawyer saw Charlie's original report, he discovered it didn't match the report Bill put into evidence. Didn't you remember thinking Bill's testifying was odd? It's usually Charlie."

"That's interesting," Jerry Watson said.

Karen knew Jerry, Bill's protégé, had the most to lose if Bill got fired. He was bound and determined to cause her trouble.

"How did this lawyer find out about the different reports?" Jerry asked. "I bet you told him."

Here it comes, Karen thought. *He's going to turn this whole place against me. There's nothing I can do about it.* After a moment, she thought, *It's better to go out with a bang, not a whimper.* "As a matter of fact, I did. Like I said,

I smelled chewing tobacco. You couldn't miss it. When the defense didn't use it, I got suspicious. I'd interviewed the Sturgis kid, and he told me he never chewed tobacco. It was the only hole in the prosecution's case. When it didn't come up at the trial, I asked Charlie Riggs if the evidence of traces of chewing tobacco was in his report, and he said it was."

Jerry broke in. "So, you went snooping around trying to find whether or not Bill had made a mistake."

"It wasn't a mistake. Bill deliberately submitted an incomplete report at the trial. If you look at both reports, it's a clear case of evidence tampering. The Sturgis trial is likely to be declared a mistrial. I don't know why Bill did it. In any event, this was no mistake."

Karen glared at Jerry. She couldn't tell how the others were reacting to the and forth between the two of them. She had a terrible feeling she hadn't won any hearts and minds. Law enforcement officers stick together. They don't like snitches, and she knew she came across as a snitch. *It was like justice be damned; we need to protect each other.*

Finally, Jerry said, "We'll see," and stalked away. The others wandered off, giving Karen long looks.

Karen returned to her office knowing the people who'd witnessed her interchange with Jerry were spreading the story. She didn't think she'd be portrayed in the best light and the outcome wouldn't be good for her. She'd become a pariah in the agency. No one would want to work with her. Some might even try to sabotage her. The fact she'd done the right thing wouldn't matter. She'd crossed a line, and her colleagues would punish her for it.

When she tried to get back to the paperwork piled on her desk, she couldn't concentrate. She thought about calling Ho but she didn't. It didn't make sense to interrupt his work. Karen still felt a little guilty about having asked him to go to the state pen the other day so she stewed and replayed her conversation with Jerry.

At four-fifteen, she heard a knock on her door. Thinking it might be a mob coming to get her, she paused before saying, "Come in." Sylvia Carmone opened her door.

Karen was thrilled to see Sylvia, her best friend in the agency, the only other female detective. They had worked together on several cases through the years. Sylvia was twenty years older than Karen, yet they'd bonded because of being together in a male world. She and her husband Tony had gone to dinner several times with Karen, Ho, and Linda. Also, Sylvia was the only one, except for Charlie Riggs, who knew what Bill Hooper had done before the news broke today.

"What have you heard?" Karen asked. "Are they calling me a snitch, or perhaps it starts with b or w?"

Sylvia sat in the chair in Karen's office. "Let's just say you aren't everyone's favorite person right now. They're saying you betrayed Bill Hooper, and now he's under the microscope. They don't have the details right. Unfortunately, I don't think it matters in this kind of situation."

Karen interrupted, "I hope you didn't stand up for me. I'm radioactive right now. It's going to be better if you don't let on you know anything about what happened."

"That's sweet of you Karen, thinking about me and not about yourself. Actually, not many people talked to me. My impression mostly comes from things I overheard. Also, I'm a little ashamed I feigned ignorance during the one direct conversation I had. I think people are avoiding me because they know we're friends."

"I guess you're putting yourself in jeopardy coming in here. Perhaps you shouldn't have."

"No, don't think that way. You did the right thing. I'm sorry everyone heard about it so soon after the troopers came for Bill. People were in shock, particularly guys like Jerry, who were close to Bill. The timing is all wrong. If they'd first learned about what Bill did and then a couple of days later learned about how the information came out, it would have been easier to take. They wouldn't be coming down on you so hard."

"Maybe you're right. Still, we can't undo history. I'm not sure I can work here anymore, no matter who they put in charge. You know how cops are. We're supposed to protect each other. There's nothing worse than a cop who reports on another cop. I'll be branded."

Sylvia sprang out of her chair, walked around to Karen's side of the desk, and put her arm around Karen. "I'm so sorry it's worked out the way it did. But just remember that you did the right thing."

Karen leaned into Sylvia's hug but didn't let herself cry. After Sylvia backed away, Karen said, "Don't tell anyone, but I'm thinking about quitting. I can see my future here, and it isn't going to be good. I'll talk it over with Ho tonight. I think I might be able to make a go of it as a private detective."

Sylvia sat back down. "You mean work with one of the detective agencies? I'd be careful. Some of those guys are sleaze bags."

"I know. I'm aware of the ones to avoid. Maybe I'll go out on my own. It can be rough, I know. Speaking frankly, Ho and I have enough money. It's amazing what he gets for one of his sculptures. My agency wouldn't have to bring in much, at least at the start."

"My God, you're smiling. A moment ago, I thought you were about to cry."

"There's nothing I can do about what happened today. When you came in, I was thinking about my future. You verified what I feared. I'm going to be *persona non grata* around here for a long time. I thought about staying and fighting. Then I figured, why engage in a losing battle? I'd ask you if you wanted to join me, but I couldn't offer you anything like the pension you're going to get if you work here another five years."

"I'll miss you. I think you'd be a good private detective. With your experience, it should be easy for you to get a license."

"I'll have to talk it over with Ho. Still, the more I think about it, the better it seems. I know quite a few lawyers in town. I might be able to get some of them to throw business my way."

Walking out of the building at five o'clock, Karen couldn't help noticing the daggers she received from several of her co-workers. Even so, she had a spring in her step. If things worked out, she wouldn't have to put up with them much longer.

When Ho arrived home from his studio in the evening, he rushed to Karen. "You wouldn't believe what I heard on the radio coming home. The governor fired Bill Hooper."

"I'm way ahead of you. I watched the state troopers escort him out of the building."

"Wow, I guess Garland's going to get his mistrial."

"You're probably right," Karen said, then she pointed to the couch. "Sit down Ho, we need to have a serious conversation."

Right then Linda came in and asked, "Can I be part of the serious conversation?"

"Sure, three of us fit on the couch. So, here's the deal. My boss, Mr. Hooper, got caught cheating, and the governor fired him. I knew about it at work and Ho heard about it on the radio. Anyway, I'm the one who caught him cheating, and I found myself in a situation where I had to explain what happened to other people at work. Several of these people didn't like what I did, and now almost everyone where I work is mad at me."

"It doesn't make sense," Linda blurted. "If he cheated, *you* shouldn't get in trouble."

"You're right sweetie, but it's not how it works sometimes, particularly with police. People who report on what another policeman does wrong aren't popular. You've heard people called snitches or tattletales before."

"Yes."

"Well, people at work think I'm a snitch."

Ho interrupted. "I agree with you, Linda. It's not right. Your mom shouldn't get in trouble. She's not the one who cheated. Nevertheless, I can see how it happened."

"It's water under the bridge now. I can't change how people reacted. You both might note that I'm not upset. Like I said, a lot of people are mad at me for no good reason. Usually, it would bother me, but this time it doesn't. See my smile? I've decided to quit my job and find another one. I was getting tired of my job anyway."

"Wow honey," Ho said. "You're quick. What are you thinking about?"

"It wasn't really quick. You know I haven't been happy about my work for a while."

"Yes, I thought Hooper was the big problem. With him gone, shouldn't things improve?"

"Given the way people reacted today, no. Anyway, I'm thinking about setting up a private detective agency. I picked up the application for a license after work. It's pretty simple. With my degree and experience, I meet all the qualifications. It'll take some money to set up my agency. I'll need to rent an office and maybe hire a secretary. I'm excited. I'm going to put in my notice at work tomorrow."

Linda and Ho were both silent for a moment, then Linda spoke up. "Are you telling us you're going to be like Sherlock Holmes?"

"Not exactly."

"No, I think exactly," Ho said. "You'll be as good or better than Sherlock Holmes. Linda and I can be your Doctor Watson."

"Yes, yes!" Linda said, bouncing on the couch. "I want to be Doctor Watson."

"Calm down, you two. It won't be easy to start as a new private detective."

"Come to think of it," Ho said. "How do you go about attracting clients? Aren't there already a bunch of private detectives in town?"

"I know a lot of criminal lawyers. I'll send announcements to all of them. Lawyers need private detective work fairly often. Even though it might be slow at the start, I think I might be able to make a go of it."

"I'm sure you will, Mom."

"Enough of this. It's time for dinner," Karen said as she rose and pulled Ho up from the couch.

Later, Karen grabbed the phone when it rang. "It's for me," she said as she stood. Twenty minutes after she disappeared into her office with the phone, she came out grinning from ear to ear. "I have my first client!"

"Details. Give us details!" Ho shouted.

"That was Garland Rice on the phone. The judge declared Kenny Sturgis's first trial a mistrial, like we thought. That means there is likely going to be another trial. Garland knows he still has a difficult road ahead. The fingerprint evidence is strong. Anyway, he wants to hire me to try to find the real killer. He never had a chance to check out all of Kenny's story. Kenny claims the girl, Maybell Wilcox, set him up. Anyway, I'm going to the prison, or wherever Kenny is, when Garland arranges for me to see him."

"How much notice will you have to give at work?" Ho asked. "If you have some leave left, you might be able to take it during the two-week's notice or whatever."

"You know, that might work. I still have some leave. I only used a few days for our honeymoon. I'll straighten it out with personnel tomorrow. I have to see what happens with my retirement funds and other details. It shouldn't be hard to figure out. Things are moving fast. I like it."

Chapter Thirty-One

Garland Rice, February 26, 1981

The judge gave Garland Rice permission to go to the state penitentiary to obtain Kenny's release. Kenny had been moved from the hospital to the state pen two days prior. Garland was thrilled the judge also allowed him to be responsible for Kenny's supervision after he'd posted bail. After driving back from the state pen, Garland drove Kenny to the cabin he'd shared with his father. They did not receive a warm welcome.

"What the hell are you doing here?" Kenny's dad shouted when they pulled up. "I can't have you living here. You have no idea what you've put me through. Police all over the place, and then newspaper reporters! I even had to deal with a television crew. It's only just turned peaceful. No, you can't be here. Get the hell out!"

"What am I going to do?" Kenny asked Garland as he put his clothes in the two paper bags his father gave him.

"Take all your stuff, and you can sleep in my house tonight."

"Thanks. What about this?" Kenny asked, holding up his rifle.

"Leave it here. The judge would probably be bothered with me taking you anywhere near a rifle, let alone taking one with you. The rifle stays with your father."

When he finished, Kenny took his two bags of clothes and a box of other stuff outside and placed them in his Jeep. His father, who'd been pacing outside while Kenny cleared his room, came up and piled on. "I can't tell you how disappointed I am with you. You've dragged our good name through the mud. I don't want to ever see you again. If you come around here, I'll shoot you like I would any other trespasser. Understand?"

Kenny knew his father, so he understood. He didn't even try to tell him he was innocent. He climbed into his Jeep and followed Garland out of the driveway.

On their way to Springfield, Garland stopped at a pay phone to call Catherine to explain the situation. He and Catherine had been married the year after they met as college juniors, and they'd been together for fifty-three years. Catherine had taught second grade while he concentrated on law school. Her income kept them above the poverty line for those three years. The first of their two girls was born during his first year as a lawyer. They'd struggled some but eventually everything worked out. Now Catherine had retired. He didn't think she'd have any problem with putting Kenny up for a while, but he thought it prudent to give her a warning. She said she'd pick up her knitting project, which she had spread all over the guestroom.

When they arrived at the house, Garland introduced Kenny to Catherine.

"I'm real grateful for you letting me stay here, Mrs. Rice. I won't be any bother. I'm used to taking care of myself."

"Come upstairs Kenny. I'll show you to your room. While it's not much, I think it will do."

"It will definitely be better than a prison cell, Mrs. Rice."

"Please call me Catherine. Mrs. Rice is Garland's mom, not me," she replied with a warm smile.

Three minutes later, Kenny and Catherine came downstairs and Kenny went out to retrieve his belongings. Catherine approached her husband.

Checking to be sure Kenny was outside, she said, "That poor boy. He told me our guest room is nicer than any room he's ever stayed in."

"I expect so. I saw his tiny room in his father's log cabin, and I think they spend quite a bit of time sleeping on cots in tents. He's never lived in a normal house."

Kenny came in the front door, halting the discussion.

Later in the evening after finishing dinner, Kenny and Catherine sat in the living room. Kenny was shocked at what he saw. Garland had cleared the table, loaded the dishes in the dishwasher, and was now washing the pots and pans. "I thought you'd be doing the dishes, Catherine. You cooked everything. Garland didn't help at all."

"It's a deal we made a long time ago. Garland gets in my way when he tries to help me with meal preparation, so I relieved him of any responsibility for cooking in exchange for his promise to clean up. It's been a good arrangement."

"Gosh, before she left, my mom cooked and cleaned. My dad didn't do anything in the kitchen. I was nine, I think, when she left, so I didn't help much. After that, my dad had to start doing everything. Eventually, he learned his way around the stove, but not like you. I really liked dinner."

"Thanks, Kenny, I could tell you liked the meal. I figured I'd be able to beat prison food."

"Yeah, I guess you're right… no, it wasn't just better than the prison food. It was great."

"Let's change the subject. Do you see your mom often?"

"No, I don't see her at all. She walked away from both my dad and me, and I haven't seen her since she left. I found out where she lives now, but I've never tried to contact her. Heck, I have a half-brother and half-sister I've never met."

"Must be awful. I wonder what's wrong with that woman. I could never abandon a nine-year-old."

"Yeah, I agree. I bet you could leave my dad though. He's a hard man. I'm here because he kicked me out. He told me never to come back. I don't know what I'm going to do long term. Before all this mess, I had a good job helping my dad, and he paid me decent too. I guess I have to hope this new trial works out better than the first one before I worry about anything long term."

Garland returned from the kitchen during Kenny's commentary with two cups of coffee and sat next to his wife. "I think you're right Kenny, the first thing to worry about is the trial. I've hired a private detective to help. She's coming over in a few minutes. You've met her before—Karen Daniels. She used to work for the state police."

"I remember her. She may have been the only one I talked to who seemed to believe me. I only saw her once. She's a private detective now?"

"Yes, she quit the state police. Remember I told you we're getting the new trial because Bill Hooper hid the evidence about chewing tobacco? Karen Daniels discovered what Hooper did, and the other cops she used to work with didn't like her telling on the boss. She, rightly I think, figured she'd be *persona non grata* in her old office, so she quit."

"All this happened very recently," Catherine interjected. "Karen is just starting her detective agency."

Garland sipped his coffee and leaned back. "Basically, we need to have her find someone who will back up your version of events. It seems like every time we turned around before, people were agreeing with Maybell Wilcox. You couldn't come up with anyone who saw the two of you together, and she had people willing to swear she was with them when you said the two of you were together. We need more than your word to go on."

Kenny closed his eyes for a moment. "Let me think on it. I guess it's weird Maybell and me never went out in public. Really, most of what we did wasn't the kind of thing you'd do in public anyway. One time we ate at McDonalds, but no one saw me. We went through the drive through in her van and then ate in the back of the van."

The doorbell rang. "Probably Karen," Garland said, glancing at his watch as he stood up.

After the introductions, Karen got right down to business. "Kenny, the way I see it, we have two options. Option one is we find out who shot Walter Cunningham. Option two is we find a way to undermine Maybell Wilcox's story."

Garland leaned forward from his seat. "Karen's right, and it's possible to work on both options at the same time."

"How you going to find out who killed Cunningham?" Kenny asked.

Karen kept her gaze focused on Kenny. "Finding the killer is a long shot. Nevertheless, the police, mostly my old unit, jumped on the fingerprint evidence so fast, they didn't do basic police work. I can think of two things right off the top of my head. They didn't check for the ownership of the rifle. Someone had filed off the serial number. It's an exotic gun and they should have tried to track it down. I'll see if I can find anything. The second thing is the car. They should have traced it through the VIN number. I can work on that too."

"I'd investigate some of Maybell's friends to find who owned the sniper rifle," Kenny said. "She got it for me to shoot. It's how my fingerprints were all over it. When she showed it to me, she told me it belonged to one of her friends."

"Good," Karen said. "Now I want you to think about who else knew about you and Maybell. Did you tell any of your friends? Did anyone you know see the two of you together? We have to do better than leave it as your word against hers."

"Garland and Catherine asked about it before, and I told them Maybell and I did what we did mostly in private. I guess entirely in private. We were either in her dog grooming van or somewhere in the woods. We did go to my house once, but my dad was in town. Also, we went out to the hunting camp. Again, no one else was there."

"You told us about the Charleston Club meeting," Garland said. "It's likely those people are in on the plot, and I guess Maybell's parents were in on it too."

Karen sighed. "Maybell's covered all her bases."

"Wait," Kenny said, "I thought of someone."

"Who?" the other three asked in unison.

"One morning, I think the morning I drove the old car, I ran into Maybell's sister, Joan, at the end of the driveway. Her boyfriend stood her up, so I gave her a ride to school."

"I don't know what our chances of turning a member of the Wilcox family are," Garland commented.

Kenny responded, "Now that I think about it, the chances might be good. Joan told me to watch out for Maybell. Nothing specific, kinda hazy. I didn't think much of it at the time. Now, I think she'd been trying to give me a warning. She said Maybell had a steady boyfriend. Given what Maybell and I had been doing, I thought Joan had to be lying. Now I'm not sure."

"Tell us about Joan," Karen said.

"Joan is the most popular girl in school. She always has a boyfriend, never the same one for long. She's a senior this year. If I'd stayed in school, I'd be a senior too. I guess she's been in one or two of my classes. I can't say I know her well. She's way out of my league."

"I'll try to interview her at the school," Karen said. "I don't think it would work if I went out to the Wilcox place and asked to speak with her."

"You're right, there's no way the Wilcoxes would let you talk to her," Garland said. "And I guess you still have your state police ID, so the school will cooperate."

"Unfortunately, I turned in my creds this afternoon. The new people in charge said they didn't need two weeks' notice. They seemed to be happy to get rid of me. I'll try to catch Joan after school."

Kenny spoke up. "It shouldn't be hard. Any kid could point her out to you. Like I said, everyone knows her."

"Sounds like a plan," Karen replied.

"What about me?" Kenny asked. "What am I supposed to do? No offense Catherine, but I don't think I want to hang around here all day."

"It's the other thing I wanted to talk to you about," Karen responded. "You met my husband at the hospital, Ho Narwhal. He has a sculpture studio in town, and he needs a helper. I think you might like the work. I can take you to the studio tomorrow. I don't think he can pay much, but as you said, you need something to do."

"Sounds great. Anyway, I don't have any other options... So yeah, I guess I'll try it."

Chapter Thirty-Two

Garland Rice, February 26, 1981

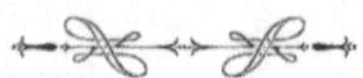

As Garland Rice walked toward his office the next morning, he mulled over the lead story in the paper that morning. The prisoners who'd been in the van with Kenny had all been killed in a shootout with the police. They'd been cornered in a mountain cabin and started shooting when the police approached. During the gun fight, a propane tank next to the cabin ignited and burned down the cabin and its inhabitants.

Deep in thought, he almost bumped into a woman waiting by the front door of his office building. The woman stepped in front of him and asked, "Are you Garland Rice?"

The question startled Garland, and he stepped back a bit. He didn't recognize the woman. She had on a nice gray coat with a big red scarf and looked to be in her late thirties or early forties. "Yes," he responded. "And who might you be?"

"Are you Kenneth Sturgis's lawyer?"

"Again, yes. Why do you ask?"

"I guess I should introduce myself. I'm Shirley Young—Kenny's mother."

"Oh, my gosh. You'd better come to my office, Mrs. Young. You might be the last person on earth I expected to see. Follow me."

In the small office, Mrs. Young unwound her scarf, hung it and her coat over the back of the chair Garland had offered, and sat down. She wore tan slacks and a red sweater. Garland thought she looked stunning. She was slim, with flawless, unwrinkled skin, prominent cheekbones, and her brunette hair shone even in the florescent lights of the small office. When he looked closer, Garland could see a resemblance to Kenny, not strong, but it was there— something around the eyes.

They stared at each other for a few moments. "I'm surprised to see you," Garland said. "Kenny told us he hasn't had any contact with you since you left his father."

She took a deep breath. "That's what his father demanded. He told me he'd shoot me if I ever came close to Kenny," she said, her voice shaking. "William Sturgis is a hard man. I believed he would kill me. Leaving Kenny was one of the hardest things I've ever done, but I couldn't stay with William. It was a horrible decision to make, and you might condemn me for it, but I had to." Her eyes filled with tears as she spoke.

"I don't know Mr. Sturgis well. I only met him once. I drove Kenny home yesterday. He'd just been released from prison. When we got there, his father wouldn't let him stay and told him never to come back. Just like you, he threatened to shoot Kenny if he ever showed his face. I have to admit, like you said, he was believable. He seemed to me to be one very angry man."

Shirley shook her head. "Like many teenagers, I was an idiot in high school. I hated my family so much that I ran away. By sheer luck, or bad luck as it turned out, William found me and took me in. Before I knew it, I was pregnant with Kenny. At the time, I was thrilled, and the first few years with the little baby were some of the best of my life."

"Wait, did you marry Kenny's father?"

"No, but the way he explained it, we had a common-law marriage."

"He's not right. Common-law marriage no longer exists in Missouri. It hasn't been possible since some time in the early 1920s."

Shirley gave him a weak smile. "I'm glad to hear it. I've always wondered. I just went ahead and married my current husband with no questions asked. I guess I was okay to do that."

"How old were you when Kenny came along?"

"I'd just turned eighteen."

"So, you were seventeen when you got pregnant."

"Yes."

"I don't know why I asked. I guess it's the lawyer in me. Sturgis could have gotten in trouble over your age. I guess it doesn't matter now. Why did you leave?"

"There were lots of things. First of all, I had trouble living like he did—hidden away from civilization. You wouldn't believe the fit William threw when he found out I'd gotten a social security card for Kenny to enter school. Second, and maybe most important, any time I did something he didn't like, he'd get incredibly angry, and our disagreements usually ended with him hitting me. It got worse the longer I stayed, but I couldn't leave because of Kenny. Finally, one of William's clients interrupted one of our squabbles. We were shouting at each other in the front yard. The guy was pulling into the driveway just when William had his fist balled up and his arm cocked. I ran to the man's car and hid behind it. I was terrified. I guess I was shaking. The man, Henry Young, he's my brother-in-law now, jumped out of his car and yelled for William to stop. After he recognized how big a mistake he'd made, William ran into the woods at the back of the house. Henry is a nice man. When he asked what was going on, I poured my heart out to him. He told me it would probably be best if I got some things together, so I could leave for a day or two to let William cool down."

"You were lucky this guy showed up when he did."

"You don't know how lucky. Henry and Wanda Young are the most wonderful people in the world. They took me in, and Wanda listened to my story and let me cry it out. I showed her the bruises on my body. William never hit me where it would show. At first, we planned for me to go back in a few days, but things got more complicated when I met Henry's younger brother, Simon. He's only a year older than me, and we had an instant attraction. It's hokey I know, but it was love at first sight."

Garland shifted in his seat and got up. "Can I get you a glass of water or some coffee? I've been a terrible host."

"Water would be nice."

Garland returned with two glasses of water. "So, you didn't go back. Is that the story?"

After taking a drink of water, she continued. "No, that's not quite right. When I decided I couldn't live with William anymore, I wanted to get Kenny. Henry and Simon went with me, but even with their help, it turned into a disaster. That's when William threatened to shoot me if I ever came back or ever tried to make any contact with Kenny. He stood there with one arm around Kenny and the other arm holding his rifle. I knew William. He's very determined when wants to be, and he's a good shot even with one hand. I had Henry and Simon back away, and we left without Kenny or any of my things."

"That's quite a story. I'm sure it confused Kenny. At nine years old, he couldn't have had any idea what was going on."

"I'm sure he didn't. The last time I saw him, he looked frightened and confused. The image has been burned into my memory. I hadn't seen or heard of Kenny since. Then I saw his picture in the papers about the murder of Walter Cunningham. After all these years, it still tore me up. I have been consumed with guilt. If I'd only insisted back then, or done something, he might have turned out differently. The way I see it, William's influence led to my son turning out to be a murderer. I cried for days."

"I take it you're here because you heard Kenny has been released from prison."

"Yes. The short story in the paper didn't have many details, but it made it sound like maybe Kenny hadn't been responsible for Cunningham's murder."

"The details are messy, but essentially, you're right. The first trial has been declared a mistrial. There is likely to be a second trial, so Kenny's not off the hook yet, but I think we might be able to clear him."

"Can you tell me what's going on?"

Garland described the way Kenny said he'd been framed by Maybell Wilcox and Bill Hooper. He concluded by saying he believed Kenny, but he cautioned her he couldn't yet prove Kenny's story. All he had so far was the chewing tobacco evidence, which cast serious doubt on the case against Kenny.

When he'd finished, Shirley said, "So the deck is stacked against Kenny. I'd like to see him. The boy needs support."

"I think it might be good. If it makes you feel better, I think you could see him without worrying about repercussions from his father. Mr. Sturgis was very angry yesterday when Kenny got home. William, that's his name, right?"

"Yeah."

"William told him to clear out and never come back. He made it crystal clear he didn't want to see Kenny again. Right now, he's staying at our house until he gets settled."

"That sounds like William. He holds grudges."

Garland handed her a piece of paper and a pen. "Why don't you give me your phone number. I'll call if Kenny wants to set up a time to meet. We'll have to leave it up to him. There's a chance he won't want to see you. The way he tells the story, you abandoned him and his father. I don't think he has any idea you left him involuntarily."

She hung her head. "William probably hasn't painted a very nice picture of me over the years. Before you ask him, tell him my side of the story. Tell him I really want to see him. Tell him I've always felt horrible about having to leave him."

"I'll give it a try, but I can't guarantee success."

Chapter Thirty-Three

Ho Narwhal, February 26, 1981

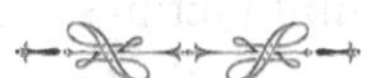

That same morning, Karen went to the Rice's house so Kenny could follow her to Ho's studio. Ho saw them coming so he stepped outside, greeted Kenny as he exited his Jeep, and waved at Karen as she drove away.

"Welcome to my studio. Come on in. You can hang your coat over there."

After hanging up his coat, Kenny looked bewildered. "What do you do?"

"I'm a sculptor. It's easier to show you than to explain with words. I have several projects going right now."

"Sorry, I guess I don't know much about sculpture." Kenny scanned the room and couldn't figure out what was going on.

His puzzled face suggested Ho should take it slow and give lots of details. "Let me explain what I'm doing, and then we can get around to how you can help."

"Thanks. I don't know nothing about this stuff."

Ho led Kenny over to the wall and showed him pictures of the animal sculptures from the exhibit in St. Louis. "These are pictures of finished products. What you see on the outside is brass. The insides of the sculptures, the bones of the animals I guess, are steel."

Kenny nodded, and after studying the pictures said, "Your animals are weird. They're all mixed up."

"Yeah, it's my thing, my niche. I'm the sculptor who does wacky animals in brass. People seem to like what I do. I guess the bottom line is people, and some museums too, buy my sculptures. Come on, I'll show you how the process starts."

Ho led Kenny to the clay modeling table and showed him the models he made of the animals. He had some old models, which he matched with the animals from the St. Louis exhibit pictures.

"Your models are smaller than the finished ones, aren't they?"

"Yes, I scale them up when I produce the final piece. The clay models are where I try things out. I want to have a fairly good idea of what I'm doing before I start welding. It's the next step."

Ho had the superstructure of an animal underway, and he showed Kenny the welding area.

"After the welding is done, I cover the steel with a copper mesh," he said, pointing to a piece of the copper mesh on a small table.

Next, Ho moved to the finishing area. "After the copper is in place, I put the brass around the copper. This area is large because I have this furnace for melting brass as well as space for the extensive polishing I do on the finished pieces."

"Wow, you have this all figured out. I still don't get it. Why make these funny animals?"

"I don't know. Actually, I'm not sure anyone knows why they get an idea. I don't quite know why I started, but I do know why I keep at it. If I succeed, my animals make people laugh. I get a real bang out of seeing people laughing at my sculptures. Some of the arty crowds are pretty uptight. I love it when they laugh."

"And I guess you make a lot of money when you sell one of these things. I bet they're not cheap. The metal alone must cost a mint."

Ho told Kenny the story of how he started out with the little tower he gave to Horace Cunningham and his good fortune of getting the commission for the hotels.

"The more I think about it, the towers made me a craftsman. I learned how to work with brass. After the first one, it didn't involve much creativity. To tell the truth, I started to get bored after ten or so, but the money rolled in, and it gave me time to think about what I wanted to do next."

Kenny filled the pause. "So, then you thought of the animals?"

"Yes. I started tinkering with the animals before I finished the last couple of towers. And I got lucky when a gallery owner in St. Louis offered to host an exhibit. The pictures are from the exhibit. My stuff there sold fast, and I've been able to get some commissions from the showing. That pretty much brings us up to date. Now I'm working on those commissions."

"So, what kind of help do you need?"

"There's some heavy lifting I need help with once in a while, and I'd like you to clean up. Once you get trained on the tools there will be more you can do. At first, I need help with the final polishing. You can start on the back end of number eighteen. It's almost finished."

They walked over to the sculpture, a deer with the head of a goose. The whole thing was odd looking, particularly because, instead of front legs, the deer had two bedsprings.

"I'm going to work on the front end, covering those springs in brass. I want you to start the polishing on the back."

After Ho showed Kenny the tools to use and gave him a demonstration of how he wanted the polishing done, they started to work.

After about ten minutes, Kenny said, "I think I'm getting the hang of it."

"Good, take your time. There is no reason to hurry."

In mid-afternoon, Karen arrived at the high school before the end of the day. When she saw the first school bus coming down the drive, she climbed out of her car and walked to the front of the school. Karen heard what must have been the final bell, and students started to spill out of the building. She stopped the first student she saw and asked him to point out Joan Wilcox.

"Sure," the kid said. He seemed happy to help.

Karen and the kid stepped toward the building as the sidewalk in front of the school started to fill with students eager to leave. About five minutes after the final bell, the kid nudged Karen and said, "That's Joan Wilcox over there, the one in the red sweater."

"Thanks." Kenny had called Joan good looking, and Karen could see why. She was petite, had blonde hair, a bright smile, and did a good job of filling out her sweater. A cluster of older kids hovered around her as she walked.

The steady stream of kids made it hard for Karen to get over to Joan's side of the sidewalk. Karen had to give way to several students who were hustling to catch a bus or some other ride. As a result, Joan Wilcox was ten or fifteen feet in front of her when Karen made it to her side of the sidewalk. Karen tried to hurry, but the crowd of students intent on leaving made it difficult. When she finally got close, Joan veered into the parking lot and jumped into a waiting car, completely frustrating Karen.

Karen hung her head and stood there watching the car with Joan get into the line of vehicles headed toward the school exit. When she turned around, she almost collided with a teacher running toward her.

"Karen? You're Karen Daniels, aren't you?" the teacher said breathlessly.

Karen stared at the woman, not recognizing her. "Yes."

"It's Fern Nichols—from high school. Actually, it's Fern Miller now."

Karen remembered Fern as a thin, brown-haired eighteen-year-old. The woman in front of her was a much older blonde fighting a weight problem. Looking closer, she saw glimpses of the Fern she knew from high school. "Oh, my goodness, Fern. It's good to see you," Karen responded finally. She opened her arms and gave her old friend a brief hug.

When they separated, Fern asked. "What are you doing here? I mean, I know why I'm here. I'm the art teacher. Have been for the last ten years."

"Oh, I remember, you were the best artist in our class. It makes sense you'd be an art teacher."

"Do you have a minute or two? We can go to my room and catch up. I want to know what's happened to you since high school. You know it's funny, I don't really keep track of any of our old high school friends."

Karen didn't have anything better to do, and it was nice to see an old friend. "Sure, lead the way."

When they arrived at the art room, Fern cleared a chair, giving Karen a place to sit. The room had several easels on one side and a similar number of desks on the other. The walls of the room were hung with what Karen thought must be the students' artwork.

"I guess I never answered your question," Karen said. "You asked me what I was doing here. The answer is: trying to locate one of your students—Joan Wilcox. Do you know her?"

"I sure do. Joan is the best student I have right now, maybe the most talented student I've ever had. Why did you want to see her?"

"I'd better explain. I'm a private detective, and I need to question her about a case I'm working on."

"Why don't you go to the Wilcox house? I'm sure she gets home later. Right now, I bet she's out fooling around with her current boyfriend."

"It's complicated. I don't think her family would be willing to let me talk to her. I have to find a way to ask my questions somewhere other than her home."

"I see… well, I guess I don't really. It does explain why you're here."

"Unfortunately, I couldn't get to her before she jumped into a car today. I was just trying to get over feeling frustrated when you ran up to me. Now tell me what you've been doing since high school. We all kind of scattered after graduation."

Fern gave Karen the lowdown on her life: an art education major at college, a firefighter husband, and three boys. Then she said, "Your turn."

Karen filled her in on Linda's birth and her interrupted college career, her work with the state police, meeting and marrying Ho, and her recent switch to being a private detective.

"Horace Narwhal," Fern said. "Isn't he a sculptor? I've read stories about him in the paper. He's a big deal!"

"Yes, in some circles I'm Mrs. Horace Narwhal, not Karen Daniels. He's a big deal, like you said. You wouldn't know it though. He's incredibly down to earth and the sweetest guy. My daughter loves him. I do too, for that matter."

Fern pushed her chair back and gave Karen an assured look. "I have an idea that might help both of us."

"Shoot."

"You want to talk to Joan somewhere out of earshot of her parents, right?"

"Right."

"And I need to find a way to spice up my art classes. I guess you wouldn't know about that."

"I'll take your word for it."

"So, if I can swing it with the principal, I can arrange a field trip to your husband's studio for my senior art class, the one Joan's in. It will give you a chance to ask her whatever you want."

"Great idea. Time is an issue. It would have to happen fast."

"Is the day after tomorrow quick enough? It fits into my schedule, and I'd only be asking for nine students to miss afternoon classes. I think I can swing it. Hold on, I'll check with the office right now. I'll be back in a jiffy."

While Fern ran to the office, Karen walked around the room, checking out the students' artwork. Two of the pieces, a pencil sketch and a watercolor, were clearly the best of the lot. Both were signed JW, which Karen guessed stood for Joan Wilcox.

Fern flew through the door five minutes later. "It's done. No problem, the students just need permission slips signed. I'll hand them out tomorrow, and they can bring them in day after tomorrow."

"Good, it'll give Ho a chance to figure out what to do with, what did you say, nine high school seniors?"

"At most nine. You can never be sure all of them will remember to get their parents to sign the permission slips. I'll forge Joan's if she forgets. I'll have the students bring their sketch pads. I expect there are some sculptures under way at the studio. We won't need a big presentation."

"You're right. He has two sculptures in process now. One is in the early stages and the other is mostly finished. I think it can work. The field trip idea is wonderful."

Karen stayed another few minutes talking to Fern about their high school friends. It turned out neither of them had kept up with many people, so the discussion didn't last very long.

Before she left, Karen remembered Joan's pictures. Going up to the pencil sketch, she asked, "Did Joan Wilcox do this?"

"Yes, and this watercolor," Fern replied, pointing to the other piece signed JW.

"You're right. She has real talent."

"Yes, and if I can get her to focus on her art instead of the boys chasing after her, I think she's good enough to go to a conservatory. I've never had a student this good."

Chapter Thirty-Four

Kenny Sturgis, February 26, 1981

Kenny knocked on the Rice's door at quarter after five. Though he'd enjoyed his day at Ho's studio, he felt tired. He figured he should have expected to be tired, since he'd just been flat on his back in the hospital. Still, he hadn't worked hard and shouldn't be so tired.

Catherine opened the door. "Oh Kenny, we should have given you a key."

Kenny walked in. "That's no problem. I'm not sure Garland would think it's right to give me a key. I'm out on bail."

"Nonsense, I'll see that you have a key before you go to work tomorrow. I guess you'll be going to work tomorrow?"

"Yes, I will. I liked working with Mr. Narwhal. It's kind of cool. Nothing like I've ever done before, but I liked it."

"You look tired. Is it hard work?"

"No, it's not that hard but I'm tired like you said. I guess I haven't been doing anything strenuous for quite a while."

"Why don't you go up to your room and put your feet up? Garland will be home soon. I'll call you when dinner's ready."

Kenny headed upstairs.

An hour and a half later, Garland knocked on his door. Kenny called out, "I'll be down in a minute."

Catherine started the conversation at the dinner table. "Tell us what Ho's studio is like."

Kenny did his best to describe Ho's sculptures and how they were made. Garland and Catherine had never seen any of the sculptures so it wasn't easy for Kenny. Eventually he decided to describe the one he'd been working on, the deer-goose with springs for front legs, and he thought they understood.

"Sounds so unusual," Catherine said.

Kenny nodded. "Yeah, it's kinda weird."

"I understand he sells his stuff for big money," Garland said. "According to Karen, he's very successful. We couldn't afford one, even if it fit our tastes."

"The ones he's working on right now are sold already. He calls it a commission."

"That's good," Catherine said. "It means you could have steady work there if you wanted it."

"I don't know about the long run, but for now I'm glad to have a job."

Like the previous night, Garland did the cleanup after dinner while Catherine and Kenny went to the living room to talk. Garland joined them when he finished. "I have a question for you, Kenny."

"Fire away."

"Let me back up before the question. I had a very interesting visitor this morning. A young lady named Shirley Young."

"My mom?" Kenny blurted.

"Yes, your mother. She had heard you were out of prison and wanted to know what was going on."

"Didn't she abandon you and your father when you were just a young boy?" Catherine asked.

"Wait, Catherine. That's not how she tells the story. According to her, she and Kenny's father weren't getting along, and when they fought, he hit her.

Finally, one day a car drove up to the house just when he pulled his fist back to slug her. The guy in the car must have seen the whole thing. To make a long story short, she went away with the guy. I don't know who had the idea, but she went willingly. When she got to the guy's house, his wife consoled her. I think the wife probably convinced her to leave Kenny's father. I don't think it was a hard sell. He beat her often. A couple of days later, your mom and the guy and his brother came to get you, Kenny, but your father wouldn't let her. He told her to leave and never come back. In addition, he told her if she ever contacted you, he'd kill her."

Kenny and Catherine sat in stunned silence.

Catherine finally spoke up. "That's not how your father described it, is it, Kenny?"

"No." Kenny stood and started to pace. "I don't know what to think. He just told me she walked out on us. That's all he would say."

"You were really young when all this happened, but I bet you could understand that your mom and dad weren't getting along," Garland said.

After another circuit of the living room, Kenny responded, "I guess so. I remember a lot of shouting. I went to school then, so maybe their bigger fights happened when I wasn't home. All I know is my father said she deserted us."

"Shirley said you were there when she tried to come and get you. It might have been on a Saturday. Do you remember that?"

"I guess I do now that you asked, but my father said it was different than that. He told me the people with my mother were there to take me somewhere awful. He told it like he was protecting me from the two guys who were with her."

"I can see it," Catherine said. "Your mom had been gone for a couple of days, and maybe your father told you she'd been taken away by some people."

"I don't know. It was a long time ago."

"That's the past," Garland said. "Now your mom would like to see you. I have her phone number. I told her I'd ask you if you wanted to call her."

"She's married now with two kids. Why would she want to see me?"

"She told me she always wanted to get in contact with you, but your father had her too scared to do anything. She believed he'd shoot her."

"Makes sense, at least for a while," Catherine said. "But for nine years? That's what it's been, hasn't it?"

"You don't know my dad. I understand why she'd be worried. Why isn't she still worried?"

"I think seeing your picture in the papers when you were arrested for Walter Cunningham's murder jolted her. She said it really upset her. She said she hadn't heard anything about you until the story about the murder. When she read the story about your release, she decided to try to make contact."

"I guess she doesn't need to worry about my father anymore. He washed his hands of me. Hell, he even threatened to shoot me, too."

"I told her about what your father said. I think you're both in the clear. You could meet her if you want to."

"Wait. What about her husband? I don't think my parents ever got a real divorce. Isn't it against the law to be married to two people?"

"She and your father were never officially married. She's not a bigamist, so don't worry. We didn't talk about it, but I bet her current husband knows about you and her visit with me this morning."

Kenny finally stopped pacing and sat down. "What do you think I should do, Catherine?"

Catherine smiled at him warmly. "It's not my place to tell you what to do."

Kenny folded his hands together and hung his head. "I need some advice, please."

"Since you asked if it was me, I'd call her. If you don't, you'll spend the rest of your life wondering what she's like."

"What do you think, Garland?"

Garland held up his hand. "I have a rule. It's never a good idea to contradict your wife." He smiled at Catherine. "In this case, it's easy to follow the rule. Catherine's right. You should call her."

After a pause, Kenny lifted his head and stared at Catherine and Garland.

"What will I say?"

"I would leave it up to her," Garland replied. "She's the one who came forward. She wants to talk to you. You only have to say who you are. She'll fill in any pauses."

"Garland's right, Kenny. She wants to contact you. Now that I think about it, I'd advise you to keep the phone call short. It's better to arrange for a time to meet. This kind of thing is better done face to face."

Kenny rose and started to pace again. After one back and forth across the living room, he stopped and declared, "Okay I'll do it, but Catherine's right. I'll keep it short."

"Use the kitchen phone, Kenny. Garland and I will go upstairs to give you some privacy. Come get us when you're through. We'll want a report."

Garland went over to his briefcase and pulled out a piece of paper. "Here's the phone number. Good luck."

Kenny took the paper and went into the kitchen. He took a deep breath and dialed the number. After three rings, a woman's voice said, "Young residence."

A child was crying in the background. After a pause, he said, "Mom."

With a sharp intake of breath, the woman asked, "Kenny? Is that you?"

The crying in the background got louder and the woman said, "Wait a minute, Courtney. This is an important phone call. Please be quiet."

"Yes, Mom. This is Kenny, but it sounds like I've called at a bad time."

"No, no. This is fine. My daughter is causing a fuss. Bedtimes are hard for her. Let me see if I can get my husband to settle her down. I'll be back in a minute."

Kenny started pacing, but the cord on the kitchen phone didn't give him much range. After what seemed like an eternity, his mother returned.

"I'm so sorry. Little kids can be so hard sometimes."

Kenny's throat clogged. "I guess. I'm a bigger kid, so I'll try to be more reasonable. Garland told me you wanted to see me. I think we ought to talk, but not on the phone. Is there a way we can meet? In person, I mean."

"Yes, that would be better. There is so much I want to say."

Kenny took a breath, hoping she didn't hear any emotion in his voice. "Let's pick a time. I'm in Springfield. That's not too far away for you. Is it?"

"No, Springfield's fine. I can get away for lunch tomorrow, if that's not too soon. What about the food court at the Springfield Mall? We don't have to eat there, but it's a good place to meet. I can be there by twelve-fifteen. Does that work for you?"

"I can make it work."

"Kenny, thank you so much for calling. It's been a long time."

At that point, the crying in the background got louder, so Kenny said, "It sounds like you gotta go. Goodbye. I'll see you tomorrow."

The next day, Kenny explained to Ho about the meeting with his mother. Ho told him to take as much time as he needed, so he got to the mall at noon. He nervously paced around the food court, wondering which direction his mom would come from. *I don't know how to act. I don't know what to say. How much of what my father told me is true?*

He was so deep in thought that he didn't see his mother until she was standing right in front of him. He stammered, "Mom?"

His mother nodded, rushed forward, and wrapped her arms around Kenny.

The hug startled him. On top of it, his mother was crying. He wanted to put his arms around her, but she had them trapped in her hug. After a few minutes, she released Kenny, opened her purse, and extracted a tissue. Wiping her eyes, she said, "I promised myself I wouldn't cry, but look at me. I probably look awful."

Kenny didn't know how to respond, so he just stared at her. He didn't think she looked awful. Her eyes were red, but he didn't care.

They both started to talk at the same time. When they stopped, Shirley said. "There's a nice pizza place down this way. Why don't we go there?"

"Pizza sounds good. There's so much we have to talk about."

After they ordered their pizza, Shirley told Kenny her version of why she left. Kenny listened without interrupting. Shirley finished by saying, "I never wanted to leave you, but your father made it impossible for me to take you."

After an uncomfortable silence, Kenny finally responded, "Sounds like him. He just told me you had abandoned him and me. I didn't know any better. I was a kid."

Shirley teared up again but controlled herself. "I know, and I felt terrible about it."

Kenny decided to change the conversation. "I guess I have a half-brother and half-sister."

Shirley smiled. "Let me show you some pictures."

Kenny was exhilarated when he got into his Jeep an hour later. After the beginning awkwardness, he and his mother had gotten along great. They had exchanged life stories, and by the time they had to leave, they were talking like old friends, and he accepted an invitation for dinner the next night. Neither of them knew how he would fit into her family, but they agreed to see what the future would bring.

Chapter Thirty-Five

Karen Daniels, February 28, 1981

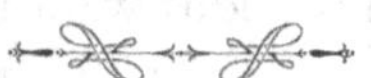

The next day, Ho and Kenny cleaned up the shop as best they could. Ho had rented ten folding chairs for the students. He hadn't done anything like this before, so he had no idea what to do. Karen had told him not to worry about preparing a presentation or anything. Fern said she just wanted the students to have a tour of the studio and then draw sketches of what they saw. Fern thought having two projects underway would make it easy.

Karen pulled up a half hour before the students were supposed to arrive.

"Everything looks good. I'm sure Fern and her students will be thrilled."

"I sure hope so," Ho responded.

"Here, let's sit down. We can eat the lunches I brought, and I can tell you what I've been able to find out."

When the three of them were assembled and opening their sandwiches, Karen couldn't help herself. "I had what I think is a breakthrough this morning. I've been tracing the VIN number on the 55 Oldsmobile. It turns out it's been sold lots of times. It didn't show up in Missouri until the late 1970s. They keep track of VIN numbers when a vehicle is licensed. I think

I located the guy who sold it to Maybell. I'm going to interview him after I greet Fern and her students."

"Wow, it could be really important," Kenny said.

"Yes, if Karen can trace the car to Maybell, it will be the first solid evidence to back up what you've been saying. It won't only be just your word against hers. Great, Karen."

"The used car dealer is here in Springfield, so I can go there and be back in plenty of time to question Joan Willcox. Kenny, why don't you come with me to the car dealer? You don't want to be here when the kids arrive. I bet some of them would know you, and we don't want to confuse the class. When we see the school bus pulling up, go out the back door. I'll pick you up by the grocery store down the street. Besides, I want to hear all about your visit with your mother."

"Sounds like a plan," Kenny said.

Thirty-five minutes later, the yellow school bus pulled up in front of the studio. Karen took the lead, introducing Fern to Ho. Ho opened the studio door and showed the students to the seats next to a partially built skeleton.

"Put your coats on the back of your chairs," Ho said. "We really aren't set up for visitors. Your class is the first ever to visit my studio."

When the students were settled, Fern introduced Ho. She'd done her homework on him, and he started to blush halfway through the too long, formal introduction. When Fern finished, the students applauded.

Ho put his hands up to stop the applause. "You're too kind, Mrs. Miller." Turning to the students, he said, "Welcome to my studio. As Mrs. Miller indicated, I'm a sculptor. I don't have any finished pieces to show you today. I do have a couple under way and pictures of ones I've done in the past. When I'm finished talking, you can wander around the studio. All I ask is don't touch anything. It's amazing how oily people's hands are. I work with metal, and the oil from a hand can make it difficult for the metals to bond the way I want them to."

Ho then explained the various parts of the studio, the clay modeling area, the welding area, and the final assembly area where the brass was applied and polished. The students appeared interested. Ho had hoped the class would ask questions. Finally, as he demonstrated the polishing process using the deer-goose combination as a prop, one of the students asked, "How do you get ideas for these weird animals?"

"Great question," Ho replied. "The answer is, I don't know quite how I decide on what combinations to use. Mostly it simply comes to me. My objective is to make animals weird, like you said. I want to make people laugh. I've been able to succeed with some people."

Next, Joan Wilcox held up her hand. "How'd you get the brass around the springs on the front legs of the deer, or is it a goose?"

"Another great question. Let's call it a deer-goose. The spring-legs were a little tricky. I took some brass piping I had and threaded it around the springs. I had to heat the brass to make it pliable enough to make all the bends. I used a blowtorch."

Ho finished up shortly after those two questions and turned the class over to Fern. Fern told the students they had fifteen minutes to wander around the studio to decide what they were going to use as the subject for their pencil sketch assignment.

Ho spoke up as the students were getting up. "I'll be walking around too. If you have any more questions, please ask."

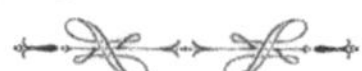

Karen and Kenny found Mac's Used Cars with no trouble. Karen asked Kenny to keep his coat on and wander around in the lot. Because Kenny's picture had been in the paper recently, she wanted to go inside and approach the car dealer by herself.

"You Mac?" Karen asked as she approached the middle-aged, balding man dressed in a rumpled suit and loose tie.

The man rose from behind his desk and walked over toward Karen. "That's me," he said as he came toward Karen with an outstretched hand.

"Karen Daniels," Karen said, shaking the man's hand.

After they shook, Karen extracted crime scene photos of the car from her bag and asked, "Do you know this car? I think you sold it not too long ago."

Mac studied the pictures for a few seconds. "Sure," he said. "I remember this one. Mostly I deal in late-model used cars. Sometimes I get ones like this. I sell them fast. No warranty, you know."

"Would you have a record of who you sold it to?"

"Who wants to know?"

"I'm a private detective working for a lawyer. We think our client has been wrongly accused of a crime, and the killer used this fifty-five Olds. We could go to court and force you to provide the information I asked for, or we could skip the formalities and you could answer my question."

Mac gave Karen a skeptical look and then said, "What the hell. I keep records. I guess you want to see them for the Olds."

"Please."

"Okay, sit over there," he said, gesturing to a chair beside the desk. "It might take me a few minutes to find the invoice."

Karen noticed Mac glancing out the window at Kenny, so she said, "The guy out there's with me. He's not really a customer."

Mac seemed to relax and turned to a file cabinet and extracted a fat file. Three minutes later, he turned back to Karen. "Here it is, the fifty-five Olds. I received a hundred and thirty-five for it. The guy didn't even haggle. I remember him pretty well."

"What's his name?

"Here it is," Mac said, showing Karen the invoice. "Kenneth Sturgis."

"Can you describe this guy Sturgis?"

"Big guy. Maybe six-four or five and had a mullet. Sometimes I chat up the customers a lot. Not this guy. He went right to the Olds. It was a no-nonsense sale."

Karen went to the door and hollered for Kenny to come in. When Kenny entered the store and took off his coat, Karen asked, "Is this the Kenneth Sturgis who bought the car from you?"

"No way. While he's tall, he's not as tall as the guy who bought the Olds, and his coloring is all wrong."

"I'm sorry, I didn't get your last name, Mac."

"It's actually Ed, Edward McNulty. Mac is a nickname. Here, why don't you take one of my business cards."

"Anyway Mr. McNulty, we might need you to testify. You didn't do anything wrong so you have nothing to worry about. If we need you to testify, the lawyers will come talk to you. It should be no big deal. This guy here is Kenneth Sturgis, and someone else, the guy you dealt with, is trying to pass himself off as Kenneth Sturgis. We will only have to have you testify that this Kenny Sturgis is not the one who bought the car."

"I guess I can do that."

"Thanks, we'll be in touch. I don't know when, or even if, any of this will happen. You've been incredibly helpful."

"I'm only trying to make an honest buck. Can I interest you in a car, Mrs. Daniels?"

"No thanks."

Karen and Kenny drove back to Ho's studio. Karen told Kenny to make himself scarce while the students were there. He understood and headed for his Jeep parked in the back of the studio.

When Karen walked in, three of the students glanced up from their drawings. The others seemed so engrossed in their work they didn't bother. Karen went to where Ho and Fern had dragged a couple of chairs.

"How'd it go?" Ho whispered.

Karen beamed. "I think we hit the jackpot. Someone, who was clearly not Kenny, bought the car using his name. The used car dealer, Mac, is sure it wasn't our Kenny Sturgis."

"Wow, it's clear confirmation. Someone tried to set up Kenny."

"Bingo."

"Is it okay if I don't know what you guys are talking about?" Fern asked.

"Sorry, I think it's best if you don't. How is everything going here?"

"Great. Ho has been wonderful and the kids are enjoying themselves."

"They loosened up after we had them get out of their chairs and let them wander around. They asked a lot of good questions, and we had several interesting discussions."

"How much more time do you have?"

Fern checked her watch. "The bus should be here in twenty minutes. My quick students are on their second drawing. My slower students have a long way to go on their first one. It's what I expected."

Karen whispered, "What about Joan Wilcox?"

"Oh, she's fast. I think she's on her third sketch."

"So, would it be okay if I talk to her?"

"Sure, come on, I'll introduce you. Ho, you come too. I think you should see what she's drawn. She's really good."

Fern led Ho and Karen to the girl. Joan blushed a little when Fern introduced her as the best student in the class.

"Here, let me see what you've drawn, if you don't mind?" Ho asked.

Joan handed Ho her sketch pad.

"Wow!" Ho and Karen exclaimed when they saw the first drawing.

Ho studied the other two drawings and finally spoke. "You've done a wonderful job. You've captured the silliness of the deer-goose. I particularly like this second drawing where you're viewing the animal from above. I saw you standing on your chair while your classmates were sitting on theirs. It's an interesting perspective."

"Thank you, Mr. Narwhal. I'm glad you like my work."

Fern took over. "Joan, Karen, Mr. Narwhal's wife, is a private detective, and she wants to ask you a few questions."

Startled, Joan backed away a step.

Karen said, "It won't take long, and it's important. Why don't we step outside?"

Joan and Karen put on their coats and went out the door. Karen sensed

Joan was a bit reluctant.

Outside, Karen got right to the point. "What do you know about the relationship between Kenny Sturgis and your sister Maybell?"

"Isn't Kenny in prison for killing the politician?"

"No, he's not. The judge declared his trial a mistrial because the police withheld important evidence. The suppressed evidence casts serious doubt on Kenny's guilt. I'm working for Kenny's lawyers and Kenny remembered one morning he gave you a ride to school, and you seemed to be giving him a warning about Maybell."

"I remember. I tried to tell him it wouldn't do him any good to hang around Maybell because she already had a steady boyfriend."

"Had you seen Kenny hanging around Maybell?"

To her credit, Joan looked Karen in the eyes when she spoke. "Yeah, I saw his Jeep in our parking lot three or four times. I don't know. I think Maybell liked leading him on. One day, after she ran back to the house and changed into jeans, I saw her ride off with him."

"Did you ever ask your sister about Kenny?"

"Yeah, I did. She got all huffy and told me to mind my own business. Oh yeah, I think Maybell invited Kenny to our house for dinner one night. I didn't eat at home that night. I had a date."

"Really interesting. I have one more question. Do you know one of Maybell's friends who is a big guy—six-four or six-five? My source described him as dark complected with a mullet. Does that ring a bell?"

Joan nodded. "Sounds like Swindle. I guess that's a nickname. His full name is William Swindler. He's Maybell's boyfriend."

"Thank you so much, Joan. If I need any more information, I'll get a hold of Fern, I mean Mrs. Miller."

Joan's brow creased. "Maybell's not in any kind of trouble, is she?"

"I don't know for sure, but it would be better if you didn't mention me or any of my questions when you get home."

When they returned to the studio, Ho came up to Joan. "Can I keep one of your drawings? I really like the one focused on the sculpture from above. If I can keep it, I'll put it over there with the pictures of my first set of animals."

Fern overheard Ho and interrupted softly, "I think it would be better if you picked Joan's picture after you checked out all the class work."

"Whoops, sorry, I guess I goofed."

"No problem." Turning to the class, Fern continued in a loud voice. "It's about time to go. Mr. Narwhal would like to see what you've drawn, and he said he might even post his favorite in his studio."

Except for two of them, the students brought their drawings for Ho to inspect. No one was surprised when he picked Joan Wilcox's drawing.

The students all shook Ho's hand as they trooped out to the bus.

Chapter Thirty-Six

Karen Daniels, March 1, 1981

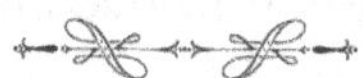

After dinner, Karen drove to Garland's house to share what she'd discovered. From the expression on her face, Garland could tell she was excited as soon as she arrived.

Karen jumped right in after Kenny and Garland were settled on the couch. "I made two breakthroughs today. First, I found the guy who sold the car. The guy, Mac, of Mac Used Cars, had an invoice showing he sold the car to someone named Kenneth Sturgis. When I asked him to describe Kenneth Sturgis, he didn't describe the Kenny we know. I then brought Kenny in, and Mac confirmed he wasn't the buyer."

"So, they, whoever they are, were trying to set Kenny up," Garland said, shaking his head. "Why didn't the police follow up on the car? This would have been good evidence."

"Bill pulled me off the case and shut down the investigation before we could get any kind of detail. When Kenny's alibi fell through, they had the fingerprints, so they thought it was open and shut."

"It's what I figured. What's number two?"

"I interviewed Joan Wilcox, Maybell's younger sister. Remember Maybell said she barely knew Kenny? Joan flat out contradicted Maybell's claim. Joan said she'd seen Kenny's Jeep at their house several times, and one time she saw Maybell get in the Jeep and drive off with Kenny."

"That's great, though we might have trouble getting her to testify against her sister."

"I hadn't thought about that. We'll have to figure something out."

Kenny clearly couldn't help himself. "See? It's like I told you. I was set up."

Garland said, "Yes son, what Karen found today sure points in that direction. The frame-up is starting to fracture. Now we need to find more evidence we can use in court. The bit with the used car dealer is very good. We can get him on the stand, and it will be great evidence. Unfortunately, the fingerprints are great evidence too. We need more."

"I have something else," Karen said. "When I talked to Joan, I asked her if any of Maybell's friends fit the description the used car dealer gave us. Mac said the guy who bought the car was big, six-four or six-five, and had a mullet. Joan said it sounded like a guy named William Swindler. He goes by the nickname Swindle. Joan called him Maybell's boyfriend."

Kenny spoke up. "I met him at the meeting. I remember the name Swindle! It's a weird name. I met a bunch of people. I don't remember any of the other names but Swindle stood out."

"Do you remember anything more about Swindle?" Karen asked.

Kenny responded after a minute. "Like you said, he's big. Taller than me, and I'm pretty tall. And… oh yeah, Swindle and the other guys his age, there were two others, they all chewed tobacco. I remember them spitting into little dixie cups all the time and I thought it was gross."

"Another thing falls into place," Garland said. "The chewing tobacco residue on the rifle stock got you out of jail. We need to find out all we can about this guy Swindle as fast as possible."

"You said there were two other young guys at the meeting," Karen said. "Do you remember anything about them?"

Kenny paused again. Finally, he filled the silence. "It's real hazy. Like I said, I met lots of new people at the meeting. I'd say neither of the other guys were as big as Swindle. One of them was pretty close. The other guy was short, sort of stocky. The taller one had one of those double names like Bobby Jo or Billy Bob. Neither of them is right. Something double, though. I don't remember anything much about the other guy. I'm not sure I could pick him out of a lineup."

"It's okay, Kenny," Karen added. "If the other two hang with this Swindle, I bet I can find out who they are."

Garland jumped up at this point and started walking back and forth in front of Kenny like he had him in the witness chair. "The meeting you went to might be the key to unraveling all this. You said they called it the Charleston Group; is that right?"

"Yeah, you're right."

"Tell me more. Where was the meeting? What did they discuss?"

"It was at the house of a guy named Lewis. After everybody did some kind of salute, Mr. Lewis gave a speech about the evils of racial mixing and affirmative action. He's a real good speaker. He had the crowd of maybe twenty people in the palm of his hand. Then his wife, at least I think it was his wife, did a rundown of who to vote for in the election. To tell you the truth, I sort of tuned her out. She wasn't as good a speaker as her husband. After those two talks, we sort of broke up, and I got introduced to a lot of people. I didn't catch many names."

"Did they talk about Walter Cunningham?"

"Probably," Kenny said. "The lady speaker talked about a lot of people running for election. Like I said, I tuned her out. I don't remember what she said about Cunningham. Sorry."

"It's okay," Garland said. "We've made great progress today. And I think we know where we should be headed. Karen, you're going to see what you can learn about this guy, William Swindler, and I'm going to see if I can learn anything about Mr. Lewis. With his strong political views, I bet I can find something about him in the newspaper files."

The next morning, Karen rose early and drove outside a small town close to Sheffield to the address she'd found for William Swindler. She parked behind a copse of trees about twenty yards from the driveway of the Swindler house. She stepped out of the car and walked up for a closer look. Through her binoculars, she spotted the license plates of two of the three vehicles parked in front of the one-story house. Two of the vehicles were pickups, and the other one was a station wagon.

She thought the house had probably started off as a double-wide trailer, but there was lots of evidence of additions. The rooflines didn't quite match, and the siding wasn't uniform. Smoke came out of the chimney so Karen figured people were up.

Twenty minutes after she arrived, an older man came out of the house and drove away in one of the pickups. This gave Karen a chance to copy down the license plate of the station wagon. Ten minutes after the older guy left, a woman about the same age drove off in the other pickup. *I must be in the wrong place*, Karen thought. *Neither of these two fit the description of the guy I'm after.*

As she'd turned to go back to her car, a motorcycle started up somewhere near the house. Quickly she focused on the bike as it came around from the rear of the house. She memorized the license plate and noted the rider was huge. Then she ran the rest of the way back to her car. She made it to the car before the motorcycle came roaring by. She did a quick U-turn and followed him. She thought the cycle was a Harley, and she had no trouble following without being too close.

About ten minutes after she started following, the motorcycle turned into a building called Kelly's Machine Shop, a one-story building with a couple of big garage doors on one side and a little office on the front. There were two cars and another motorcycle in the parking lot. Karen slowed and saw the rider get off the Harley and remove his helmet. It was Swindler, no question about it—mullet and all.

It didn't make any sense to stake out Kelly's Machine Shop, so Karen went to find a place to have something to eat. About a mile down the road, she saw a diner and pulled into its parking lot.

The diner was empty. She'd thought it might do a big breakfast business. After sitting at a booth for two near the front door, she scanned the place. Only four of the ten booths were occupied, and no one was at the counter.

The waitress, a pretty twenty-something, put down a glass of water and handed Karen a menu. "I'm Eunice," she said. "Want any coffee?"

"Yes please. With cream."

"Coming right up."

When Eunice came back with the coffee, Karen asked, "Is it usually this dead in the morning?"

"Yeah. This is nothing unusual. We do a great business at lunch and pretty good at dinner. Breakfast is almost always slow. I asked the owner why he bothers to stay open before eleven. He told me he thought breakfast would pick up eventually."

"An eternal optimist."

"I guess so. What can I get for you?"

Karen ordered the waffle with whipped cream and strawberries.

The waitress, Eunice, went behind the counter, handed the cook Karen's order, and came out and leaned on the counter across from Karen. She seemed incredibly bored.

"Worked here long?"

"Two years. It helps pay for community college. I go at night. I wasn't very serious in high school, but I'm doing real good in my college classes."

"Are you planning on transferring to a four-year school?"

"Yes, they have a program with the university. If I keep up my grades and take the right classes, I'm guaranteed admission. The only problem is figuring out how to pay for it. I don't want to have to borrow money, but I might have to."

"It doesn't seem like you'll get rich from tips from the breakfast crowd."

"You're right. I do all right at lunch though. There are some regulars, guys who work around here. They come in almost every day. I'll be honest. I flirt with them, and they tip quite a bit."

"Any of them work at Kelly's Machine Shop?"

"Yeah, and lots of other places. Why do you ask?"

"I'm interested in talking to one of the Kelly guys, William Swindler. Do you know him?"

"I'm pretty sure he's one of the chrome guys. What do you want to talk to him about?"

"Chrome guys—I don't understand."

"I guess chrome guys is our slang. A bunch of guys who own Harleys all tricked out with lots of chrome order takeout during the week. They roar up on their bikes at a little after twelve and one of them comes in to pick up their order. I think they've been doing the same orders for at least a couple of years. It was already going on when I started working here."

"So, if I wanted to talk to this Swindle guy, it wouldn't work. He's on his lunch time motorcycle ride every day."

"What do you want to talk to him about?"

"It's private. I'd rather not say."

A bell rang in the kitchen, and Eunice perked up. "There's your waffle."

When she returned to the table with Karen's breakfast, Eunice said, "You know, if I wanted to talk to Swindle, I'd try the Road Station at night. I go past it almost every night I have a class. I see a bunch of Harleys parked out front almost every time. It's a honkytonk bar two miles east of town. Big parking lot out front. You can't miss it."

Eunice heard another bell from the kitchen and ran off to deliver the order to one of the other booths. Karen dug into her waffle, disappointed the strawberries had been frozen. After she thought about it, she figured it's what she should expect in March in Missouri. As she ate, she started to formulate a plan for the evening.

Chapter Thirty-Seven

Karen Daniels, March 1, 1981

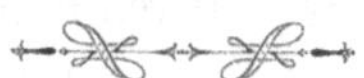

*I*n the evening, Ho drove to the Road Station with Karen. She didn't want there to be any chance her car would be recognized. She didn't think Swindle had paid any attention to her car but being safe seemed sensible. Only one motorcycle was in the parking lot when they rolled in.

"I guess we just have to hope that motorcycle belongs to Swindle," Ho said.

"No, we're early, and this is better. I bet we can identify the owner of the cycle by his clothes. If we grab a booth or table beside him, when his friends get here, we might be able to hear what they're saying."

"If the friends get here."

"Don't be such a pessimist."

The Road Station turned out to be a typical small-town hangout—dim lighting, sawdust on the floor, and the smell of stale beer in the air. There was an area for hosting live music, probably on weekends, and a small dance floor. The only music came from a jukebox in one corner. A couple of servers in tight jeans and Road Station t-shirts were hanging out by the bar. There were six patrons—two couples sitting at small tables, a guy at the bar, and an obvious motorcycle rider sitting alone in a big corner booth. Ho and Karen, who'd put her hair in a ponytail, sat in the booth next to the motorcycle guy. When one of the servers came up, they ordered a small pitcher of beer.

After they'd been there fifteen minutes, a second guy in black leather pants and a black leather jacket entered the bar with a helmet under his arm. He came over and sat in the booth with the other motorcycle guy. Karen shook her head and mouthed, "Not him."

Ho and Karen continued their discussion about Ho's plans for his next show. They had decided earlier on their topic of conversation, so they'd look more natural. Two more similarly attired men joined the motorcycle group before Swindle came in. When she spotted Swindle, Karen smiled and gave Ho a wink.

A large girl accompanied Swindle. One of the guys jumped up and gave her a hug. "How you doing, Maybell?" he asked.

Karen smiled at Ho again.

"Fine, Billy Ray, and I'm thirsty," Maybell responded as she slid into the booth beside Swindle.

The waitress came up to the booth. "Here, let me put those helmets somewhere. You hardly have space for your drinks."

After she made a couple of trips with the helmets, which she placed on an empty table, the waitress took the newcomers' drink orders and dinner orders for the group. Apparently, they weren't expecting anyone else.

Ho and Karen decided to order food too, so it would be easier to linger. They didn't want to have to order another pitcher of beer.

The conversation Karen could overhear didn't turn out to be very interesting. They talked a lot about their bikes and a concert they were planning on attending the upcoming weekend. There were also gripes about bosses and talk about how one of their friends had recently broken up with his girlfriend. It was a messy breakup. The two had been living together for a couple of years, and they had furniture and stuff they'd jointly purchased.

As Karen was getting bored listening to the chatter in the next booth, the guy at the bar went over to the jukebox and selected a few songs. The music made Karen's task considerably more difficult. She could no longer hear every word, especially when the person on the far side of the booth spoke.

Finally, the songs came to an end. As the last song finished, she heard, "—notice for a package from the post office. I'm going to pick it up tomorrow on my morning break. I'm sure it'll be the new rifle."

Karen strained to hear more. She couldn't tell which person was speaking, which frustrated her. Someone in the group asked if he'd have a chance to shoot his new rifle soon.

The guy responded, "I'm going to the shooting range Saturday morning before leaving for the concert."

Karen's eyes got big when she heard Maybell say, "Duncan, I'm sorry you had to lose your old sniper rifle."

"It's okay, this new one will be better. Thanks for paying for it."

While Karen wanted to turn around so she could identify Duncan, she didn't dare. The conversation at the other table changed topics, so Karen relaxed a little and concentrated on finishing her hamburger.

After the waitress cleared the dinner plates from the motorcycle guys' table, Karen smelled a familiar odor—chewing tobacco. The talk at the table turned to bikes, and Karen figured she'd learned about all she could expect. After another ten minutes, Karen and Ho decided to leave so they signaled the waitress for their tab.

Before Ho finished paying, one of the motorcycle guys stood up, retrieved his helmet, and left the bar. Karen overheard the group saying goodbye to him. They called him Jim, not Duncan, so she still didn't know which one was Duncan.

Karen decided to go to the ladies' room before leaving. On her way back, she walked slowly and took a good look at everyone in the booth. She knew Swindle, the one Maybell called Billy Ray, and Jim, who just left, so Duncan had to be one of the other two. One, a blonde, was tall and skinny, and the other one was darker, shorter, and a little plump.

When they left, Ho and Karen decided to hide around the corner of the bar to see if they could learn anything when the group left. All the Harleys were in view from their hiding place. They hoped they wouldn't have to wait long because of the cold. Ten minutes later, the entire group of bikers came out. Karen and Ho overheard some goodbyes, and they were able to identify Duncan. It didn't help much because they all had on helmets. Still, Karen was pretty sure Duncan was the shorter, stockier one. Given her investigation inside, Karen had a good guess about what he looked like.

As the motorcycles roared off, Karen watched closely to see which way Duncan turned from the parking lot. Fortunately, Duncan was the only one turning right. "Let's try to follow him," Karen yelled as she started running toward the car. Ho jumped in the driver's seat and turned the way Duncan headed. At Karen's urging, Ho drove fast trying to catch up with the motorcycle, but it must have turned off, because they never saw it again.

"I think we lost him," Ho said.

"I'm afraid you're right. But we learned something. He must live near here. It's useful information. It will give me a better chance to stake out the correct post office tomorrow. I couldn't get his license plate tonight. I bet I can get it when he comes to pick up his package."

"You'd better tell me what you're talking about. Remember, I was too far away to hear the things you heard."

"Sorry," Karen responded. On their ride home, she told Ho all she'd learned when eavesdropping.

At nine-thirty the next morning, Karen parked at the post office she thought Duncan would use. She felt conspicuous sitting in her car checking out the people coming and going from the post office. But she didn't have to stare at the people or do anything objectionable, so she pretended to read a newspaper. She only wanted to get the license plate of Duncan's motorcycle. She didn't need anything else.

After thirty very boring minutes, she changed the position of her car by driving to the convenience store across the street. She could still see the post office parking lot even from inside the store. She ducked into the store and ordered a coffee. When she came out and got back into her car, a police car had pulled into the post office lot. No motorcycles were in sight.

Luckily, no one had taken her old parking spot, so she parked there again. Immediately after parking, she perked up when the policeman came out and loaded a long package into the back seat of his cruiser. Karen figured the package was large enough and about the right shape to hold a rifle. When the policeman turned to get in the driver's door, Karen had a good view, and, while she couldn't swear to it, she thought the policeman was Duncan—the size, shape, and coloring were right.

She had no reason to follow the police car. She could easily get a list of the members of the Sheffield police department. If nothing else, she could call Sylvia and ask for a favor. She headed to Springfield with one more piece of the puzzle.

When Karen arrived at Ho's studio, she found Ho and Kenny sitting in the office in a deep discussion.

"Oh, good Karen, you're the person who can help." Ho said, getting up from his chair and greeting Karen with a hug and a kiss.

"What can I help with?" She smiled at Ho when he brought her a chair.

Kenny spoke up. "Wait. Did you find anything in Sheffield?"

"As a matter of fact, I did," she said, sitting. "Duncan is a policeman. I'll be able to find his full name and address easily."

"Wow, a cop," Kenny said, shaking his head.

"It's not too surprising. Some cops are bent. The pay isn't great, so some of the people who sign up aren't from the top of the pile. Also, some people are attracted to police work so they can boss people around. They aren't the best cops. In any event, we'll be able to find out quite a bit about him. Oh sorry, I interrupted. What were you talking about?"

Ho returned to his chair after scooting it closer to Karen. "Kenny wondered what he's going to do if he's cleared."

"I'm starting to think it's when, not if," Karen said.

"I guess the question's the same. When I get cleared of the murder charge, I still need to have something to do with myself. My dad's not going to take me back. He made it clear as can be. He told me I dragged the family name through the mud, and he never wanted to see me again."

Karen stood, went to Kenny, and put an arm around him. "Even if we get you cleared, and I think we will, you'd think he'd forgive you. Maybe not. You said he's a hard man, not used to forgiving people."

"You have him pegged right."

"Also," Ho added, "when you were captured and when you were convicted, it made big news, headline news. As usual, the story about the mistrial turned out to be much smaller. I'm surprised your mother saw it. If we can convince the district attorney to drop the charges, it will result in an even smaller story. The thing that will stick in people's mind, the thing your father will probably remember, will be the first headlines."

Karen returned to her seat. "Ho's right Kenny. It's terrible. Unfortunately, it's the way things work. First impressions are important, and big headlines make big impressions. I think it's pretty unlikely you'll be able to go back to work for your father."

"What about your mother and her family?" Ho asked. "You told me you had a great meeting with them when you went to their house for dinner. They seemed to have welcomed you."

"Yes, I really liked it, but I can't just hang out at their house. Simon, he's my mom's husband, is a doctor so he's real busy, and my mom has Courtney. She just turned three. It's great to have them, but I'm going to need a job."

Ho gave Karen a look, and she nodded. "I have a proposition for you, Kenny. If you are cleared and you want to continue here, I'll take you on."

Kenny reacted. "I barely know what I'm doing around here."

"You've done a good job on the things I've asked you to do, and I think you're capable of learning. There's one other thing. If you start working with me, you'll have to get your GED before the first year is out, or you'll be let go."

"That's pretty harsh, Ho," Karen said.

"No, I don't think so. It's one of the conditions Horace Cunningham put on me when I started work in his brass bed factory. It turned out to be good for me, and I think it'll be good for Kenny."

"You were a high school dropout?" Kenny asked.

"One of the stupidest things I ever did. I did poorly in school as a teenager; I wasn't mature enough. But still, I shouldn't have dropped out. I should have stayed with it. I would have had so many more options."

"You're a big-shot sculptor. You make loads of money, I bet," Kenny countered.

"I'm the luckiest guy in the world. You're right though, not everyone who is successful is a high school graduate, though I guess I am. I have the GED Cunningham made me get. Anyway, being a high school graduate opens doors. While you didn't need to graduate high school to work for your dad, that's a special case. On average, high school dropouts are on the bottom of the economic ladder."

Karen nodded. "Ho's right, Kenny. He's doing you a favor by forcing you to get a GED. As he said, it will open doors for you. You're young, and there's no telling how many doors you'll be knocking on before your life's over. I can tell you're smart. It shouldn't be difficult for you to pass the GED."

"I'll give you time off if you need it to study."

Kenny took a deep breath. "Okay, I'll think about it. I still have this murder rap hanging over me. I've got to beat it before we talk about me working here on a permanent basis."

Karen stood up and headed toward the door. "You're right, and I'd better get to work clearing you of this thing."

When she made it to her office, Karen called her friend Sylvia. After they caught up with each other, she asked if Sylvia could search the state's files for the members of the Sheffield police force. She explained she only had a first name, Duncan, and she needed the full name and address.

"It should be easy," Sylvia said. "I'll call you back in a few minutes. Actually, you'd better give me your phone number. I don't have your office phone. While I'm sure you sent potential clients an announcement about your new business, you skipped me."

"I didn't figure you'd need my services," Karen said and then gave the phone number.

"I'll get right back to you."

Ten minutes later, Sylvia called. "I found him: Duncan Lewis. He's been on the force for four years and he lives at the Stratford Arms Apartment, Unit Three in Sheffield."

"Great Sylvia, it's exactly what I needed. I owe you one."

"No problem. Always willing to help a friend."

Later in the afternoon, Karen went to a gun shop to buy a pistol. She'd had to hand in the one the state issued her. She didn't know exactly what she wanted, so she searched slowly. Finally, she settled on a Glock very similar to the one she'd carried before. She bought several boxes of ammunition and sound-suppressing ear protection so she'd be able to spend quite a bit of time at the shooting range the next morning. She figured Duncan would get there early to try out his new rifle. She didn't know how early, so she planned to be there when the place opened. Having a new pistol to try out would make her appearance seem perfectly natural.

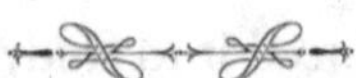

Saturday morning, Karen brought her new pistol to the shooting range in Sheffield. She arrived right as the guy unlocked the front door. She chatted up the guy at the counter. His name was Matt and he liked to talk. She had him admire her new gun.

After their discussion, Matt assigned her a lane in the pistol range. She took her time, even dawdled a bit before shooting. She enjoyed shooting and was good at it. It had always been easy for her to qualify when she had to. As she finished her first target, she heard a motorcycle pull up out front.

Karen waited until she figured the motorcycle person had made it to the desk and then headed for the restroom. As she expected, Duncan was at the front desk showing his new rifle to Matt.

"Impressive," Karen said as she walked by. The two men glanced up and watched her go into the restroom.

When Karen came out, she saw Duncan headed to the rifle range.

"Matt, I bet you don't have a long enough range for a guy with a rifle like that," she commented. "It's like some kind of sniper rifle."

"Actually no, we don't have anything long enough to really challenge him. We only have small targets. I expect he'll be obliterating the center of them when he gets the thing sighted in. It's brand new."

"Sounds like you know him. This must not be his first sniper rifle."

"No, it's not. He used to have an older one, some kind of German rifle, I think. I don't know what happened to it. Anyway, he sure is proud of this new one."

Karen went back to the pistol range and shot up another target.

Just when she'd settled at the counter, Duncan Lewis came in with his new rifle. Karen turned and walked past him out to her car. She didn't have anything else to learn.

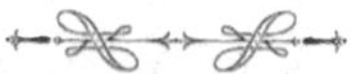

Back at the counter, Duncan asked Matt, "Who's the chick?"

"Don't know. She sure can shoot though. She has a brand-new Glock, and she was real good with it right from the get go."

"She looks familiar. I can't place where I saw her."

"Lucky you. I'd like to be familiar with a chick like her."

"She paid with a card, didn't she? Can you find her name? I might want to know who she is," Duncan said with a wink.

As he walked away from the desk with Karen's name, it came to Duncan. Though she had fixed her hair different, he thought for sure Karen Daniels was the same chick he saw checking him out at the Road Station a couple of nights ago. He didn't like it.

Chapter Thirty-Eight

Duncan Lewis, March 3, 1981

As they walked toward their bikes after the concert, Duncan pulled Maybell and Swindle aside. "Something's bothering me."

They stopped walking. "What's up? You've seemed jumpy all day."

"It's probably nothing, but I think a chick is following me."

"So?" Maybell said, "I'd think you'd like a chick following you."

"No, it's not that way. I think she's a cop or something. You remember the older couple sitting next to us at the Road Station a couple of nights ago?"

"You go on," Swindle yelled to the rest of their group who'd stopped, wondering why the three of them had fallen behind. "What about the couple? They seemed ordinary enough."

"It may be nothing. I thought the woman was staring at me toward the end. You remember when she went back to her table after she visited the john? I didn't think much of it at the time. Then I saw her, at least I'm pretty sure it was her, at the shooting range this morning."

"Did she act strange this morning?"

"No, it was only a brief encounter, but it bothered me. I don't believe in coincidences. I think she might be a cop. I got her name from Matt at the range. He had it from her credit card receipt. I'm going to see what I find."

"I bet it's nothing," Maybell said.

"Still, you're probably right to check into it," Swindle added. "Let's hustle. I think we can catch up to the rest of the crew."

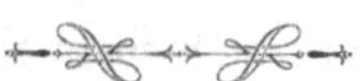

Monday morning, Duncan got to the station early to see what he could find about Karen Daniels. As he'd expected, there were several Karen Daniels with driver's licenses in Missouri. He checked the listings of police officers and found a Karen Daniels in the state police roster. He called a state trooper friend of his, Willard, and asked him if he could track down any information.

Duncan had to go out on patrol before Willard returned his call. He didn't like the way things were happening. The whole thing was starting to fall apart, and it made him nervous. The guy they'd set up, Kenny Sturgis, had the first trial thrown out, and Bill Hooper had lost his job. Everyone had told him to calm down but he couldn't. His rifle had been the murder weapon, and even though they had filed off the registration numbers, it was an unusual gun. Duncan was afraid Matt might have told the Daniels chick about his old rifle. Finding someone named Karen Daniels working for the state police made him even more nervous.

When he returned to the station, there was a note on his desk to call Willard. Duncan tried Willard right away. All he could do was leave a message.

"What's bothering you Dunc?" Jimmy asked. "You seem jumpy."

Jimmy, the station busybody, had the desk right next to Duncan's. Duncan didn't want Jimmy poking his nose into what was going on.

"Nothing. I'm trying to reach a friend of mine. It's nothing important."

Late in the afternoon, Duncan finally connected with Willard. Luckily Jimmy had stepped away from his desk, so he could speak freely. He didn't like what he heard. Willard told him Karen Daniels didn't work for the state police anymore. The person he contacted told him she quit because she'd somehow been behind Bill Hooper's firing.

Duncan was shaking when he finished the phone call. He had to get himself under control. When he saw Jimmy coming back, he stood up and headed for the restroom. As he sat in the stall, he tried to convince himself he'd been jumping to conclusions without evidence. Karen Daniels was a common name. He learned that much from the driver's license information. He didn't have any idea if the woman he saw was the Karen Daniels who used to work for the state police. That thought didn't calm him down. He had a terrible feeling everything would fall apart.

When he finished work, he tried to call Swindle. No one answered. Next, he tried Maybell, and he had to leave a message. He paced around his apartment, getting more and more frantic. He extracted a TV dinner from the freezer and heated it up. Just as he finished dinner, his phone rang.

"It's Maybell. What did you want Dunc?"

"I found the woman who I thought might be following me, and I don't like what I learned. I'm getting nervous."

"Calm down and tell me about it."

"So, the name Matt had from the credit card imprint was Karen Daniels. There are quite a few Karen Daniels in Missouri, including one who works for the state police, or at least used to. That Karen Daniels had something to do with Bill Hooper getting fired. If it was her following me, she's involved in the Cunningham case. I don't like it at all."

"I can tell, and I guess I understand." Maybell paused, then she started in again. "Duncan, you don't even know what the Karen Daniels who worked with the state police looks like. Also, you don't know if she's the woman you saw who was following you. We gotta get more information before we jump to any conclusions."

"How do we get more information? My sources are tapped out."

"Hold on for a few minutes. I'll call Bill Hooper. He'll know the Karen Daniels who worked for the state police."

"Call me when you find out something."

"Will do."

While Duncan tried to calm down, he couldn't. Nothing on TV interested him. He paced around his apartment. Finally, Maybell called him back.

"Duncan, Bill has some pictures of his unit with the state police, and Karen Daniels is in a couple of them. It's okay with him if we go to his place in Springfield to check out the pictures. Swindle and I will be over in fifteen minutes. We can take the bikes."

"You know where Bill lives?"

"Yeah, I've been there a couple of times."

"Good, I'll be ready."

An hour later, the two motorcycles pulled up in front of Bill Hooper's house. The front door opened before they had a chance to knock.

"I heard you coming. We don't get many Harleys in this neighborhood. Come on in."

"We're sorry to bother you, Bill," Maybell said. "Like I told you, Duncan would like to see your pictures of the people you worked with."

"Sure, I've got a couple of them laid out on the dining room table. Here, put your helmets on one of these chairs and follow me."

Duncan scanned the two pictures and pointed. "It's her. That's the one who I think has been following me."

"Karen Daniels," Bill said.

"What can you tell us about her?" Swindle asked.

Bill finished his discussion about Karen Daniels by saying she recently married a sculptor with a funny name.

"Horace Narwhal?" Maybell asked.

"Yeah, you're right."

"How do you know the name, Maybell?" Duncan asked.

"My bratty sister couldn't stop talking about the sculptor her art class visited. This guy Narwhal liked a drawing my sister did and put it up in his studio."

"Did your sister meet the sculptor's wife?" Bill asked.

"I don't know. I sort of zoned out when she got into the details. I think we should go home and have a talk with Joan. She might have been the one who opened her big mouth."

"I told you I had reasons to be worried," Duncan said.

"Yeah, I guess you were right to be nervous," Maybell said.

"I think it's a good idea to talk to your sister, Maybell," Bill said. "Keep me in the loop if you find anything important."

Maybell, Duncan, and Swindle arrived at the Wilcox house at eleven o'clock. Joan had already gone to bed. Maybell went down the hall and pounded on her bedroom door. "Come out Joan, I need to talk to you."

Maybell didn't hear any noise from Joan's bedroom, so she pounded on the door again. Finally, she heard her sister moving, and the bedroom door cracked open.

"What do you want? What time is it?"

"We need to talk."

"Give me a minute," Joan said. "I need to put on some clothes."

When Joan appeared in the living room, Maybell stood up and the two men stayed on the couch. Maybell closed in on Joan and shouted, "Did you talk about us to the sculptor, Horace somebody?"

"No, what are you talking about?"

"How about his wife? Did you talk to her?"

Joan gasped, and Maybell stepped closer. "You did talk to her, didn't you? What did you tell her?"

Joan stepped back, not knowing what to say. She stammered, "I… I told her I'd seen Kenny Sturgis's Jeep here a couple of times, and you went off with him once. What of it? I told the truth."

Maybell slugged Joan on the side of the face, and Joan stumbled back, whimpering.

Maybell shouted, "Don't you ever talk about my business with anyone!"

Joan cried out and held her face where she'd been hit.

Just as Maybell balled up her fist to hit Joan again, her father came into the living room. "What's going on in here?"

Joan ran back into her bedroom and slammed the door. She tried to stop crying so she could hear what they were saying in the living room. What she heard frightened her to death. Maybell shouted at her father, telling him Joan had blabbed to a private detective and now she, Duncan, and Swindle maybe were going to be in big trouble. Joan heard her father trying to calm Maybell down. Eventually he did. When Maybell started explaining everything she knew to her father in a calmer voice, Joan couldn't quite hear it all, but she heard enough to know she had to immediately leave the house. She'd left through her window plenty of times, so it wouldn't be difficult. She grabbed a few things, put them in a gym bag, and climbed out the window.

Joan started to develop a plan as she headed for the road. She'd go to Mrs. Miller's house. She lived back toward town a couple of miles. Her parents and Maybell didn't know Mrs. Miller. Nobody ever went to those parent-teacher conferences. Based on what she'd overheard, several of her parents' friends, as well as Maybell, Duncan, and Swindle, were trying to put something over on the police. She thought maybe they were mixed up in the killing Kenny Sturgis had been charged with. While she didn't know the details, she knew they were very worried about being discovered. The more she thought about it, the more she understood innocent people aren't worried about being discovered. It was all confusing to her. As she walked through the night, the one thing she knew was the importance of running from the house and hiding from them.

It was after midnight when Joan arrived at Mrs. Miller's house. She knocked, and eventually the porch light came on. Mrs. Miller's husband cracked open the door and asked what she wanted.

"I've run away from home. I need a place to stay."

Mrs. Miller appeared behind her husband. She asked, "What is it dear?"

"I think it's one of your students, and I think someone's hit her."

Mrs. Miller shoved her husband out of the way. "Joan. What's happened dear? Come on in."

Joan gave a quick explanation of what had happened, and Mr. and Mrs.

Miller were shocked. It was obvious someone had hit her, and she would probably develop a black eye before the bruise disappeared.

When Joan finished her story, Mrs. Miller said, "Certainly, you can stay here tonight. We'll make up the couch in the living room. We'll have to figure out something more permanent later. Do you have any relatives close by you can trust?"

"No I don't. They're all in Virginia, both sides of the family."

"Don't bother her about relatives now, Fern," Mr. Miller said. "Let's get a pillow and some blankets. I bet she's tired. I think she walked here. I definitely didn't hear any car pull in."

"Yes, I walked. I don't have a car."

"Oh gosh, it must be at least two miles," Mrs. Miller said.

While the Millers made up a bed on the couch for Joan, she went into the downstairs bathroom. She shrieked when she saw herself in the mirror.

Mrs. Miller knocked on the bathroom door and asked, "What's the matter?"

Between her sobs, Joan mumbled, "I'm hideous."

"You're not hideous. It's true you have a nasty bruise, but bruises fade. You'll be beautiful again."

Joan came out of the bathroom with tears streaming down her face. "How long will it take?"

"I don't know, dear."

Fern took a close look at Joan's face. "I don't think the skin's broken, which is good. It's a deep bruise, and there's some swelling. I'll get an ice pack. It should help with the swelling. Unfortunately, I think you may develop a black eye."

After holding the ice pack to her swollen face for half an hour, Joan laid down. She found it difficult to sleep. Thoughts kept racing through her head. *My father is mixed up in whatever Maybell did. What am I going to do? Where will I stay? What did Maybell do?* Confused and incredibly worried, eventually sleep came, but she had a restless night.

Chapter Thirty-Nine
Karen Daniels, March 6, 1981

The next morning, Fern Miller let her surprise guest sleep. From what Joan had divulged last night, she decided to call Karen Daniels. The mess with Joan's big sister had something to do with Karen.

Joan roused herself as Mrs. Miller and her kids were getting ready to leave for school.

"Joan, I've called Karen Daniels, the sculptor's wife. She's coming in an hour or so. I think you ought to talk to her."

"I guess you're probably right," Joan murmured.

"I need to run to school. Fix yourself something for breakfast. I've left out some cereal boxes, and milk is in the refrigerator. I think there's still coffee in the coffee pot. I put a towel on the chair over there for you if you want to shower. And looking at your face, I think you should use the ice pack again. It's in the freezer."

"What about school?"

"I'll cover for you today. Don't worry about it."

When the doorbell rang an hour and a half later, Joan jumped. She feared her family had found her. She was relieved when she peeked out the front window and saw Karen Daniels waiting by the door.

Joan unlocked the door, opened it, and said, "Come in." She scanned the front yard and street before closing the door.

Karen eyed her, staring at the nasty bruise on her cheek. "Fern, I mean, Mrs. Miller didn't have time to give me many details," she said. "So why don't you tell me what happened, and we can figure out what to do."

Joan was a little wary. Waiting for Karen, she'd decided to ask some questions before she said anything.

"Okay. Why don't we take those chairs over there?"

After they were settled, Joan said, "I'm willing to talk. First, can you tell me what this is all about? Why are you interested? Who do you work for? I feel like all of a sudden I'm in the middle of something, and I don't know what it's about."

Karen leaned back in her chair and looked like she was considering what Joan had said. "Okay, you deserve to know what's going on. I'm a private detective like I told you when we first met. I'm working for a lawyer, Garland Rice. His client is Kenny Sturgis. As you know, the police accused Kenny of killing Walter Cunningham, the guy who was running for governor."

"Didn't Kenny eventually get off?" Joan interrupted.

"Not quite. His first trial was declared a mistrial, and there is likely to be a new trial. I used to work for the state police, and I was on the scene at the shooting. In fact, I discovered the rifle the shooter used. It was in his getaway car, an ancient Oldsmobile. It looked like the car crashed, and the guy stashed his rifle in the car before he ran off. We never located him. The crime techs found Kenny's fingerprints inside the car and on the rifle."

Joan shifted in her chair, trying to keep her injured cheek out of view. "And Kenny was a good shot. At least his old girlfriend told me."

"Yes, it didn't help him. The killer made a long shot. Not everyone would have been capable of hitting a shot from that distance. When the police picked up Kenny, he said he hadn't been anywhere near the shooting. He claimed he was out with your sister Maybell for the whole day. The police called Maybell, and she said she barely knew Kenny, and she'd been grooming dogs on the day in question. Two of her dog grooming clients backed her story. In the final analysis at the trial, Kenny didn't have an alibi, and his fingerprints were all over the gun and the car—an open and shut case as far as the police were concerned."

"I can see that. So, what caused the mistrial?"

"When I found the rifle, I smelled chewing tobacco on it. Kenny told me he never chewed tobacco. He thinks it's a disgusting habit. The head crime tech also smelled the chewing tobacco, and he included it in the report he wrote. The head of the state police, Bill Hooper, left any mention of the chewing tobacco evidence out of his testimony and the report he placed in evidence. To make a long story short, I noticed the omission, and we took the original report from the crime tech to Kenny's lawyer, Garland, and he convinced the judge to declare a mistrial."

Joan stood up and paced around. Finally, she spoke. "Let me tell you what happened, and how I wound up here with this awful bruise on my face."

"Yeah, it's your turn."

"Last night after I'd gone to bed, Maybell started pounding on my door. She was there with her boyfriend Swindle, William Swindle, and another one of Harley guys, Duncan Lewis. When I went out to the living room, Maybell accosted me, demanding to know if I'd talked to you. When I said I told her I saw Kenny's Jeep in our yard a couple of times and I'd seen her ride off with him once, she hauled off and punched me right in the face. I guess I look like I've been punched."

"It's not pretty right now but it will go away. What happened after she hit you?"

"Luckily for me, my father came out right after she hit me. I guess he heard Maybell yelling at me. I ran back into my room. I wanted to get away from her."

"How'd you get to Fern's house?"

"When I made it back to my room, I listened at the door. Some of what I overheard from them makes more sense after what you told me. Anyway, I could tell my dad knew what Maybell had been doing with Kenny Sturgis. Swindle and Duncan are mixed up in it too. They seemed really worried about what I told you. Duncan found out who you were somehow. The way I see it, they're all involved in something illegal. I didn't want to have any part of it, so I put some stuff in a bag, jumped out my window and walked over here. I don't know what I'm going to do."

Joan turned away and started to sob.

Karen came over to Joan, took her in her arms, and rubbed her back. She stopped crying after a while and broke away, wiping her eyes.

Karen filled the ensuing silence. "I'm sorry you're involved in this, Joan. I never expected you to get in trouble with your family. It's all water under the bridge now. The question we have now is: what are we going to do?"

Joan and Karen sat back down and discussed the options. There were lots of issues involved: Joan's schooling, protection for Joan, a place for Joan to stay, and what Karen could do with what Joan had learned. They decided Joan could stay with Karen in Springfield for a few days, so they folded the blankets and straightened Fern's house. They left a note for Fern telling her Karen would call in the evening.

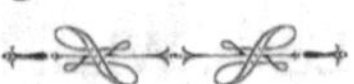

What they had learned the night before at Bill Hooper's and at the Wilcox house really upset Duncan. He was even more upset when he received a call from Maybell telling him Joan seemed to have run away. Everything had started to unravel. He didn't like thinking about it. Maybe he should head for Mexico or somewhere.

He hadn't been paying much attention as he patrolled the streets. Very little happened in Sheffield anyway. When he got to the city limits, he turned around and headed back to town. Just as he got started, he almost jumped out of his skin when he recognized a car coming the other way. It was Karen Daniel's car. He'd memorized it, a black Subaru license plate LRB 722. The car had two people in it. In his quick glance, Duncan thought he recognized the Daniels woman driving. All he could see about the person riding in the passenger seat was she was a blonde. It could have been Maybell's sister. He couldn't tell for sure.

Duncan didn't know what to do. He thought about turning around, putting on his lights and siren, and chasing the car. It wouldn't work. They were already out of the city limits. What's more, he didn't know what he'd say if he did stop them. All he could think to do was to cool it and tell Maybell and Swindle what he'd seen.

When he returned to the station, Duncan left a message with Maybell's answering machine and with Swindle's mom. In both cases, his message said for them to meet him outside the Road Station as soon after five as they could make it.

A few minutes after five, Maybell showed up in her grooming van followed by Swindle on his Harley. Duncan was still in uniform in his patrol car. Maybell and Swindle walked over to Duncan, who climbed out to meet them.

"You'll never believe who I saw driving out of town late this morning," Duncan said.

"Come on Duncan. Don't make us guess," Maybell pleaded. "I hate it when people do that."

"Okay, I'm pretty sure I saw Karen Daniels leaving town, at least it was her car, and I'd bet a million bucks your sister was in the car with her."

"Oh my God," Maybell blurted.

"Are you sure?" Swindle asked.

"I'm sure about the car. I had the license plate memorized from the other night. I'm less sure about Joan. The one in the passenger seat was a blonde. That much I know. If Joan hasn't shown up anywhere else, I figure it was her."

"As far as I know, Joan hasn't shown up. When she didn't come to breakfast this morning, we checked her room and found her window open. Apparently, she ran away right after I hit her. You know, it felt good to clobber her.

She's such a conceited bitch. Anyway, she didn't show up at school; my mom checked. And she hasn't come home, at least not yet. I bet you did see her in Daniels's car."

"What the hell are we going to do?" Swindle asked.

"We'd better find out where Daniels lives. You can do it, can't you Dunc?" Maybell asked.

"I can find out the address on her driver's license. People move around a lot. Let's hope she's still at the same address. I remember the license isn't very old, so the address might be good."

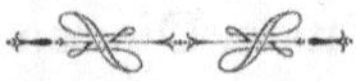

Earlier that afternoon, Karen and Joan met Garland at his office. They had stopped at a mall for lunch and bought Joan a new outfit and some personal items since she hadn't been able to bring much with her when she rushed out of the house the night before. What she saw in the mirror in the dressing room horrified her. There was nothing she could do about it, so she tried to ignore it.

In Garland's office, Joan replayed her encounter with her sister the previous evening. What she'd overheard after she returned to her bedroom particularly interested him.

"I was still shaking, and my cheek hurt so bad, and I guess I was crying, so I didn't hear anything too clearly, especially after they stopped shouting. Mostly I have impressions. They were scared something might be unraveling. That's one word I heard, 'unravel,' and my father was involved somehow. I knew Maybell had been doing something funny with Kenny. Like I told Karen, and Kenny too I think, Maybell has had a boyfriend for a long time. It wasn't only Maybell involved from the way they were talking. All of them, even my father, were talking like they were guilty of something, and people were starting to find out about it. That's all I can figure. Mostly I heard random words."

Garland looked up from the notes he was taking. "You're very savvy, Joan; your impression is right on the mark. Kenny has always thought he'd been the victim of a big conspiracy, and we're starting to agree with him. Your sister played him. She got his fingerprints on the rifle used in the shooting and on the getaway car too. You don't remember your sister having an old car, a big Oldsmobile, do you?"

Joan thought for a moment, then said, "Yes, I guess I do. It wasn't around long, maybe a week or so. I thought it didn't fit. It was sort of a wreck, not the kind of thing Maybell or her friends would like. Her van is new and she always keeps it shiny. Swindle and his friends have Harleys all covered with chrome, and they are always polishing the stupid things."

"Would you recognize the car if you saw a picture of it?" Garland asked.

"Maybe. I don't know. Like I said, it wasn't in the yard for very long."

"You never rode in it or drove it or anything?" Karen asked.

"No, Maybell kept it over by her van. I guess I never saw anyone drive it. Oh wait, I'm wrong. I saw Kenny Sturgis drive it. He only went to the end of the driveway and turned around. I thought it was weird at the time. When Kenny came back in his Jeep, I had to ask him for a ride to school."

Chapter Forty

Maybell Wilcox, March 7, 1981

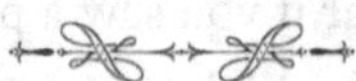

Maybell woke up early the next morning and drove to Springfield, arriving before eight. She drove her parents' car. She couldn't take her van—that would be way too conspicuous. Though he'd offered, she didn't want to go with Swindle on his motorcycle. Again, too conspicuous. She didn't know what she'd do if she spotted Karen Daniels or Joan. The others had urged her to make this only a reconnaissance mission. She guessed they were right. After they had an idea of the lay of the land, they'd figure out what to do.

The address Duncan gave her led to a townhouse. She saw the car he thought was Daniels' out front, so she hadn't moved after all. Maybell found a place to park around a corner and got out of her car. She walked back to a spot with a view of the townhouse and found a hedge to hide behind. There weren't many people around this early, so she thought it was a reasonable place to stay, at least for a while.

Twenty minutes later, a car left a townhouse three doors down from Daniels' place. Maybell went back, climbed into her car, and moved into the space the car had left. She slumped down in her seat and continued her surveillance. Luckily for her, no one came out to get in the cars on either side of her.

Maybell almost jumped when the front door to the Daniels' townhouse opened. She saw Karen Daniels and a little girl carrying a backpack. They entered Daniels' car, backed out, and drove off. Maybell decided not to follow. She wanted to see if anyone else came out of the townhouse. She had a sneaking suspicion Joan might be in there.

Ten minutes later, she discovered she was right. A guy, Daniels' husband, Maybell figured, and Joan came out of the townhouse and drove away. It pleased Maybell to see Joan had a big bandage on one cheek. *Good. I thought I hit her pretty hard.* After the car backed out, Maybell started her car and followed them. She let a couple of cars get in between them, so she didn't think they would know they were being followed.

Unfortunately for her, after a few minutes, the car she was following turned out to be the last one through a green light. Maybell was trapped behind a car because it stopped at the yellow light. When the light finally turned green again, she zoomed past the two cars at her first chance. Luckily the car with Joan and the guy had stopped at the next light. Maybell didn't want to be right behind them, so she pulled over to the curb to let a car pass her.

Joan and the guy turned right at the next cross street, and Maybell slowed before she followed them. Two blocks after the turn, she saw his car stop in front of a building. She slowed as Joan and the guy climbed out of the car and went into the building. *This must be the sculptor guy's studio or workshop or whatever*, Maybell thought.

She shuddered as she recognized the other car parked in front of the building—Kenny Sturgis's Jeep. Maybell noted the address as she slowly drove past the building. She didn't want to linger. Joan might recognize their parents' car. She parked a couple of blocks past the building, got out, and walked back toward it. She didn't want to get too close. But she had to get a better sense of the place before she called Swindle to report on what she'd found.

When she got closer, she could see the building had a funny sign. It was metal piping bent in the shape of a bizarre looking fish. It looked like a unicorn fish. The word studio came after the fish. Maybell wondered what the hell Kenny Sturgis was doing at a sculptor's studio. She'd figured Daniels had stashed Joan there, because they didn't have anything else to do with her. Kenny baffled her. She didn't know why he'd be there.

Kenny glanced up when the studio door opened. He was surprised to see Joan Wilcox walk in with Ho.

"Hi Kenny," Joan said.

Ho laughed. "I don't think he expected to see you, Joan."

"Well, I sure didn't," Kenny retorted.

"Come sit down, and we'll tell you what's been happening," Ho said.

After Ho and Joan filled Kenny in on the recent events, he had two questions. "What are you going to do, Joan? And what do you think will happen next?"

"God Kenny, I don't know. For now, I'm going to stay with Ho, Karen, and Linda. They've been nice enough to let me stay. I'm taking it one day at a time."

Ho interrupted at this point. "Given what Joan has told us, Maybell and her friends are starting to think their plan is unraveling. They'd planned to pin everything on you. Since it didn't work, they think they're going to be in trouble. If I were them, I'd run."

"Where? And how many of them are there?" Kenny asked.

"You're the one for the two-part questions this morning, aren't you, Kenny."

"Well?"

"Okay. As for where, first I'd go to where I had relatives, someone who'd put me up for a while. I'd use my time there to make more permanent plans. Does your sister have a passport, Joan?"

"Yeah, she had to get one for our trip to Cancun last year."

"That opens up a few possibilities for them, or at least her. What was your second question?"

"How many of them are thinking about going?"

"Maybell for sure, and probably the two guys, Swindle and Duncan. We're pretty sure the sniper rifle belonged to Duncan, and Swindle bought the car, and one of them did the shooting. There are others—the people who lied to the police about Maybell grooming their dogs on the day Cunningham got shot. I forgot their names. I don't know if it's enough to make them want to flee. And there's Bill Hooper too. I don't know how much trouble he's in."

"What if they don't run?" Joan asked. "You guessed that's what you'd do. What if they don't think like you?"

"I guess then maybe they'll try to come after us. They might think we are a small enough group. Maybe they'd try to kill us. I don't know. They might think there's not much difference between one murder rap or four or five. So far, the only ones who've put this all together include Karen, Garland, and the three of us."

Joan started to shiver, and Kenny went over and put his arm around her.

Joan leaned into Kenny. "I'm scared. It's just like my sister to want to kill us. She'd see it as taking revenge on me."

Following breakfast at a fast-food place, Maybell wandered around a mall until it was time for her call to Swindle. He congratulated her on finding Joan and told her he liked the idea that she'd found Kenny Sturgis too. Swindle decided he and Duncan would go to Springfield later in the afternoon. They had to get rid of the problem. Swindle told Maybell to return to the studio and do another, more thorough recon job, and then they decided on a place to meet at three o'clock.

Maybell returned to her old parking place. She walked around and investigated all sides of the studio. She couldn't see much because the only windows were too high for her to see in. She guessed the high windows provided nice light for the studio, but they were no help for her.

She scoped out the surrounding buildings and saw one perfect for them to watch from. It was a two-story building across the street and a block away from the studio. The front of the abandoned place had a sign indicating it had once been a furniture store. If they could find a way to get on the roof, they'd have a clear shot at anyone coming out of the studio. At the back of the building, she found a fire escape she thought Swindle could grab. It was perfect.

After surveying the other structures, Maybell realized none of them were nearly as good as the flat roofed furniture-store building. Now she had a lot of time to kill. Before she left, she thought, *If I go close, maybe I can hear something inside.* She gathered her nerve and tiptoed to the side of the building. All she could hear was pounding and whirring sounds she couldn't figure out. As she was about to give up, she heard a car coming, so she ran away as fast as she could.

Karen pulled up to the studio and caught a glimpse of someone running away from it. She jumped out of her car to see who it was. She ran to the side of the building and saw a girl running to a car parked a couple of blocks away. The girl hopped in the car and drove away. All Karen really saw clearly was the car. It was an older, dark blue Ford. The car roared off and Karen decided not to follow.

It pleased Karen when she had to knock and wait for Ho to come unlock the door. She'd told him he had to take precautions. Knowing somebody had been snooping around made her sure she'd been right.

After everyone greeted Karen, she said, "I think I spooked someone snooping around the studio. She ran off when I came up and hopped into a car, an old dark blue Ford. Does anyone know who might be driving a car like that?"

"My parents have a dark blue Ford Fairlane," Joan volunteered. "It's old, maybe ten years or so."

"It's the right color but the person driving away wasn't either your mother or father. It could have been your sister. I couldn't say for sure, too far away."

Ho pulled four chairs together. "Come sit down. We need to talk."

When they were all seated, Joan spoke up. "Before, when the three of us were talking, we thought Maybell and her crew had two options. If she was snooping around, it doesn't appear they are taking the option to flee."

"What's the other option?" Karen asked.

"To murder us all," Kenny answered.

Ho broke in, "Maybe they think they're in for a murder rap already, and there's little cost to getting rid of the bunch of us. There's only a small group who's figured all this out."

"You don't think they would, do you really?" Joan asked.

"I think it's a long shot," Karen replied. "But it's not impossible. These people are dangerous. They hatched a very sophisticated plot leading to the murder of Walter Cunningham, and they came very close to pulling it off. If Ho hadn't gone to Kenny's trial, they would have gotten away with it. They had Kenny in a very tight frame-up."

"Can't we go to the authorities and tell them what we know?" Joan asked.

"Oh, I almost forgot why I came. I was so hung up on the person I saw and her car. Garland and I have an appointment at three-thirty this afternoon. We're going to present our findings to a friend of mine at the state police where I worked. I think we have enough for them to start an investigation of Maybell, Swindle, Duncan, and the others."

"Oh, and I thought you came to take us to lunch," Ho said with a smile.

"Oh yeah, you're right. That too."

Ten minutes later, when Kenny was opening the door to Karen's back seat for Joan, he looked down the next block at the flat-roofed building. *Boy, if I wanted to ambush us, it would make a perfect spot,* he thought. He kept his thoughts to himself and ran around the car to get in the backseat with Joan. He'd never thought he'd be sitting this close to her. Even with the big bandage on her cheek, she still looked beautiful.

Chapter Forty-One

Kenny Sturgis, March 7, 1981

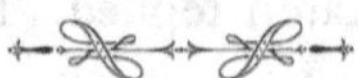

Karen dropped Joan, Kenny, and Ho off at the studio after lunch and left to get ready for her appointment. As he stepped out of Karen's car, Kenny glanced at the flat-roofed building again and saw nothing. He shook his head. He was being paranoid.

Later in the afternoon, Karen felt uneasy about returning to her old office again, so she waited outside for Garland. In some way she thought he'd provide cover. Most of the office doors were closed, so it didn't feel as awkward as she had feared. Still, she felt much happier when they made it to Sylvia Carmone's office. Sylvia had invited John Marsh to the meeting, and he showed up shortly after Garland and her.

Garland started the discussion by describing how Kenny claimed he had been framed. He explained how, at first, he'd found the idea far-fetched, so he hadn't brought it up at the trial. There were too many people lined up on the other side. First, Maybell flat-out denied Kenny's story, and she had people who backed up her claim about grooming their dogs on the day in question. Also, the fingerprint evidence appeared convincing, and Kenny seemed to have the same response for it—Maybell had tricked him.

Karen picked up the story next. She said they had uncovered several witnesses who made Kenny's story seem much more plausible. She had tracked down the car, the fifty-five Oldsmobile. The person who sold the car had a bill of sale showing he sold the car to a Kenny Sturgis, but when he described Kenny Sturgis, the description didn't match. In fact, it fit Maybell's boyfriend, William Swindler. Next, she described how she learned Duncan Lewis, another friend of Maybell's, picked up a new sniper rifle at the post office and Maybell and his friends told him he had a good reason for losing the old one. The guy at the rifle range had described Lewis's old sniper rifle as being similar to the one used in Cunningham's murder. Finally, she explained what they had learned from Joan, Maybell's sister. She told them Kenny and Maybell knew each other well. She'd seen them driving off in Kenny's Jeep one day, and she saw Kenny driving the Oldsmobile used in the murder.

Garland summed up. "Our conclusion is Kenny was in fact framed like he said. One more thing—two of the families who backed Maybell's story about grooming their dogs have the same last name as Duncan Lewis and William Swindler. I certainly didn't believe it at first, but I'm convinced this girl Maybell Wilcox set Kenny up. He turned out to be the perfect victim. It's easy to get a seventeen-year-old boy hooked on sex, and he didn't think it was odd they never went anywhere where anyone would see them. I'm sure they targeted him because he was known to be a great shot with a rifle. They had someone with the necessary skill. They were able to get his fingerprints to the scene two ways, and given Maybell's testimony, he didn't have an alibi."

Sylvia, who'd been taking notes, looked at John and said, "The chewing tobacco evidence makes this whole case screwy. I say we should follow up on the leg work Karen and Garland have done. What do you say John?"

"I agree. Where can we find the people you've talked to?"

"Joan, Maybell's sister, is at my husband's studio today. If we hurry, we should be able to get you there before they close for the day."

Ho was pleased with the progress the three of them made in the afternoon. Joan had turned out to be very adept at polishing and even helped mold some of the wire mesh. He knew she was a good artist, and her skill in two dimensions transferred to the third. Kenny had also learned a lot, so they were ahead of where he expected to be. If he kept these two helpers, Ho figured he could be ready for his next show sooner than he thought.

At four-thirty, he told Kenny and Joan they had reached a good stopping place and could knock off for the day. They put up their tools, and Kenny gave the floor a final sweep before they stepped out of the front door.

Outside, Kenny checked out the flat-roofed building. "Get down!" he yelled. He grabbed Joan and pulled her behind his Jeep. Two loud shots rang out, and two bullets struck the stucco on Ho's studio behind where Joan's head had been less than a second ago.

Ho dove behind his car. "What's going on?"

"Somebody's on the roof over there," Kenny said, pointing down the block. "I saw a rifle barrel. I think there might be two of them."

Another shot rang out. This bullet went into Ho's windshield and scattered glass on him.

"What are we going to do?" Joan asked.

"We're pinned down. I say we sit tight. Some neighbor is going to call 911 to report the shooting. If we expose ourselves in any way, we'll be picked off."

Two cars pulled up. The state police officers had heard the shots, and they quickly sized up the situation. John stepped out of his car, used his door as a shield, and fired his pistol at the roof across the street.

John's shots gave Karen and Sylvia the cover they needed to run behind Karen's car. Karen shot at the roof a couple of times, and then ran to Ho who still hid behind his car. "Are you all right?"

"Yes," Ho answered. "Kenny saw them and had us get down before the shooting started."

"Give me some cover," yelled Sylvia. "I'm going back to John's car to call this in."

John and Karen started shooting at the roof, and Sylvia scrambled into the car.

After two minutes of silence, a siren blared. Kenny grabbed Joan's arm. "Someone's running toward a parked car. Is it your sister?" he asked.

"Yes! I think it is!"

A police car came up the street with its siren and lights on, and an additional police car screamed around the other side of the building.

"Let's go get Maybell," Kenny said as he jumped in the Jeep. Joan followed and they roared off.

"What's he doing?" yelled Sylvia.

"He saw one of them getting away, so he's following," Ho reported.

Sylvia backed John's car out of range of the building and conferred with the local police. The others stayed behind their cars, too afraid to move. They were trapped in place.

❧❧

Kenny's Jeep easily caught up with Maybell in the Ford. "You think she has a gun?" Kenny asked.

"I doubt it. She usually carries a knife."

"I think I can force her off the road," Kenny said as he pulled up beside Maybell. He pulled in front of her and yanked his Jeep to the right, forcing Maybell to the shoulder. Kenny could see panic in Maybell's eyes as he forced her car further off the road.

Maybell lost control of her car, and it came to a sudden stop in a ditch and turned over. Kenny maintained control of his Jeep and stopped off the road. Joan finally let go of the death grip she had on the Jeep's door handle.

"Let's see what happened to her," Kenny said as he got out of the Jeep and cautiously approached the overturned vehicle. He went around the car to check the driver's side and Joan stayed back. Kenny bent down and looked into the car. Then he straightened and shouted, "She's not in there!"

A slight noise, or some instinct, caused Joan to turn. Maybell, her head covered in blood and her clothes torn, stumbled toward her with clear intent. She gripped a knife in her right hand. When Maybell reached her, Joan made a quick pivot, stuck out her leg, and tripped Maybell. Her sister crashed to the ground and the knife flew out of her hand. Kenny ran over and jumped on Maybell's back, securing her and putting her in a hammerlock.

Two minutes later, a police car, lights flashing and siren blaring, came to a screeching halt in front of them. Joan ran up to the police car to tell them they had captured one of the people involved in the shooting.

"Who are you?" the policeman asked.

When he wrote down her name, he returned to his car.

A couple of minutes later, the policeman returned to Joan. "I have the story. You're good. And I suspect that is Kenny Sturgis is over there."

"Yes, and he's holding down Maybell Wilcox."

"Check. We're supposed to take her into custody. Is your car in any shape to drive?"

"Yes, it's the Jeep. It's okay, but I don't think Maybell's car's so good."

In the Jeep as they drove toward the studio, Kenny marveled at how calmly Joan had tripped Maybell. "I was scared to death for you. I couldn't help from behind her car. All I could see was she had a knife, and she was headed toward you fast."

"I've lived with her all my life, and this isn't the first time she's come running at me with evil intent. I've tripped her before. The funny thing is, she never learns. She never sees the trip coming."

They ran into a police blockade two blocks from Ho's studio. Kenny parked on the side of the road, and he and Joan made their way to the front of the roadblock. They could see things were calming down. Lots of people were milling around, which they wouldn't be doing if there were still active shooters.

Joan elbowed Kenny. "Over there," she said, pointing. "It's Ho and Karen. It looks like they're okay."

Chapter Forty-Two
Ho Narwhal, June 21, 1981

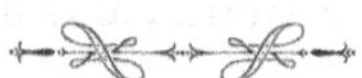

Even though he'd been through this before, Ho paced nervously. The gallery had everything set up, and it looked great. Still, he couldn't help being on edge. His first showing had been a life-changing success. He didn't think there was any way this one could be as well received. He'd lost the element of surprise. Most of the people who'd been invited knew what to expect. He'd never been good at being the center of attention. He guessed he'd never get over feeling self-conscious.

Kenny and Joan were giving Ho a wide berth. Even though they couldn't understand why, they sensed his nervousness. The animals were wonderful, and the way the art gallery had arranged them showed them off splendidly. The polished brass contrasted nicely with the light blue walls.

Joan felt good about how well her cheek had healed. If she looked closely, she could still see a little bit of discoloration, but she could easily hide it with makeup. The way Kenny and the other guys working on the set-up kept staring told her she must look good in the green outfit she'd picked out. Joan knew she'd be on display a little. She had designed the show's poster, and it featured one of her drawings. She thought the name for the show was great—Brass Menagerie II.

Kenny felt uncomfortable in his suit. He'd only worn it twice before, at the trial and at the ceremony for the GED graduates. He'd done some studying, but the test hadn't been hard. He passed it after only three months of work. Ho had given him a raise, and he'd been able to rent a small apartment in town. Garland and Catherine had been great to him. And he liked his new place, even though the food wasn't as good.

Kenny glanced over at Joan walking beside him. During the school year she worked on weekends at the studio, and for the last two weeks she had been there full time. They'd become friends. She was so beautiful, and she was nice too, not at all stuck up like he'd thought before. All things considered, Kenny liked having Joan as a friend and not anything more. He'd made a big mistake getting mixed up with one Wilcox sister. He didn't need another one. She planned to go to an art college in Chicago next year anyway. She had a big scholarship.

Karen and Linda walked into the gallery ten minutes before the official start of the show. Karen thought about her first meeting with Ho at his earlier show. A lot had happened since. When Linda left to talk to Kenny and Joan, Karen sidled up to Ho and gave him a big hug. "Nervous?"

"Yeah, a little. You know some of these things fall flat. The headline might be, same old stuff from Narwhal or something similar."

"Don't worry, everything is spectacular. Given the reputation you've developed, this show will be a smash like the first one."

"I hope so. Did you hear anything from Garland? It's pretty coincidental. My show is the same day as the preliminary hearing for Maybell and her crew."

"Oh yeah, I was so overwhelmed at how nice everything looks I forgot to give you my latest report. Maybell's still in jail. The judge denied the motion for bail. Duncan Lewis is the only one who's out of jail. Apparently, he's turned state's evidence. He admitted he owned the rifle used in the

Cunningham shooting, and that he took some shots at us. Swindle was the one who actually shot Cunningham, so they're going to throw the book at him. Maybell will also have a tough time. She lied to the police and was an accessory to murder. We'll find out how many of us will have to testify later. Maybe no one."

As they finished their talk, the first few visitors wandered into the gallery. The Youngs, Shirley and Simon, were in the first group. They walked up to Kenny, and Ho watched him introduce them to Joan. He spent most Saturdays with his mother and her family, and he had reported he liked being a big brother.

As Ho observed Kenny and his mother, MacElroy Jenkins rushed up to him.

"I want you to meet a couple who are very interested in Number Fifteen. The combination goose and kangaroo." As Ho followed MacElroy, Karen gave him a knowing grin.

"Charm them dear," she said.

Ho enjoyed most of the show. He knew several of the guests this time, and he didn't mind mingling as much as he had at the first show. There were a few art snobs who rubbed him the wrong way, but he'd learned how to deal with them. *Just smile and nod.* He grinned to himself. He spent quite a bit of time with Fern Miller and some of her students who'd made a summer field trip to the big city. Also, he was getting more comfortable with Karen's parents. They brought several of their friends to meet him and seemed very proud of his work.

Horace Cunningham had brought a couple of his co-workers from the brass bed factory. Ho had a wonderful time catching up with them. Despite their suits, they were different from most of the other people there. Spending time with his old work friends reminded Ho how much he still straddled two worlds. Even though he'd become a big success in the snooty art world, and could be comfortable there, he still had connections in the world of everyday, blue-collar workers. It was odd.

While he wasn't sure which world he lived in, he concluded it wasn't the one his father talked about. People weren't out to get him. In fact, most were trying to help him. Kenny, Garland, Karen, and even Joan, all helped him. If anyone should have thought the world was out to get him, it would be Kenny, but in the end it hadn't worked. Ho's dad was wrong. There was no guarantee that being decent and hardworking would pay off, but it often did. There were people out there who would help.

The show turned out to be a big success. Seven of the fifteen pieces on display had sold signs on them by the end of the evening, and MacElroy told him representatives from two out-of-town museums had asked him to reserve a couple of others. They took pictures of Ho's pieces to show to their acquisition committees.

"Another smashing success," MacElroy concluded. "Also, the little blonde cutie who did the poster got some exposure. I saw her talking to several guests. She even signed posters for a few people. She is quite the artist. Wherever did you find her?"

"Don't try to poach her, Jenkins. She's working in my studio this summer, and then she's off to art school in September. Some big-time talents come from small-time places. Remember her a few years from now."

After the show, Ho and Karen hosted a private get-together in a hotel meeting room. Kenny and the Youngs, Joan, Garland and Catherine, and Sylvia Carmone and her husband joined. Fern Miller and her husband arrived later. They'd had to help the chaperone get the students settled. The group wandered around chatting with each other and had small desserts and sparkling wine.

Five minutes after the Millers arrived, Karen gave Garland the signal, and he clinked his glass to begin his job as the master of ceremonies. "Ho and Karen asked me to say a few words. This little party is for two people. First, it is for Ho to celebrate his new show, which looks to me to have been a smashing success. Second, it is for his assistant Kenneth Sturgis, who, I'm happy to say, is a completely free man. Today, with the indictments of William Swindle and Maybell Wilcox, the state has officially dropped all charges against Kenny. We've all known this was coming, but it is now official, making this a great day."

About the Author

Robert Archibald was born in New Jersey and grew up in Oklahoma and Arizona. After receiving a BA from the University of Arizona, he was drafted and served in Viet Nam. He then earned an M.S. and Ph.D in economics from Purdue University.
Bob had a 41-year career at the College of William & Mary. While he had several stints as an administrator, department chair, director of the public policy program, and interim dean of the faculty, Bob was always proud to be promoted back to the faculty.
He lives with his wife of 50 years, Nancy, in Williamsburg, Virginia.